A Feast of Longing

a feast of Longing

Sarah Klassen

Edited by Sandra Birdsell.
Cover image: "Floating Woman" by Kamil Vojnar, Getty Images.
Cover and book design by Duncan Campbell.
Printed and bound in Canada by Friesen's.

National Library of Canada Cataloguing in Publication Data

Klassen, Sarah, 1932-
A feast of longing / Sarah Klassen.

Short stories.
ISBN 978-1-55050-357-9

I. Title.

PS8571.L386F43 2007 C813'.54 C2007-902256-1

10 9 8 7 6 5 4 3 2 1

2517 Victoria Ave
Regina, Saskatchewan
Canada S4P 0T2

available in Canada and the US from:
Fitzhenry & Whiteside
195 Allstate Parkway
Markham, Ontario
Canada L3R 4T8

The publisher gratefully acknowledges the financial assistance of the Saskatchewan Arts Board, the Canada Council for the Arts, the Government of Canada through the Book Publishing Industry Development Program (BPIDP), the Association for the Export of Canadian Books and the City of Regina Arts Commission, for its publishing program.

For John & Martha

contents

All of us are better when we're loved.

– *Alistair MacLeod*

Adelia

When I arrived in Winnipeg that fall for my first year of university, a woman was standing at the end of Aunt Helen's driveway when I pulled up, as if she'd been waiting for me. Her uninhibited gaze nailed me while her mouth opened to expose a forward-tending tongue. A dribble of saliva quivered on her lower lip and slipped in a liquid string lazily over the edge, landing on the flowery summer dress that hung slack and stained on her short, squat body. She held a bunch of green leaves in one hand, a scrunched up Kleenex in the other.

"Hello there." Her voice came from somewhere deep, as if obliged to make its way through layers of thick liquid before it could reach my ear. Her movements were slow. Awkward.

I hoisted my bags down from the back of the pickup truck, wondering who this reception committee of one might be. And how I should respond.

"That your truck?" the thick voice asked.

"Uh huh."

When I took out the key Aunt Helen had mailed me – she and Uncle Ralph would both be out when I arrived – the woman asked, "Take me for a drive in your truck?"

I set down the suitcase and the backpack I had grabbed and turned to look at her. "Who are you?"

As if in answer, another woman, also small, but older, in navy shorts, a broom in hand, called from the driveway across the street, "Adelia! Adelia, come home. Come," as though she were calling a very small child or a favourite cat. The voice was resonant and slipped musically over "Adelia," lending the name a sensuousness. It was a seductive kind of voice and I wasn't surprised that the shapeless woman turned to follow it.

"Everybody calls her Dillie," Aunt Helen said at supper. "A nuisance, that one. Always wandering off to the neighbours. Always underfoot. Last week they found her in the Blockbuster Video up the highway. Could of got killed crossing over. They should do something about her. She's so repulsive with her drooling. And her tongue always hanging out like a dog's. Has light fingers too, gotta watch her. Her kind shouldn't be inflicted on the general public if you ask me." Aunt Helen spoke with the fervour of someone on a "Clean up Your Neighbourhood" crusade.

"Now, Helen," Uncle Ralph said, though without insistence. "Where should she go?"

Uncle Ralph's role in life, I came to understand, was to support Aunt Helen's actions and opinions in a blanket sort of way, do the yard work and, after that, keep out of sight. On the whole he deserved top marks for the way he fulfilled this mandate. He would glide in noiselessly after work, and when supper was finished he'd scuttle down the basement stairs to read the paper or watch TV. On weekends he spent hours cutting and raking grass, in winter shovelling snow, his careful attention to lawn and driveway a sharp contrast to the casual yard care across the street. Uncle Ralph was never underfoot. Mild, was the way I summed him up. Easy to forget.

Aunt Helen had agreed to provide board and room my first year at university. "After that, we'll see." Although I was registered for history, it was women's studies I had in mind. I didn't tell my father this. He had loaned me the money for fees and books, for board and room at Aunt Helen's, in spite of a disastrous year for farmers in the southwest part of the province. I had worked on the farm for a whole year after high school, and as part payment for postponing university he let me have the truck instead of selling it or keeping it for trade-in.

Not that he was against women, but the women's studies courses I had registered for would have seemed to him a very vague field. "Wishy washy," he would have said. "What will you do with that?" So when I spoke about my arts program, I emphasized the Canadian history course. He liked that.

Dillie's education, I soon discovered, had ended at about grade five and she had no concept of university.

"Where you off to every day in that truck?" she'd ask, already up and on the prowl when I left for classes, checking out the trees and hedges for unusual leaves, for fruit she expected to find hanging from the branches. For stray cats. Her fingers itched to probe, touch, stroke, gather. Her mouth was moist.

My defence against Dillie was to avoid looking directly into her blue eyes. They possessed a child's ability to see straight through you. Sometimes they held unveiled hunger, other times they turned wary as if no one was to be trusted, or dark as if concealing unspeakable things.

You'd think assignments and new friends – I met Logan in my first class of Canadian History – could provide me with lots of reasons for forgetting Dillie, but Dillie would not be forgotten.

"Gonna' take me to the Dairy Queen after supper?" she would say in her thick, unclear voice, or "Can we have a hamburger?" And sometimes, "I've got a *great* idea! Let's go to the mall! Nobody ever takes me to the mall."

"Adelia, take it easy."

The admonishment, and my rescue, always came from the neighbour, Dillie's sister, the woman with the seductive voice. I felt sorry for Gracie who had to keep track of the street's *persona non grata*. Her husband Mike was rarely to be seen and anything to do with Dillie was left up to her.

"She just can't cope, that Gracie," Aunt would say, with a contempt that implied her neighbour was to blame for everything to do with Dillie. "Thinks she has to take the whole disgraceful business on her shoulders. Well, you can see how hopeless she is. As if there aren't other places for the likes of Dillie."

It was Gracie's complete loss of freedom that appalled me. Her obvious love for her sister, the desire to make her life better, kept her always on duty, always on call. She fluttered around like a mother hen stuck with one helpless chick, except that no real mother hen I had seen would bother so long with such a failed offspring.

I soon felt that I too was losing my freedom to this disabled woman with her constant questions and childish requests. "Why you wear those black pants? Got a cat at home? When is it your turn to take me for a walk?"

"Just don't get involved," Aunt Helen warned. She was curt with Dillie, applying her sharp tongue like a whip, quick to lash out against what she labelled, wholesale, Dillie's impertinence. Whenever the phone rang and it was Dillie, Aunt would say, "You know you shouldn't call people. You shouldn't bother them, it's impertinent. I don't want you ever to call again." She would bang down the receiver with such venom it made me cringe. But Dillie was undeterred. She would call again and I would get a follow-up demonstration of how to handle a public nuisance.

"Otherwise she'll attach herself like a leech," Aunt would say. "You've got to discourage her from hanging around."

Uncle simply cleared his throat when Aunt looked to him for his usual assent.

"She leaves a messy trail of wadded Kleenexes and you've got to clean up after her," she said with a shudder, as if that clinched everything.

"Kleenex is dangerous?" Uncle said before he scuttled out.

I found myself dreading Dillie's hungry gaze when I pulled onto the driveway. I felt mean and guilty for ignoring her, for escaping into the house with my books before she could come close. Her tongue increasingly insisted on pushing its way out and her hands had begun shaking.

"It's the medicine," Gracie apologized.

My year in the city had hardly begun and already Dillie weighed on me like a millstone. I began to resent that I couldn't afford to live in residence or in an apartment close to campus. I longed for winter, for short cold days when Gracie would have to keep Dillie indoors.

Early October I decided to clear the whole matter from my conscience once and for all. I would do what I had been determined not to do: I would take Dillie for a drive. This would be a one-shot deal. But where to go? Not to the Dairy Queen where she would dribble saliva and ice cream on her dress and over the seat of my truck. Her thick, protruding tongue would turn my stomach. And not to the mall where I might meet someone I knew and be totally embarrassed. A drive north of the city to Birds Hill Park – I had been there with Logan, from my history class – and all the way around the circular drive should satisfy her. We wouldn't even get out of the truck. After that I would have done my duty. My conscience would be free for the rest of the winter.

So the next time Dillie asked, "When are we going for pizza?" I said, "We're not. We're going to the park."

"I'll tell Gracie," she said, her mouth wet with excitement, her body beginning its awkward shuffle to the house. "I'll get my jacket."

"Hold on," I said. "We're not going *now*. Not *today*. We're going Saturday morning." Naming a place and time convenient for *me* left me feeling I was in control, a feeling that Dillie's persistence had begun to erode. I was already anticipating the relief when the outing would be safely over, my obligation done with.

Sometimes I wondered what Logan would think of Dillie. Logan seemed blessed with all the confidence I lacked. His words held conviction and his movements were underpinned with amazing fluidity and grace that made it hard to tear my eyes away from him. Everyone seemed to like him. He joined committees, spoke up on campus issues and dashed off snappy articles for the student paper criticizing fee hikes, funding cuts, campus parking regulations, incidents of racism, abuse involving faculty or students, the latest genocidal war in some African country or in Eastern Europe. Students stopped him when we walked across campus, complimenting him on some idea or a potent phrase in his latest article. I was flattered when he wanted to discuss these matters with me over coffee or a beer. But nervous too. I had little experience discussing concepts and ideas and possessed a dread of being found wanting.

When someone said, "You've got them rattled, Logan," or "Go for it, man. Take 'em by the throat. Kick ass," he loved it. But I also noticed his restlessness when he didn't get attention and I found myself saying flattering things about his articles even if they didn't particularly interest me. You might say it was a way of paying for, or ensuring, the share of spotlight that fell on me as his friend. When you're from a rural place like I was, and shy, any boost to the ego is good news.

Logan was not the first guy I had ever been involved with. High school had been a sort of sexual apprenticeship, a groping and fumbling toward experience that had not passed me by. Not entirely. Sex, I had decided, was designed for guys, and it annoyed me that the girls in Valley High accepted their rules for the game. It *seemed* like a game. I lost my virginity with the help of some inconsequential town boy who quickly stepped out of the picture and became a blur on the periphery of my unremarkable life. When our brief, unprotected sport had ended and my periods continued to happen on schedule, I felt relief and gratitude. Like others before me, I discovered that I could absorb this initiation and go on with life. But I stayed clear of entanglements and when the usual anxiety about "Who will I go with to the grad dance?" began to spread its frantic tentacles, I organized a table for "singles." We convinced ourselves that we had more fun than our friends with their anxiously acquired dates.

But on campus, the security of a steady male friend was not easily resisted and by the time I was reading Virginia Woolf, and also Naomi Wolfe, in women's studies courses, I was comfortable enough with Logan to want to discuss their ideas with him.

"What, exactly, is feminism?" he asked, and I assumed he was teasing.

"It means being *for* women," I said, lamely.

"Well, that's settled then, isn't it?" he said. "That's one issue we've resolved, wouldn't you say?" He sounded certain and patronizing. I could tell he wanted to shift the conversation to some campus event or issue closer to his heart and that irritated me, though I went along with the shift.

The sun hung low over the trees when I arrived at the park gates with Dillie. She had removed her scarf and mitts and the pink toque she had pulled down over her forehead when I stumbled out of the house, coffee mug in hand, and found her waiting for me beside my truck. Even before I had backed off the driveway she was opening the plastic container she carried.

"Treats," she said. "Sugar cookies. I made them yesterday. Gracie showed me."

"No thanks," I said. "Too early."

"You have to eat too," she begged, her mouth full. "Please?"

When I saw that Gracie had packed each cookie neatly in foil, I relented.

Dillie had a comment for everything in the park: the bare skeletons of trees, the speed bumps, the crow that swooped down from an oak branch to perch ominously on the fence. When she spotted a flock of wild turkeys huddled at the road's edge she was jubilant as if she had come upon something exotic. Her hands moved restlessly and her incessant nattering threatened to unhinge me.

"Where are we stopping?" she asked. "Let's walk. Let's go in the bush. Bushes got paths. Let's look for berries."

"It's almost winter, Dillie."

I could see that my plan of not getting out of the truck would have to be modified. Completely without enthusiasm I pulled into the road that led to the stables where horses were being saddled for a late autumn trail ride. Dillie waddled over to the wooden rail fence, an outburst of amazement burbling thickly up from her throat. I followed, picking up the mitts she had dropped.

"Can I ride? I wanna ride."

"Before you ride, you'd have to get *on* the horse," I reminded her.

"I can get on, easy." She spoke with a cocky bravado, her eyes glowing with the prospect of being carried off on the back of a steed.

"It's not so easy." I pointed out a woman struggling to mount a black horse.

"They could get me a ladder."

As we watched the riders leave through the narrow gate of the corral, Dillie fell silent. The fire in her eyes faded, giving way to unconcealed longing as she let her gaze follow the string of horses along the bush trail until the poplar trees swallowed them. Her hands gripped the wooden railing.

"They walk when they start out," I said, "but afterwards they trot. And even gallop."

"I *know* that."

"You'd be flung off. You'd get hurt."

"No I wouldn't." But the steam had gone out of her.

We returned to the truck and completed the drive around the park in silence, Dillie's dejection palpable. I wondered for the first time what was really going on in her head. Had she imagined that she could leap lightly into the saddle, fling her short leg over the horse's back and ride off across a green field?

"We had horses," she said. "My Dad had horses. On the farm."

I didn't know if I should believe her – it was the first I'd heard of a farm.

"Did you ride them?"

She shrugged. "Maybe my brothers." Her voice was unnaturally high-pitched. She was fiddling with her scarf, twisting and twisting it into a rope. When she was done she let it go with a laugh that was shrill and thin. "I can neigh like a horse. Wanna hear me?"

Just before the park gates, the road forked. Straight ahead led to the highway; turn left and we would follow the circle again. I slowed the truck, considered repeating the drive to lengthen Dillie's outing, but essay assignments justified keeping straight ahead, though I left the perimeter highway and took the slower route through the city. Dillie emerged from her gloom and commented on billboards, waved at pedestrians, especially those with dogs. We were home before lunch.

"Next time, longer," she said when she climbed out of the truck.

Gracie was waiting at the window and came rushing out jacketless, calling: "Adelia, Adelia, I missed you. Come, I've got hot chocolate." Dillie was bundled into the house. At the door, Gracie turned and called back to me with her musical voice: "Thanks. Thanks ever so very much."

I had already switched mental channels. A half-finished paper was waiting. "The Future of Feminism: Problems and Possibilities."

The drive to the park was inconsequential, I knew that, but even so I felt a sense of accomplishment, even virtue, and I wanted to talk to someone about it. Not Aunt, who naturally thought I was an idiot for paying any sort of attention to Dillie. Uncle, who rarely stayed around to be talked to, stopped to say, "Dillie's life, it's not been easy. Not many rides to the park for her, I dare say."

With Logan I didn't talk much about my family, about the farm where I grew up. Over the autumn weeks my mother's flower beds, the willow-shaded creek behind our barn and the evergreen shelter belt had begun to blur like an old memory. After the first few weekends, I rarely drove home and seldom pictured my mother at work in her kitchen, stripping the garden before winter, hanging bed sheets on the line. Or in her coveralls getting ready to take her turn on the tractor, completing some fieldwork essential to our existence. In good years, the grain would turn to warm yellow in August and, barring frost or heavy rain, there would be a harvest, sometimes abundant, sometimes adequate. In recent years heavy rains and floods meant almost no crop at all. It was painful to conjure the figure of my father standing in a field of meagre grain that should be chest-high and golden as sunlight, crumbling an almost-hollow head of wheat in his hand, assessing the implications of another failed crop.

Logan didn't speak about his family either and though I wanted to ask, something held me back. We were friends, but also strangers. As fall moved into winter, he became subdued and his frenetic energy subsided. I assumed he was preoccupied with his courses. He no longer greeted me with, "Hey, let's just see how the world unfolds today." One week the student paper rolled off the press without a single article by Logan.

We never talked about Aunt and Uncle, though Logan had met both when he picked me up for a movie or an occasional football game. So why would I introduce Dillie into our conversation? She was not a campus problem, not of political interest. Not of any interest at all, and yet I had failed to rid either conscience or consciousness of her. I was not free.

The next Saturday, the last fine weekend of the fall, Dillie and I were on the road again. Gracie had packed donuts, but I wasn't up to them. When I offered Dillie the choice of where to go, she said, "Same place," and moments later added, "Please." I assumed she was remembering the horses but I was unable to face her longing to ride so I didn't turn in at the stables but headed toward the artificial lake instead. A straggle of Canada geese floated on the water and others hunkered on the sand close to the water's edge where thin ice had begun to form. Dillie scrambled out of the truck and started toward them.

"I'm coming," she called out, her arms reaching ahead of her. "I'm coming."

"Wait, Dillie," I yelled, but she continued her clumsy progress toward the lake. The geese, alarmed by her noisy arrival, started up from sand and water, filling the air with their ungainly flapping wings and their querulous honking.

Dillie, her face raised to the ascending geese, didn't stop, but kept her course doggedly, stumbling over stones, over her own feet, until she fell face down into the shallow, icy water. It seemed to happen in slow motion with a sort of inevitability. Horrified, I ran to the lake, bracing against the shock of the cold water. I waded in, tugged at her, heaved her onto her back, then knelt in the frigid lake and held her head above the water.

"Get up, Dillie," I begged. "You've got to help me." I was panicking. I had to get her out before she became chilled through.

We struggled while the geese veered uncertainly above the lake, their squawking a frantic cacophony. Straining and pulling, I finally had Dillie turned over, then up in a sitting position, and I held her there. She was soaked, her lips blue, her whole body shivering. With mutual resolve we struggled again, Dillie grunting while I pulled or prodded until I managed to coach and shove her onto her knees. From there I got her more or less upright. We stumbled across the sand, dripping water and clinging to each other. Once we were in the truck I turned up the heat, found a blanket to wrap around her shoulders and headed for home. Dillie shed water like a drowned rat, whimpering and shaking uncontrollably. My legs and arms were numb.

"She'll get pneumonia and die." Aunt was both predictably smug and alarmed.

"It's not her fault," Uncle said and I wasn't sure whether he meant me or Dillie.

Gracie said she'd ply her sister with poultices and hot milk laced with brandy and put her to bed. "She's getting better," she assured me when I dropped in that evening. Dillie lay asleep, her mouth open, her breathing a laboured rattle. We stood a while at her bedside, Gracie and I, not speaking, just listening. Gracie stroked her sister's hair as if she were administering a blessing. "Sleep, Adelia," she crooned. "Sleep."

Dillie did not die. It was Gracie who surrendered some weeks later to a harsh strain of flu that had moved in on the city. She was buried only weeks before Christmas; Dillie had already been moved out. I drove Aunt to the funeral. "It's my duty, I guess," she said. Since Gracie's death I'd seen her at the kitchen table or the stove, her hands idle, her eyes downcast or pensive, seemingly removed from where she was and what she should be doing. There was no criticism now of Gracie. Or of Dillie.

Uncle declined to go to the funeral, suggesting I should take his place because naturally I'd want to see Dillie. And I did. Word in the neighbourhood had it that although she had recovered from her icy baptism, her brain functioned even less willingly than before.

Dillie came to the funeral escorted by a largish woman, a relative I guessed, who guided her firmly and expeditiously along the aisle to the front. Dillie sat facing the casket stoically, her mouth open, her tongue almost touching her chin. Afterwards, she wrapped her arms around me and pressed her wet mouth to my cheek. She didn't speak, and it seemed to me the familiar longing in her eyes was overlaid by fog. But it hadn't been extinguished altogether.

"I'll come visit you," I blurted. She looked so pathetic I couldn't help myself. I wondered then if Gracie's amazing love for her sister had begun as pity.

In the parking lot Aunt announced that we would drive to the cemetery. This was not according to plan and I wasn't delighted, but I didn't object. "Gracie was a good woman," Aunt said, as if she intended to convince me. We stood together on the periphery of the mourners. I waited for the only words I could remember from earlier funerals, *ashes to ashes, dust to dust*, but the words the priest read were unfamiliar: *What is sown is perishable, what is raised is imperishable...what is sown in dishonour is raised in glory.* It made me think of the way my Dad would take a handful of seed wheat and study it for quality.

I told Logan about Dillie, about her illness and Gracie's death. He considered the information, then said, "Well, that's life, isn't it? You're motoring along more or less on track, then WHAM" – and here he brought his hand down so hard on the counter our mugs jumped and coffee spilled on the table – "some horror slams you down hard. Maybe you'll pick yourself up, maybe you won't. It happens to lots of people. This time it happened to – what's-her-name?"

"Dillie," I said. I found his answer unfeeling and I told him so.

"Do you expect *me* to do something about it?" he asked. His look of mixed anger and desperation took me off guard.

I mourned then for the confident, energetic Logan I had first known and regretted mentioning Dillie. I consoled myself that, after the stress of exams and assignment deadlines, the Christmas break would refuel him and he would be himself once more.

I meant what I said about visiting Dillie but after the last, overdue, term paper I had to buy presents for my parents and finish Christmas shopping for Mom. Before I left for home there were parties Logan and I had slotted in, though he had become oddly indifferent, even resistant, and mostly I went alone. Once, at a classmate's apartment, I saw him standing by himself at the bookshelf, not even a beer in his hand, a sad figure. I started toward him, but when he turned and noticed me there was a chill in his eyes.

"Are you okay, Logan?"

"Why wouldn't I be?" He stared at me as if I were an unwelcome intruder. A short time afterwards he left. I caught a ride back with Bill, Logan's on and off roommate.

Next day Logan called and I waited for him to explain, if not apologize, but he said little of anything. I had planned to ask him to drive out to the farm with me to meet my parents, but his strange dejection and aloofness left me uncertain. My parents did not need more gloom. He promised to call me over Christmas but remained vague about how he would spend the holiday.

The morning I drove back to Winnipeg for the second semester, the crisp and brilliant Christmas weather had given way to overcast and snow fell in thick, mesmerizing flakes over the monochrome landscape. "Better wait until tomorrow," my father had advised at breakfast. "They're forecasting strong winds." But I was impatient to get to the city.

My mother had roasted the usual turkey for Christmas and steamed a pudding, but the year's farm failure had hung like a verdict over our celebration and I kept thinking guiltily that I was inflicting on my hard-pressed parents the additional burden of a costly university education. An education I wasn't sure how I would put to use. I was disappointed that Logan hadn't called; it would have brightened things for me. Dad looked weary even though he slept a good part of each day. This was the slack time for farmers, the time to think about a vacation in Florida or Texas or the Caribbean. The time for being re-created, re-energized. For my father, it was a time to brood, and I wished I could cheer him up.

Mom's hair had begun to grey. She had worked all her life on this farm, a full partner in the shared hopes and setbacks. It had never seriously occurred to me that she might have had aspirations beyond the farm, and I asked her if she'd ever wanted to train for a career or go to university. She was at the counter making perogies for dinner and kept pinching dough, pinching dough and saying nothing. I thought she hadn't heard. Then she brushed the flour from her hands into the sink and spoke to the snow-banked driveway beyond the window, "I'm just glad you can go. If you're happy, I'm happy." I wasn't willing to prod at what her words might be concealing.

Snow streamed toward the truck, a silent onslaught that prevented daylight from ever quite arriving.

About halfway to the city, the wind my father had warned of blew up, increased quickly and flung gusts of new snow across the highway, threatening to obliterate the landscape. Several cars had slid off the road and sat eerily in the ditch. Slippery patches were forming; I gripped the steering wheel and concentrated on the way ahead.

It was a relief to reach the city where the streetlights cut through the afternoon gloom and everything seemed safe. The storm, and the release of tension afterwards, had purged me of my Christmas melancholy and dulled my worries about the farm; already I felt removed from it. Turning in at Aunt's snow-clogged driveway I caught myself expecting to see Dillie, who should be waiting for me or looking for dead leaves and berries in the snowy hedge. I wondered how Mike had spent Christmas, his first without Gracie. I had given up despising him for not helping her with Dillie. What did I know about his life? His sadness or his hopes?

I arrived early for my first class, Canadian history, and looked around for Logan. He wasn't usually late. I kept turning toward the door long after latecomers could no longer be expected. After the lecture, when the others grabbed their books and dashed off, I remained where I was, irresolute, until the next class began piling in. I grabbed my things then and left too.

"You're waiting for Logan." It was Bill. He was standing outside the lecture room and his soft voice startled me. I was embarrassed that anyone should see me so obviously forlorn. He pulled me out of the busy corridor into a quiet corner.

"Logan won't be back," he said. "He wanted me to tell you. Winter's a bad time for depression." When he saw my distress, he explained, "It came back, this time pretty bad. There's no way he can handle classes, so he's dropped out for this semester. It's tough. He needs help."

His words swirled around me, sucking me into a cold wind tunnel and I couldn't speak.

"You didn't know." It was a statement rather than a question.

I steeled myself against his concern, dismayed that I had somehow provoked it.

"Logan's got a history of mood swings, it runs in his family. Mostly he handles it, but sometimes...well, he should've gone for help earlier. I thought maybe you knew. You were going out with him. He liked you, obviously."

I was ashamed that I had known so little about Logan. I had been attracted to his confidence and energy, coveting them for myself, wanting to draw strength from him, never learning of his need. I had failed him, and at the same time I felt betrayed.

During the course of the winter I occasionally and reluctantly visited Dillie in the group home where she now lived. If she was up to it we'd go for a drive, though never again to Birds Hill Park. Her speech had slowed, her brain seemed sometimes to be shutting down, her steps increasingly unsteady, but when I least expected it her spirit would flame up out of the dullness that shrouded it and there would be some new revelation. She had grown up on a farm north and west of the town I came from, with Gracie and several brothers who were now scattered over the world. London, she might say, or Seattle or New Orleans or Regina. I suspected she had no idea what they were doing. They had not come to Gracie's funeral. Her parents were "long, long, gone," as she put it. When I asked if she had visitors, she said, "They don't want me," and lowered her eyes. Her hands were restless, twisting her Kleenex into tight, short ropes and then pulling bits off the end. The floor was covered, as if with confetti.

On brighter days she would say, "I used to pick berries. Saskatoons, with my Mom." Or she'd tell me she could shell peas "real good."

Sometimes she would turn to me with that old hunger and ask, "Do *you* want me?"

"Dillie, you say such comical things."

I admitted to myself that I did not want Dillie either, with her naked need. Her sloppiness. Our visits left me downcast. Life would be simpler if she had no part in it. I could not imagine myself ever hovering over her like Gracie. I wanted Logan back, to offer a distraction from Dillie. I waited for Aunt to tell me not to get involved, but although she knew about the visits she never discouraged me. In fact, her voice and glance implied approval. "Tell her hello from me," she'd say, and when she mentioned Gracie, "A saint, that one."

Uncle would push a few loonies into my hand. "Get a treat for Dillie. Poor thing, there can't be much in her life to make her happy."

I couldn't imagine Dillie happy, and I resented Aunt and Uncle's assumption that I had accepted some sort of responsibility for her well-being. My major paper on feminist theory could not shut out the unwelcome sense of duty, and I kept up the visits.

I had this vague idea that if I built regular time with Dillie into my schedule maybe the visits would get easier, I might get to know her better and one day I would be able to say with a measure of truth, "Yes, Dillie, I want you." If I kept at it long enough, I might one day call her "Adelia" in a voice as musical and full of love as Gracie's.

But that didn't happen. Late April, after exams and just before going home for the summer, I arrived at the group home intending to take Dillie for a drive to Birds Hill Park where the furry petals of the first crocuses were poking through the grass. The previous week I had taken Aunt, who had never seen crocuses growing wild, and this made me wonder if Dillie remembered them.

But Dillie wasn't there. Transferred to Regina, a nursing assistant told me. A relative had come for her. I should go to the office if I had other questions. I didn't ask questions. When I walked to the truck, sadness slowed my steps, but I also sensed relief – a load lifted. That afternoon I packed, said good-bye to Aunt and Uncle, and as I drove home, guilt replaced the relief as I knew it would.

Driving west from the city I pictured Dad readying the equipment for another spring seeding and Mom carrying boxes of tomato and pepper seedlings out to the yard where the sun could shine on them.

The Wind Blows Where it Chooses

It was one thing after another that morning: the election canvasser at the door earlier than she had expected; the philodendron dry as bone; the metal clasp to be cleaned on the brown leather shoulder bag she had found at the Watt Street Thrift Store for one dollar. She would have liked to speak to the canvasser, a woman who seemed friendly enough but in a hurry once she had obtained her information. The metal polish for the clasp took a while to find and consequently the radio did not get turned on until long after the funeral announcements were over. A good thing someone at the church had called to remind her that the service for Sheila Soderstrom was scheduled for one-thirty this afternoon. She would have to rush to clean up the breakfast dishes before she left. Better to come home to the reassurance of clean counter space.

Six blocks to the funeral chapel. Though the wind was brisk the September sun shone warm on Verna the entire way. The windows at Safeway screamed out promises – large eggs two dozen for two dollars, chicken legs a dollar twenty-nine a pound. Should she stop in on her way back? A forest of election posters had sprung up on the boulevards. She wondered if this might present a traffic hazard. Verna had owned a car once, but long before the doctor had removed her cataracts, before she had retired from her job at Sears and begun the monthly waiting for the pension check, she had sold it and discovered that she could walk to most places. Her life slowed down.

It had been, all along, only a matter of time for Sheila Soderstrom. Her heart was giving out, people said, though last Sunday an announcement from the pulpit had assured the large and not entirely indifferent congregation that her condition was stable. The funeral had caught Verna off guard, but she had not for a minute considered staying home.

The foyer in the funeral home opened onto a lounge designed for comfort and consolation: sofa and chairs in muted rose, navy and grey patterns; on the gleaming coffee table a giant flare of white silk roses with feathery green fern; opposite the window a painting – three sails on a tranquil sea. It was all familiar to Verna.

And there, signing the guest book, was Linda Hertz. How lucky, Verna thought. She would like to sit with Linda because, as usual in a gathering of people, she felt nervous, alone. She walked up to Linda: "Hello. A shock, isn't it?"

"A shock? More like expected, I'd say. Excuse me, dear, I have to find one of the ushers." She handed Verna the pen for the guest book.

Verna stared at it for several moments before signing her name. She knew a snub when she met it. A good thing life had given her a thick skin. Anything other would be useless if one was to go on, and Verna had gone on, more or less, for seventy-two years. She signed her name, put down the pen and made her way to the chapel looking for a place on the aisle, a place she could slip into quietly beside someone, not an empty row where she'd be obvious. Ushers tended to seat you too far forward; she waited until they were busy.

Three girls – teenagers or almost, relatives of Sheila's most likely – had left an aisle spot free. Verna moved toward it but when she was about to sit down one of them said, "We're saving it, actually," and she had to squeeze past several pairs of knees in the next row up. Not that she needed to squeeze past anyone, the chapel was mainly empty. She felt foolish, an intruder; when she sat down she was breathless. She caught the movements of the three girls and heard them giggling, obviously still amused that she had tried to sit with them. She put the girls out of her mind and watched as a few latecomers straggled up the aisle toward the front where the coffin already stood.

Now that she was seated there was nothing further to do but wait for the minister and family to file in. Most important was the family. Who were they? Were there daughters? Sons? Unlikely that anyone would be grief-stricken. Verna assumed there was no husband, he must be long gone, if he had been there at all. Organ music, slow and sombre, filled the chapel. When Verna turned slightly to check on the aisle spot behind her, it was still empty.

Sooner or later at every funeral Verna's mind moved back to her husband's burial twenty-two years ago, his inert body in the closed coffin, the spray of pink roses and white carnations the funeral director had suggested. She did not think of Frank with any sorrow; he had left her so long ago that he seemed even less familiar than Sheila Soderstrom. Unless she had recently come across his picture in one of her albums, it was difficult to conjure his face. But at funerals, waiting, enveloped in soothing organ music, she allowed memories of him to surface. Nothing, however, that might make her sad. Funerals were not sorrowful occasions for Verna, who throughout the decades had shed plenty of tears over loss and disappointments. Those tears had dried up; she would not dab her eyes like some of the other women. Loneliness, she had concluded long ago, was inevitable, and therefore a state to be embraced, not shunned. She believed that. Most of the time.

Everyone stood now while a short entourage began making its way to the front. Verna caught glimpses of a discreet navy hat, a flame of gold-red hair, a bald head, a brownish floral print – all of them moving toward Sheila Soderstrom in her modest daisy-and-fern-bedecked coffin occupying the place of honour at the base of a small podium.

When everyone was once more seated, a trio of women sang, "I Come to the Garden Alone, While the Dew is Still on the Roses," and Verna wondered if the song had been a particular favourite of Sheila's. For her part, she considered it far too sentimental, but she liked it all the same. She was determined not to forget that besides Psalm twenty- three the minister had read "The wind blows where it chooses..." – she couldn't remember the rest – before the meditation. She would try to find it in her Bible at home and reread it. Her mind had a way of wandering during the service and if anyone should ask her for details later she would recall very little. As it happened, nobody ever asked.

Verna had come cradling the small hope that Linda Herz would offer her a ride to the cemetery for the interment; it would be something to do in the interval between the service and the reception. It would take her out of the city, even just a short distance. After the rebuff at the guest book she knew enough to let go of that hope. She could think of no one else she could ask to take her. But it did not really matter.

While the others left in twos and threes for the parking lot, she made her way, as she had often done, to one of the chairs in the lounge and settled her body into its floral cushions. She had learned to take simple pleasures where she found them. While she waited she relished the comfortable solitude, the white almost-real-looking roses, the three calm sails on blue water. She picked up a brochure from a pile on the table. *Difficult Decisions in a Time of Sorrow*, the front page read, and under the caption there was a photograph of the lounge with the words *The Rose Room* in a delicately scrolled script.

A woman in a navy pant suit – it resembled a uniform – came into the lounge and looked around the way someone with confidence, someone who is at ease anywhere, looks around. She sat down on the sofa opposite Verna. An elderly man, slight and greying, strolled past them, turned, walked back and sat beside the woman.

"Haven't I seen you at Grace Manor?" the man asked the woman.

"I'm a volunteer. Janice Sparke. I used to visit Sheila Soderstrom."

"I'm the chaplain at Grace. Bill Winter." They shook hands.

"Guess it wouldn't be wrong to say it's a blessing she could go," Janice said.

The chaplain paused before agreeing. "You might say that."

"I mean she's been there forever, it seems like. How long can a body exist like that? I mean, exist is all she did, wouldn't you agree? I have no idea how long."

"Eight, nine years, probably. At least that. I remember when she was admitted. Rather dramatic actually." The chaplain hesitated, unsure, and Verna felt him glance at her.

She turned a page in the pamphlet. Other people's conversations were dear to her, but she knew about being discreet. She studied the picture of a gleaming brown oak coffin with the four-digit price in small numbers and in parentheses, (*casket, with earth burial.*)

The chaplain continued in a lowered voice: "She was removed, you know."

"Removed?"

"That's when a person is forcibly taken out of their residence. Police and everything. They forced her door. Brought her here kicking and scratching."

"The police?"

"Oh, believe me, she resisted. Yelled and called them bloody bastards. Furious as a cornered fox, that one. They couldn't do anything with her. *I* couldn't do anything. She was exceedingly ornery for two years." He chuckled, remembering.

"And then?"

"And then she sort of withdrew. Wasn't really there, if you know what I mean. Like she'd given up – people do that sometimes." The chaplain shrugged, a gesture that seemed to acknowledge helplessness in the face of the inevitable. "If she hadn't had a set of pretty tough vital organs, my guess is she'd never have lasted this long."

"A shame. Poor Sheila. I've only been visiting her six months. She never said much. Such a lost creature."

"They had no choice about bringing her to Grace. She'd given the home care people a circus of a time. She'd accuse them of robbing her. Of trying to poison her. They said her place was a royal mess. There was no other way but removal."

"Far as I know, nobody visited her but me," the volunteer said. "Once in a long while someone from her church."

Verna had leafed twice through the pages of the brochure with its pictures of various caskets: cloth, veneer, hardwood. For Frank's funeral, she had selected from the medium price range. She had not visited the grave in years.

The final two-page spread showed the reception room located past the lounge, with a close-up insert of the buffet table covered with plates of dainty sandwiches and small square cakes in pink paper cups. It was the photograph she looked at the longest.

"She had no children," the chaplain was saying.

All this about Sheila was news to Verna. She had not really known the woman, only the snippets announced Sundays from the pulpit or printed in the bulletin: "Let's remember to pray for Sister Soderstrom at the Grace Manor Personal Care Home. She is failing." Or "Let's remember Sheila Soderstrom before the Throne of Mercy. She is completely bed-ridden." From these appeals she gleaned that sooner or later there would be a funeral. The thought that she should visit Sheila Soderstrom, that Sheila might need or want her company, had not occurred to Verna until now.

The man and woman opposite fell silent, mulling over the sad existence of the deceased woman in their own way, Verna imagined, letting their thoughts roam in the wide pastures of fantasy. She paged once more through the brochure, reading a phrase here and there.

"I think they're back from the interment," the chaplain said, rousing himself. And then, as if an explanation was owed, added, "I would have gone, except for the wind. Not good for the asthma." He tapped his chest as he hoisted himself up from the soft sofa.

Verna placed the brochure back on the table and straightened her skirt. Her black shoes were dusty from walking and she wiped them with a tissue. When she looked up, funeral guests were dribbling in through the door. The three young girls came in together and stood close to Verna's chair.

"Stupid wind out there. Do I look like hell?"

The long blonde hair of the one who spoke was wind-tangled. She began combing it with her fingers. She wore the most astonishingly brief skirt Verna had ever seen. The short girl beside her had taken out a lipstick and began working her lips with incredible accuracy. Verna couldn't help staring.

The third, a chubby one, said: "Well, that's it for Great Aunt Sheila."

"Now if only she'd left a fortune. I'd be rich."

Verna would not have expected the blonde one to be sarcastic, there was something sweet about her pale face. She wondered if she had ever visited Aunt Sheila.

"Forget it, Dee Dee. She'd have left it to me. I've even got her name." That was the short one.

The other two, surprised, said, "No way! You serious? No way you've got her name."

"Yep. I'm Sonya Sheila Soderstrom. So if I wanted to I could be Sheila Soderstrom. Naturally I don't want to. Sonya's evil enough." Her companions laughed.

"I'm starved," the chubby one said. "Let's go."

Sonya and Dee Dee. Verna rose, settled the strap of her newly-acquired handbag on her shoulder and followed the others. She wondered what the name of the chubby one might be. Jennifer? Emily? She liked Grace, but people didn't name their daughters that any more.

The exhilarating aroma of fresh coffee wafted through the doors leading to the reception room. Verna breathed it in greedily and felt her spirit quicken, her flesh and blood come alive. She wondered why the people ahead of her were so unhurried. Didn't they feel drawn as she was by the aroma? Bunched into a shifting queue, chattering, gesturing, they seemed more numerous than in the chapel. Verna closed her eyes and tried to imagine the table they were moving toward. There would be tea in china pots, but she would have coffee from the large electric urn. At the last funeral – whose was it? She couldn't remember – there had been warm sausage rolls, but it would be foolish to count on such bounty. Once, there had been a spectacular array of salads – potato salad, salmon salad, coleslaw with carrots shredded into delicate slivers and the dressing exquisitely seasoned. Verna remembered suddenly the pastor's reading, "You spread a table before me in the presence of my enemies." Odd, to think of eating in the presence of enemies. What could that possibly feel like?

She thought of Sheila, who was now beyond the pleasure of this table. Sheila, whom she had never visited. Whom she hadn't known. She felt a small twinge of remorse.

A gap had appeared between her and the people ahead, while the queue behind her remained a patient murmur of conversation. With a few quick steps she closed the gap and occupied herself with imagining the generosity of today's table. Cubes of cheese yellow as the sun. Fresh white Kaiser buns split in half and covered with three or four slices of pink ham, wads of shaved corned beef glazed with mustard, mounds of creamy egg salad, salmon generously blended with mayonnaise. Here and there a savoury touch of green onion or dill or parsley. Bowls of fruit – translucent green grapes, wedges of apple, strawberries surprisingly red for September, a bit of greens and stem left on.

The reality, when Verna reached the table, was more modest. The ham and lettuce sandwiches were thin and slightly limp. The Danish pastry, cut in halves, had lain too long uncovered on platters and would be dry at the edges. But the pickles looked fresh; Verna was sure they would be crisp A rush of gratitude enfolded her. She approached the table and took a white plate from the stack.

Even before she had filled the plate, a small, perverse cloud cast its shadow across her pleasure. Where would she sit? The round tables in the dining area ahead of her were always set for six. Today, because Sheila's was a small funeral, fewer had been laid with white cloth and instead of the usual navy or deep maroon linen napkins – she liked the maroon best – there were plain paper serviettes. Verna could see Linda Hertz moving toward a table in the centre of the room, a table where the chaplain and the volunteer were already sipping their coffee. Although there were three chairs left, Verna stayed clear of Linda's table and instead, after adding one more ham sandwich and one more pickle to her plateful, claimed a place on the periphery at the only laid table that was still completely empty. When she had put down her plate and steaming coffee cup, pulled her chair into a good position, she felt exposed, an elderly woman sitting alone, though of course no one was paying the slightest attention to her. She resolved to put the entire room out of her mind. She would enjoy her food at leisure. She wanted to pray for Sheila

Soderstrom, to whom she suddenly owed something, but the minister had said Sheila was in a better place, so her prayers would be after the fact. Futile.

The three girls had loitered long at the buffet table and seeing no better opportunity set their overloaded plates down opposite Verna, leaving the safe distance of the table's diameter between them. Verna gave her full attention to her heaped plate and the steaming coffee into which she had poured a good measure of cream. Any possible conversation that might drift her way was welcome too.

"Megan , you pig. Look at your plate." Dee Dee, the blonde, pointed in theatrical outrage to the mountain of ham sandwiches and pastry on the chubby girl's plate. Her own was piled almost as high.

"So? I'm starved."

"Stuffing yourself at poor Great Aunt Sheila's funeral. Shame." Sonya snickered.

So. Megan. Verna sank her teeth into the ham sandwich. She had never had to concern herself with weight gain. Right now her thin body was settling into a state of well-being that was expansive enough to tolerate the silly chatter going on across the table.

"My Dad says that now she's dead there's one less person leeching hard-earned money from the taxpayers," Dee Dee said.

"That's mean." Megan spoke with a mouthful of sandwich. "She prob'ly didn't want to be in a nursing home."

"I'd swallow poison before I'd let anyone put me in one," Sonya said. "In grade five, my teacher made us go every month to visit the old people in a home down the street. She said we were 'The Happy Gang.' We sang for them, 'You are my sunshine,' stuff like that and then she made us find at least one shrivelled body and talk to it. They were mostly, like, out of it. Totally. No way I'm going into a place like that."

"Maybe no worse than getting beaten by your husband."

"Who?"

"Aunt Sheila. Great Uncle Alex beat her. Don't your parents tell you anything, Sonya? He had a mean temper when he got drunk."

"Prob'ly did all sorts of ugly things to her in bed, too."

The trio exploded in laughter. Megan choked on her sandwich, causing bits of ham and lettuce to spatter the white cloth. She wiped it with her serviette.

"I bet Aunt Sheila had tons of visitors," Dee Dee said. "From the church. That's what they do."

Verna was not appalled, not at the girls' coarse talk about their dead relation, nor at the sprayed tablecloth. Few things had power to appal her. Certainly not the revelation, even if it was true, about Sheila's abusive husband. She thought of Frank. He had never hit her. At first she had believed him shy, a man who didn't quite know how to show his feelings. Or maybe he was just reserved. Hard to say when she had absorbed the fact that her husband cared little about the things that gave her pleasure: the new lilies in her perennial bed, the way light poured mornings through the kitchen window, the melting snow in spring. He had never been enthusiastic about anything. They had never discussed separate beds, but toward the end he left her entirely alone. There had been no children. No daughters. Sitting opposite the three girls, Verna wasn't wishing for daughters, not seriously. The passing years had long since put an end to that.

It was Sonya's description of the nursing home that lodged in her mind, the details gathering into a hard knot inside her. Some day she would be a resident in such a dismal place.

"You a friend of Aunt Sheila's?" the chubby girl asked, her sandwich poised mid-air.

The question startled Verna. She finished chewing the bit of pickle with a slow deliberateness, swallowed, dabbed her lips with the paper napkin. Then she looked up, right into Megan's large eyes. They were astonishingly blue and in spite of their boldness, innocent looking.

"Yes," she heard herself saying. "Yes. I knew her." And after the briefest of pauses, "I visited her at Grace Manor. Every Tuesday."

All three girls were looking at her now, expectantly, curiously. "Did you think she was, like, weird?" Dee Dee asked.

Verna hardly hesitated with her reply. "Seemed like she almost wasn't there," she said, astonished at her calm words. "You know what I mean? As if she'd given up. People do that sometimes when there's no hope. But she was brave. Yes. Very brave. I could see that."

"Brave?" Sonya said.

"Yes. Really brave. I mean the way she faced the police."

"Police?" All three girls had stopped eating. Their young faces, turned toward Verna, had a kind of blankness about them. She dabbed her mouth once more, wondering what she should say next, when she saw the chaplain go over to a mike set up next to the buffet table.

Verna leaned toward the three girls who leaned further toward her. In a lowered voice she said, "They brought her to the nursing home in handcuffs. Dragged her down the corridor." After a pause she added, "They had her in a straitjacket."

"Can I have your attention, ladies and gentlemen." The chaplain said. "We are here to pay tribute to Sheila Soderstrom."

Verna took a sip of her coffee. She liked this part, when people stepped up to the mike and talked about the deceased. Nobody ever said anything the least bit unkind. Sometimes they shared interesting things. Once a woman said her father, whom they had just buried, always prepared Sunday dinner and it was always the same: baked beans, baking powder biscuits and chocolate pudding with whipped cream. That was Verna's favourite story. Frank had never cooked anything.

Verna, of course, had never stepped up to the mike, had never spoken into it at any funeral. What could she have said? She turned so she could see the chaplain who stood waiting patiently at the mike. At some funerals, a line of people wanting to speak formed quickly, but today no one was coming forward. No one from the table near the chaplain – she assumed they were relatives – was pushing their chair back in preparation for getting up. There was no clearing of throats. No movement from Linda Herz. You would think the volunteer would have something to say, but she was deep in a whispered conversation with Linda. It seemed that no one was going to say a good thing about Sheila Soderstrom. Verna could feel the embarrassment spawned by the long silence.

As she turned back to her almost empty cup for one more sip, her eyes once again met Megan's. Verna saw a challenge in those intense blue eyes, or it may have been a plea. She wanted to turn away from that gaze, but the thought that Sheila Soderstrom, who lay freshly buried somewhere not very far away, would have no testimony from those who remained behind still able to enjoy sandwiches and coffee, seemed suddenly unfair. Obviously Megan thought so too, or at least appeared to, Verna believed. She knew with a sudden sense of inevitability that today she would walk up to the mike and speak into it, and there was little time to think about what she would say.

As she made her way awkwardly past tables to the mike, words came to her mind, a small parade of them. *Brave* was one. *Lonely* another. *Forgotten. Kind. Long-suffering.* A pathetic enumeration of weaknesses. An inadequate summary.

The chaplain smiled, relieved that someone, anyone, was going to speak about Sheila Soderstrom. He stepped aside to give her space. Suddenly shaky, Verna noticed she held in her hand the bunched up strap of her brown bag which she must have grabbed instinctively when she stood up from her chair. Embarrassed, she looked around, and finding the depleted buffet table right beside her, she placed her handbag on it. Then she reached out nervously for the neck of the mike. She cleared her throat. From this vantage point the audience before her seemed formidable. Her mind went blank. The assembled guests blurred before her eyes. Somewhere in that blur she could see the three girls, their bodies twisted round so they all faced her. She thought she saw Dee Dee place her hand over her mouth to stifle a giggle. Sonya's face was expressionless, Megan's sky-blue eyes more imploring than ever.

"Sheila Soderstrom," Verna began, her voice unsteady, thin. "Sheila Soderstrom was a good woman. And I think...." Here her thread-like voice faltered, threatened to turn traitor. But she went on, finding the words, "I believe she is sitting somewhere at a table, like this one, here." She gestured weakly in the direction of the table, and noticing how empty it was she added, "Only, her table, it's piled high." She made a motion with her hand as if tracing the outline of a modest hill. She stood there shakily for a time and then added as an afterthought, "And there aren't any enemies. Not even one."

Verna let go of the mike, turned her back to the funeral guests and began walking past the buffet table, through the lounge, through the foyer and into the street. The wind had gained force, the elm branches above her whipped the air furiously, scattering brown and yellow leaves. She wished she had brought a coat. Leaning into the gusts, she set off resolutely. She would not stop at Safeway, she would go directly home. If she kept a good pace her blood would circulate and her body warm up.

Verna had walked almost a block when she heard running steps pounding on the sidewalk behind her. She moved aside to let the runner pass.

"You forgot your handbag."

If Sheila had had a choice, she would have wanted it to be Megan who had pursued her, but it was Dee Dee, quite out of breath, her long blonde hair yanked about by the wind. She held out the brown bag whose long strap was bunched in her hand.

Verna took her forgotten possession. "Thanks. Thanks for bringing it."

Although Dee Dee was breathless, it was clear she had something more to say. Looking boldly at Verna, her grey eyes almost defiant, she said, "I visited Aunt Sheila too." She stopped, still struggling to catch her breath. "Not every week, but often. Very often. Every month when my parents drove into the city."

Verna didn't believe for a minute that Dee Dee had ever visited Sheila Soderstrom. It just wasn't the sort of thing she could imagine her doing. But she said nothing, just nodded her head slightly. "I hadn't even noticed," she said, indicating the handbag.

"All that about the police," Dee Dee said, "and the straight jacket. That's not true, is it?"

"Oh, it's true all right." And to herself, "It very well could be."

Dee Dee seemed to be thinking it over. "Well, goodbye," she said after a while, raising her hand chest high and wiggling her fingers in farewell.

Verna had walked a short distance before she knew that she should have said something more. If Dee Dee were her granddaughter she'd want her to have more, even from a stranger. She was not sure whether that something should be encouragement, a smile or a stern word of admonition. Apology? What if Dee Dee *had* visited Sheila Soderstrom? Indecision slowed her steps. She stopped, turned round. In the distance she could see Dee Dee's thin, flailing arms and the pale wild halo crowning her slender form. The girl was moving quickly away from her, but then, as if drawn by Verna's gaze, or as if she too realized the need for something more, she stopped and slowly turned.

The distance between them was too far for conversation. Verna raised both arms and moved them in a sweeping motion so vigorous it sent a searing stab of pain into her shoulder and the brown handbag dangling from one hand bumped against her side. In the distance Dee Dee too raised her arms and waved back to Verna. To any passerby they might have looked foolish. As if they were flagging down traffic. Or as if they were children pretending to be trees blown by the wind.

Eye of the Moon

The summer I turned seventeen someone dropped a chocolate-covered ice cream bar in the middle of the sidewalk along Donwood Drive. Impact with the pavement had flattened it into an off-white oval shape with an irregular brown border that bled into the creamy middle. It resembled a sloppy flower, the wooden stick its short stem. Pedestrians on their way to work or to the bus stop, cyclists who insisted on using the sidewalk, joggers – that was my jogging summer – all had to make a detour around the mess or jump over. When the sun rose, the sweet substance attracted an obscene buzz of flies.

The end of the school year always coincided with my birthday, and that year it also coincided with my grandmother's corneal implant. A small piece of translucent, quivering, jelly-like substance removed from the eye of someone newly-dead was meticulously stitched into Nana's right eye under a local anaesthetic. Nineteen tiny, tiny stitches, the surgeon told my mother, and five times a day they would have to be lubricated with medicated drops. Like watering a seedling.

I had completed grade eleven and was to get a summer job. "No reason she can't help with her university costs," I remember mother saying anxiously. She was always thinking of my future. Dad, who ever since my fifteenth birthday had become convinced that all youth was headed for hell in a hand basket, agreed. "Won't hurt her one bit to get a feel for work." They had a habit of speaking about me in the third person, as if I wasn't there. Or as if I was deaf. Or still a child. The habit had solidified; maybe the indirectness offered Dad a buffer against the awkwardness of dealing with an adolescent in the volatile process of becoming a woman.

At seventeen, a job looked appealing. Jody and Claire, my closest friends at that time, had found jobs after grade ten, and the benefits of time away from parents, not to mention the extra money, weren't lost on me. I put in applications at Domo Gas and Wendy's and the library, but before anyone wanted me for an interview the hospital called to say a cornea had become available and Nana had to be there right away. Nana got so excited you'd have thought it was early Christmas instead of someone wanting to slice her eye with a laser, implant an object from a barely-dead stranger's face. She was a tough bird, Nana, and within a week she was back in her apartment at the seniors' housing. The public health nurse would come first thing in the morning, but that left four more applications of eye drops daily for five weeks.

Nana, at eighty, kept track of her arthritis medicine, time of day, the changing seasons, birthdays. "I've got all my marbles thank God," she'd say. But she couldn't manage to squeeze the eyedropper without first shutting her eye, and my mother couldn't change her vacation which she'd booked for September.

"She'll have the rest of her life to work." Dad was looking sideways at me, talking to Mother. "Why does she have to start this summer?"

He was expert at shifting position. For years he had berated the government for spending a fortune on rehabilitating criminals: "Spending my sweat-earned money on that scum." But then someone from the city office where he worked got him involved in Open Circle, an organization that matches would-be visitors with prison inmates, and now Dad was driving out to Stony Mountain every week to visit the Lifer he'd been assigned. A murderer.

"Was it a family member he killed?" Mother asked. "His wife?"

Dad wouldn't say.

I was dying to know had he raped his victim? Was he tattooed all over? Did he look evil? But Dad spoke only in generalities about his Lifer.

"There's things in this world you don't know anything about," he'd tell Mother in a voice that hinted he'd become privy to a whole new world.

To be fair, my parents didn't force me into doing the eye drops. They let me choose – a job or Nana. And they would pay me, though not as much as a job, if I chose Nana. If she'd been a complainer and fussy, like

Dad's mother, I might have balked. But Nana and I got along, though we weren't as close as when I was little and she'd sing me to sleep, or later when she taught me to make cat's cradles and play cards. She was firm and she was fun.

It would be a fifteen-minute jog to Nana's each way. I would climb the stairs to the sixth floor and maybe by the time school resumed in fall my body would have acquired a sleekness I could maintain for my graduation next year. Besides, the stretches of free time between eye drops held tempting possibilities.

"Weekends you'll be off," Mother said. "That's when your Dad and I will take care of Nana."

The mess on the sidewalk must have been new my first day of duty. It was a morning in late June, the sun brooding luridly behind the smog that hung above the shopping mall. There was no wind and I felt sticky. I didn't see the splat staring up at me until the last minute and had to take a flying leap over it to save my new runners from getting mucked up. In spite of the heat it felt good to be running and I imagined the excess flesh melting from my thighs. The chickadees were nervously busy in the trees, kids lounged in front of the 7-Eleven, and on the south side of a small white bungalow a cat lay stretched out in the sun.

"What are you doing for summer holidays?" Nana asked after I'd made her tip her head way back, then pulled her eyelid up with my thumb the way the nurse had shown me. I positioned the dropper correctly above the bloodshot, sutured eye, steadied my hand and squeezed out a tiny globule of liquid that fell more or less on target. I removed my thumb and the wrinkled eyelid fell shut like a china doll's. I dabbed away the moisture at the corner of the eye with a cotton swab and taped gauze over it, proud of myself and relieved I'd actually done it alone for the first time.

"I said, what are you doing this summer, Julia?"

Nana was pretty sharp, as I've said, but she hadn't grasped that this year, *she* was my project. In the beginning I hadn't felt locked into a schedule. Starting before ten every day, wind or calm, humidity or unrelenting sun, I would jog at three hour intervals the two blocks down our street, across the highway at Springfield Avenue, then along that winding stretch of the Donwood Drive sidewalk past the murky ice cream splat to Donwood Manor where Nana lived. The route would be as familiar as my own breathing before summer was over, a summer when everything would become desperate for rain.

"There's lots to do, Nana," I said. "Fringe Festival starts next week, I might go. They're doing *King Lear*."

"Hmm," she said. Nana hadn't read much Shakespeare.

I wasn't expecting Nana to be filled with gratitude every time I came to do the drops. Still, I thought I was making a sacrifice, even if it was small, and I wanted it to be noticed. Nana simply assumed I had come for a long visit. "Leaving already?" she'd say, totally astonished.

No point in telling her that Brendan Haverluck, who had just graduated from River East High and therefore stood on the threshold of the future, was playing the part of the fool, or that the tragedy would be condensed –

ninety minutes was max for the Fringe. This was all beyond Nana's world.

The previous winter, Brendan had played John Proctor in *The Crucible*, our school's major production. He always got substantial parts and I always got, "Julia, you'll be one of the stage hands, OK?"

"That's important," Brendan would assure me. "Stage hands are important." His earnestness had melted my inexperienced heart. Brendan was kind, and at that point in my life any kindness I encountered made me stop short. It comforted me, as if I'd come home.

A teenager playing John Proctor is bound to be at a disadvantage. I doubt if Brendan had ever grappled with questions of betrayal and integrity any more than I had. But after the show everyone said he'd been great in the role, and now he had a small part in *King Lear*.

By the time the Fringe opened, the nurse said Nana's eye was doing fine, keep up the good work, these next weeks would be crucial. The mess on the sidewalk had shrunk significantly under the relentless sun, and I had begun to fantasize running in cool rain. Dad spoke of global warming. "Scientists agree on that. There's evidence. By the time our offspring grows up, who knows." Mother, when she came home from work at five-thirty, went directly to the basement, the coolest place, and spent the evening watching TV, sipping cold beer. "Go ahead, make yourselves something," she'd tell Dad and me. "Pasta. Salad." Heat tended to reduce my energetic mother to a rag doll.

The opening of the Fringe was scheduled for Friday, more or less all day. I decided to bike down to Market

Square between the ten o'clock and one o'clock eye drops, not only because Brendan might be there, but because the novelty of the four daily trips to Donwood Manor was beginning to wear thin, Jody and Clare always seemed to be working when I was free and the days of summer vacation were running past without anything happening. Time was slipping like water through the cracks of every day.

The bike ride was not a good idea. I arrived at Market Square hot and sweaty, in no mood for the stage show that turned out to be not worth my effort. I bought a Diet Coke, found a shady place on the grass near the stage and let my eyes scan the crowd. Brendan wasn't there.

"You going to Fringe your face off?" The guy who'd sat down next to me was grinning. I wasn't impressed with that pep phrase, "Fringe Your Face Off." It was everywhere, on programs and posters and T-shirts. On the button on this guy's baseball cap. I considered it all second rate, I could easily have come up with something less juvenile.

Disparagements came easily to mind those days, less easily to my tongue. Just as I coveted a sexy body, I longed for self-assurance and poise. When I see the whole spectrum from insecurity to cockiness in every new class of nursing students I teach, I remember my callow self that summer I turned seventeen.

At Market Square that morning I wasn't interested in the guy behind the dark glasses who said that his name was David and what was mine? He was probably in his mid-twenties. Maybe even thirty. Unemployed, he said later. I wanted to move away from him, but the shade was too comfortable to give up, and when he pulled a navy nylon jacket out of his knapsack and spread it out for me, I shifted my butt onto one small corner of it because even on the hottest day grass is slightly damp. That move was a mistake.

The stage show was disorganized. Between local bands performing with dogged bravado, someone would call for volunteers to come up and make fools of themselves. David went up too. They made him lift a huge tuba to his mouth and blow. What came out sounded very much like an amplified fart and of course everyone laughed.

"So what plays you gonna' see?" he asked when he'd returned to his jacket and stretched out beside me.

"Not sure," I said. I could tell he was fishing for my plans. I wasn't ready to leave, but I sure wasn't going to trust this guy. At seventeen I was determined not to be naïve.

"Shakespeare," he said. "That's what I've got to see."

His choice surprised me and I turned to look at him for the first time. His shades hid his eyes but his tanned face was clean cut. Strong. Someone who appreciated Shakespeare might be okay.

"A play's only good if it's about the big things," he said somewhat grandly, taking off his baseball cap, revealing damp, straw-coloured hair plastered to his head. "The philosophical things. Like good and evil. Like gaining self-knowledge. Insight. *King Lear* – that's the play to see."

David stared up into the sky, his sun-browned hands clasped at the back of his head. I observed him with growing interest. What did he know of good and evil? What self-knowledge had he managed to acquire? Another rookie band rocked Market Square and we didn't speak for a while. I couldn't tell if David was absorbed in the music or in his own thoughts. He wasn't following the beat with his body, and if he was humming along like I was, I couldn't hear it.

"My friend's got a part in *King Lear*," I said when the modest applause had died down. "Friend" was not the right word. Brendan knew I existed, but we weren't actually friends.

When David said, theatrically, "*The stars above us govern our condition*," it took a few seconds for me to realize he was quoting from the play. I came back with, "*Oh! that way madness lies; let me shun that.*"

We both laughed and before I biked back to Donwood Manor, only fifteen minutes late for the one o'clock drops, we had arranged to meet on Tuesday for the seven-thirty performance of *King Lear*. I would cheat a little, give Nana her seven o'clock drops early that day so I'd have time to make it. The play would be over by nine, I calculated, and afterwards I'd take the bus and get to Nana's well before ten o'clock.

"You're not going alone to the Fringe," my mother said, after I'd informed her that I was.

Most Fringe venues were located in an area of rundown warehouses, shabby hotels, cramped art galleries and hole-in-the-wall cafes near Market Square, an ambience that left Mother uneasy.

"We'll get your Dad to pick you up afterwards," she said, but Dad was going to see his Lifer and afterwards for a drink with another volunteer from Open Circle. "I can't be at her beck and call," he complained and Mother, drained of energy by the humidity, said nothing more.

"*King Lear*." Dad was looking past me as usual. "Isn't that the one about the mean daughters?"

I wanted to tease him by reciting, *Trust not your daughters' minds/ By what you see them act*. I wanted to tell Dad the play was really about a foolish father. I had been rereading *King Lear*, preparing myself for the performance. At that moment, I felt sure I possessed more sophistication than my parents. It was convenient to forget how quickly I could be overcome by a crushing sense of my own shortcomings that sometimes left me bewildered. Or in tears.

At the School of Nursing where I teach now I am well acquainted with emotional meltdowns; our department has developed a variety of strategies to deal with them. We remind ourselves that we must be patient with our students, that maturity comes with time and experience. Of course it can also be precipitated more abruptly, even brutally.

That Tuesday evening, I arrived early at Venue #3, an old commercial building where a line had already formed at the ticket table just outside the door. I had expected to find David waiting for me but he was nowhere in sight. I got in line; he'd show up any minute.

Alone in a string of strangers, I felt exposed and wished desperately for Jody and Clare beside me, chattering about their work. Their boyfriends. Even my mother's company would have been a comfort. It was hard to feel confident while sweating in my carefully chosen black pants and T-shirt.

"I'm expecting a friend," I said to the couple behind me to prepare them for David barging into line.

David didn't barge in. The line crept slowly toward the ticket table where I would have bought two tickets if I'd had that much money. I wasn't naive enough to expect David to offer to pay for me. I bought my ticket and followed the others into the building where we waited for the elevator that would take eight people at a time to the fourth floor. Surely David would get here before it was my turn. Should I wait for him if he didn't?

When I got off the elevator I was pushed into the tail end of a queue snaking back from the theatre entrance down the crowded hallway almost to the elevator. The heat hung over us like a lid. I felt suddenly claustrophobic. Panic gathered in my stomach and threatened to rise to my mouth. I shut my eyes and imagined myself jogging the morning route to Nana's apartment, the air not cool but bearable. The slowly desiccating ice cream mess floated before me and turned into the circle of small stitches that kept Nana's new cornea in place.

A door creaked open to my left. I opened my eyes in time to see a costumed actor step out, bizarre in what looked like a toga, a sword in his hand. "Hey, thanks for coming," he said. It was Brendan. He had spotted me and was addressing *me*, not the entire queue. At that moment I should have said, "Break a leg," but I was too miserable to think of it. I considered pushing my way back to the elevator but the congestion ruled that out.

Someone near me was muttering about safety codes and some one else said the play had better be worth it.

When the doors to the makeshift theatre finally opened, the fringers poured like lava into the room and scrambled for front seats. I was glad for a little more space and looked around me until I spotted two places halfway up, in the middle of a row. "These taken?" I asked and a woman shook her head. I pushed my way in and sat down, placing the program someone had given me on the empty chair. I half turned so I could watch the door. The possibility that David would not show angered and alarmed me. I'd never been alone in any audience; surrounded by strangers, I was sure all eyes were watching me.

Just before curtain David appeared at the entrance. For exactly two seconds I considered ignoring him, then I stood and waved. When he slid in beside me his shoulder rested against mine and I didn't pull away. Relief at having someone familiar beside me was greater than the heat, greater than my anger, even greater than the queasiness that ebbed and flowed.

"Couldn't find a parking spot," he whispered. I had assumed that unemployed meant no car. I considered this new element as the curtain went up on *King Lear*.

It was an amateur, truncated version of the tragedy with none of the ugliness omitted. The cruel daughters, a scheming bastard son, the old, foolish King. Everything was exaggerated: malice and madness, violence and deceit. Even though I'd never seen the play on stage, I knew this show was crass. All that sordidness added to the heat intensified my nausea. I wanted to escape, but squeezing past the row of knees between me and the dark aisle was more than I could manage.

"What's the matter, Julia?" David whispered.

I shrugged and tried to concentrate on the fact that the heat must be ten times worse for the actors, for Brendan, than for me.

Brendan, besides playing the fool, was also a servant and when he came on stage with a sword, I knew that one of the daughters would grab it and gouge out the eyes of the good Duke of Gloucester. I rose to my feet.

"Excuse me," I said and blundered my desperate way to the end of the row then along the dark aisle to the exit. David caught up with me at the elevator.

"You'll be okay," he said when we were finally out in the street. I wanted to pull free of David's arm, hot and heavy around my shoulder, but I couldn't muster the strength.

"I'm parked near Market Square, just a block away. Can you make it?"

His truck was an old pickup, rusted and the metal broken. When David fumbled with the keys I pulled away from him. I felt I was about to enter a danger zone. "No," I said. "I have to have fresh air."

He looked uncertain then, or annoyed, but I didn't care. As we walked the short distance to Market Square, David put his arm around me once again. By now I was too shaky to resist. I recall that a band was playing; the concession stands were busy. We found a bench and David brought me a ginger ale, a beer for himself. My nausea subsided.

"Sorry," I said. "You're missing the play."

"It wasn't any good," he said and kissed me on top of my head, innocuously. My stomach heaved and I vomited some of its wretched contents, splashing his arm.

Although I was embarrassed I didn't altogether miss the hilarity of this ridiculous situation: a poorly played Shakespearean tragedy, the summer's liquid heat, my upset stomach, girl and guy. It was all of little significance, I consoled myself, as were the leaps and gyrations of the vocalist performing on stage. His howled words of lust and longing would give way in time to the next act which might be better, might be worse.

We sat there at the edge of Market Square, neither of us certain what to do or say next.

"I wonder if they cut Lear's last line," was David's awkward, or maybe gallant, effort at ending our uneasiness. By now I was sure he wanted to get rid of me and didn't know how. I couldn't recall Lear's last line so I said nothing.

"No one should cut it, it's so simple. So great. '*Look there, look there!*'" David's words were so intense I looked around before realizing he had caught me with King Lear's last words, words that should have evoked for me the tragically dead Cordelia. But at the moment they were only words. When he grinned, I responded with a sickly twist of my mouth.

"You ready to go?" David asked, toying with his truck keys. He was no longer close to me.

Another wave of queasiness welled up and I said, "Not yet."

And then a new group arrived at the square, the actors who had played *King Lear*. Brendan came with a laughing black-haired girl I recognized as one of the mean sisters. Definitely too young to know anything about life.

"Hey, Julia," Brendan said. "Hope you didn't suffocate in that hole of a theatre."

"You were great," I said, with an effort at enthusiasm. "A wonderful performance. Really."

He responded with a forced smile, as if he knew my praise was not warranted. "Are you okay, Julia?" he asked. "You look kinda pale."

Before his concern had a chance to undo me, the black-haired girl tugged at his arm. "I'm dying for a beer. I'm totally wilted." They left hand in hand.

"Let's go," I said and David led me to the truck.

"We'll go for a drive," he said in a voice intended to reassure me. "It'll clear your head."

We drove past the lights of the city, past the suburbs towards the provincial park. Some sort of denouement seemed inevitable and I didn't fight it. As I rolled down the window to let the air settle my stomach, I felt a new excitement grow inside me.

The sky was partly overcast and a full moon moved in and out of thin, breeze-driven clouds. Inside the park, David turned down a side road. He stopped the truck and we got out. He led me by the hand to an opening in the trees. In the centre of the clearing there was a shallow dip in the flatness, the grass mostly worn away. He's been here before, I thought, and felt oddly curious. He spread out his navy nylon jacket; we lowered ourselves onto it, and sat silently together. In the coolness that came with the breeze his arms around me were welcome and I didn't seriously resist until he pulled me down. Then disbelief and outrage roiled inside me and I wanted to strike out, break free, run, but I couldn't. Steeling myself, I looked past David's shoulders and saw the pale moon. The eye of God, Nana had told me when I was little.

That eye, cold and brilliant and crossed by streaks of cloud, watched as David hunched over me and his hands began staking out the territory. The smell of his sweat threatened to trigger my queasiness. I tried to rally against it, and against the fear I could no longer deny. I began to object, to push away, but David muttered, "It's too late for that." I shut my eyes then, gave up my small struggle. Behind my closed lids appeared the grotesque form of the violated, sightless Duke of Gloucester.

It was not yet midnight when David turned down Donwood Drive. My head was perfectly clear – my brain racing, my body numb as if it didn't belong to me – and my stomach was steady. I felt no emotion except relief, as if something unpleasant but necessary had been accomplished and was over with. I could have been abandoned under the dark trees in the park or dumped at the side of the road. Instead, David's rusted truck was delivering me back to where Nana waited with her sutured eye. In some foolish way I was grateful to him for not being rough. For bringing me back to Nana. We didn't speak.

By the time I got out at Donwood Manor thick clouds covered the moon. Instead of buzzing Nana, who might be in bed, I let myself into the building with a spare key I always carried and, scorning the elevator, climbed the six flights. Nana was still up, waiting for me in the big brick-red chair, her white night gown shining eerily in the dim light. The room was warm and airless, and she looked crumpled. I don't think she noticed my disarray. I opened the windows wide before reaching for the eye drops.

"Sorry I'm late, Nana."

"Your mother called. She's worried."

"I'll call her right away."

Nana's eye stared straight ahead from beneath my unsteady thumb as I held back the eyelid. It looked tired but watchful and the bloodshot redness was almost gone. I bent closer to see the nineteen small stitches that with time would dissolve, unassisted, and the implanted cornea would become part of Nana's eye. I squeezed the eyedropper too hard: three drops spilled over Nana's cheek and rolled like tears toward her chin. I didn't hit bull's eye till the third try.

"You better stay for the night," Nana said, her drowsy words conveying what seemed to me incredible wisdom.

The phone rang.

"Julia, where for godsake were you?" It was my father, his voice agitated and high-pitched. "We've been calling since ten. You're mother's going crazy."

For once he was actually speaking to *me*. Directly and only to *me*. I couldn't reply.

"You there, Julia?" he said, desperate. "Say something."

"I'm here, Dad." And then I added, my voice steady, "I'm staying overnight with Nana. Don't worry, I'm fine."

Later I would learn that Dad had returned home early because his Lifer had escaped from Stony Mountain that afternoon and the police search was on. Had he run on the spur of the moment, this murderer, driven mad by the humid heat? Or had he planned meticulously, timing his escape to coincide with the full moon? He could have been mingling with the noisy Fringe crowd at Market Square, or spying on ticket line-ups from a dark lane between warehouses, or hiding out in the provincial park under the moon's vigilant eye.

I had some crazy idea that Nana would know what I had experienced and would speak soothingly as she used to when I was little. Her words would be warm and everything would be all right. When she finally spoke it was to say she wanted to go to bed. Her nightdress was soaked with perspiration.

"You need a shower, Nana."

"A good soak in the tub," she said. "I never shower."

I wasn't sure I could manage getting my drowsy grandmother in and out of a tub. "It's okay, Nana," I said. "I'll help you."

I turned on the shower, adjusted the temperature before I struggled to get Nana's uncooperative body into position and pulled a plastic shower cap over her eyes to keep the bandage dry. I peeled off my soiled, sticky pants and T-shirt and looked down at my own pale body that had lain, warm, on the forest floor with David.

I think it was then that a bolt of panic shot through me. What if he had AIDS? What if I was pregnant? Panic gave way to remorse and at that moment I would have given anything to restructure the day. To start over. But *What's done cannot be undone.* Macbeth.

Nana was waiting in the shower. I forced myself to turn from the incident in the forest and step into the bath with her. We held on to each other as the water poured down, astonishing Nana with its bracing onslaught. Her breasts sagged to her waist, the flesh on her thin thighs hung in draped folds. It was sobering to think that in time my unwelcome roundness might be replaced by such slack and wrinkled flesh. As the water streamed sharply down, washing us both clean of the day's heat and grit, I felt anger, not fierce but sad. Against David for approaching me at Market Square and Brendan for letting the dark-haired girl lead him away. Against time that moves relentlessly forward and always forward and can't be turned back.

"You refreshed me, Julia," Nana said, when I towelled her down and helped her to bed. "You refreshed me all over. Give me a hug, now." Her gratitude and her touch released the sorrow and fear I had been fighting back, and the cheek I held against hers was wet. Nana was too sleepy to notice.

As I turned off the lights, I could feel an assertive breeze moving in. Avoiding the too-short couch, I settled into Nana's brick-red chair. The air blowing in carried the first distant grumble of thunder. And then lightning, flash after flash, each one increasing in brilliance and followed by cracks of thunder that grew vicious as the storm rushed in, bringing the longed-for rain. It pounded down outside the window, a deluge that would soak the city, pouring onto Market Square with its deserted food stalls, on the stage and the empty benches. Fringers lingering in the beer tent would be drenched and in the hollow in the park where I had lain with David the ground would be slick with mud.

Next morning the congealed ice cream on Donwood Drive was finally gone, the air fresh as I headed home, not jogging, but walking slowly. I was alive, but heavy-hearted, although all around me shrubs were dripping, the sidewalk still wet. Sparrows chirped and fluttered ecstatically.

I can't say that I entered my last year of high school with increased confidence or insight, but I remember thinking that time, though it could not be stopped or reversed, seemed able to expand and offer the bounty of another day.

Wednesday is Adoration

Egon climbs out of the car and heads down the sidewalk toward the church, briefcase banging against his thigh. Slow down, slow down, he tells himself, but he doesn't know how. On his left, the familiar clipped hedge is followed by a wire fence, then pickets of weathered wood and finally the concrete curb that marks the edge of the parking space for church staff. Everything's dusty. The traffic rushes by on his right. He shifts his briefcase. Why did he bring it? It's just another appendage. A prosthesis.

Egon settles into a pew mid-way up the sanctuary to the left, where the dusty afternoon light seeps through the coloured window. He loosens his tie and prepares to empty his mind. Not an easy undertaking. Not a brief-case he can turn upside down so its guts spill to the floor. His mind is a warren of compartments. Where to start? He starts by fixing his gaze on a mass of lilacs adorning the altar. Their colour is a deep purple, no sign yet of fading, and if he were closer there would be that familiar, cloying scent that always recalls his childhood, the long lilac hedges that flanked the sidewalk approaching the entrance to the school Egon attended as a boy. The white and purple hedges became boundaries, barricades that separated enemy teams. Once, he had been a child with no greater worry than defending himself against the other side. How did he ever get from there to here?

Egon first came to Adoration when winter had begun melting into spring, weeks before the lilacs were in bloom. The discomfort of sitting idly for an hour after work had appalled him. Doing nothing when there was so much to be done. Karla nagging him to get the lawn mower repaired before the grass started growing, to have the young cat spayed right away, to file his income tax return. Lately, she's been harping on the roof; it absolutely has to be replaced this year. She sounds frantic about the roof, but Egon knows it's really Josh she's worried about, and the burden of her anxiety on top of his own made him listen when one of the secretaries at work told the other that at her mother's church, Wednesday was Adoration. All day. Everyone welcome.

"What's it for?" the other secretary asked.

"Some kind of meditation, I guess."

"But what's it *for*?"

"Well, peace of mind, of course."

Of course.

Lately, Rachelle has been begging him to take her fishing. Personally, Egon is itching for golf, for the satisfying thwack of a good drive, the open fairways, the male cameraderie. When do we get to beat you at golf? Ed Barnes keeps asking.

How could a man possibly say to his wife or daughter or colleague: I'm going to Adoration after work. It would sound ludicrous, completely out of keeping with anyone's concept of what's normal. Instead, he tells Ed he's got to see about a new roof, or the lawn needs cutting, or he's got a dental appointment. He warns his family that from now on he'll be working late on Wednesdays to catch up on a backlog.

Egon suspects it's possible to shove all thoughts of warped shingles, unspayed cats and perfect golf greens out of his mind although he hasn't succeeded so far. Much harder to turf out his fear about Josh. It's entrenched. Sometimes he believes his family is doomed to live out their lives under the weight of the blow they have been dealt.

The pews are oak. Hard. Designed to keep the body erect, the mind attentive. Something like the screwed-down wooden desks when he started school, a fearful, chubby six-year-old. Incredible that he's still fearful, as if the years have taught him nothing. He lets his attention wander from the lilacs to a bank of lit candles. Should he light a few before he leaves? The candles waver steadily as they burn down, their light modest but faithful. Egon supposes they represent that other Light, the eternal Light that is illuminating the world. Does it flicker erratically like these almost-spent candles? And why for God's sake is the world still so filled with darkness?

During his school years Egon had often felt misplaced, as if he stood apart from the other children. Only in drawing class, holding a paint brush or a pencil in his hand, had he been happy. Not that he was good at drawing, but he remembers that he felt he had a small chance of becoming good.

Egon's flitting thoughts are not Adoration, not what he came here for. He searches for a phrase he can recite. The words that come to mind are not *Praise the Lord O my soul*, or *The Lord is my shepherd, I shall not want*. Both are recommended in the pamphlet he picked up when he entered. He's recited them on previous Wednesdays. Or tried to. Today the words surfacing from somewhere deep down are from a novel he read at university: *I want, I want, I want*. The words balloon out, demanding to be used, and he repeats them like a confession.

Two months ago, Josh was charged with break and enter, unlawful possession, and theft, and taken to the Youth Centre. He's still there, his case making its snail's progress through the sluggish judicial system. Everyday routine goes on, but life, real life, has been put on hold. They are all – Egon, Karla, Rachelle, and Josh too – kept in a state of uneasy waiting for the outcome, an outcome he suspects will bring them neither comfort nor joy, only the end of waiting.

Adoration Wednesdays are times of waiting too. Egon is not yet sure for what. For whom. Is he hoping for a miracle? Helplessness replaced by insight? Power to act? Solutions? He hasn't had a good night's sleep in weeks.

It would be easy to blame the others involved in the B&E and the theft of the van. They are older, but Egon knows his son is no slouch, he would have been front and centre in the action, and in any planning too. Anything Josh sets his mind to he usually carries out. Egon has left no stone unturned instructing Josh that success comes to those who act, who take initiative, who strike out with conviction and confidence. It slips through the fingers of the faint-hearted. Egon remembers himself hovering on the periphery of action, observing, never leaping into the fray. And he is still faint-hearted.

Josh was the one driving and he didn't pass the breathalyzer test any more than the other two. Thank God no one was killed. Only one passenger in the other car had to be hospitalized. There was a weapon too. Egon knows that Josh has had guns before, who knows from where. Guns, and Josh only sixteen, only grade eleven, for God's sake! And this is not his first time out of favour with the police.

Remembering why he came, Egon forces aside all thoughts of Josh. He closes his eyes and, resting his hands palms up on his knees, begins to breathe evenly, deeply, counting each breath. By the time he gets to ten he's become aware of an uneasy sensation of being watched. Is it the painting behind him on the balustrade of the balcony? He doesn't have to turn his head to see it, the scene is imprinted in his mind from previous Wednesdays. A white dove spreads its immaculate wings like a canopy over the crucified Christ. Egon guesses that God the Father's presence is implied, completing the trinity. The feeling of being watched by the Holy Trinity brings to mind skiing with Rachelle in La

Barriere Park when their lives were still fairly normal, though the signs of trouble were multiplying – Josh, sullen or lippy, disappearing for days, then suddenly reappearing, refusing to say much of anything. It's not uncommon, at his age, the police said. What the hell do they know?

The sky was brilliant, the snow a field of diamonds.

When they came into the wooded stretch, the trunks of aspen and birch cast thin blue shadows across the trail. Egon, angry that Josh had refused to come with them, set a good pace. The two moved swiftly, silently, past silent trees, then out of the woods into a depression in the landscape, a sort of bowl edged with trees, its base dotted with snow-covered stones that reminded Egon of white loaves. He looked up and stopped short, gesturing for Rachelle to be quiet. Ahead, three deer, arranged at different levels along the slope, stared at them with dark, unflinching eyes. They were elegant, motionless as stuffed museum pieces placed against a diorama of bare birches and fresh snow. Captivated by the perfection, and by the unequivocal scrutiny of six animal eyes, Egon felt his anxiousness ebb. The deer eventually turned and disappeared into the trees, a few snapped branches marring the ethereal silence.

Rachelle was elated, and Egon too, at this unexpected glimpse into nature's sentience. The quiet grace of the animal trio. When they continued down the trail they abandoned speed for leisure.

"Father, Son and Holy Ghost," Egon murmurs.

"It's peaceful, huh?" The voice comes as a rough whisper.

Egon's eyes fly open, his whole body jerks to attention as if he's been dealt a sharp, unexpected reprimand.

"Didn't mean to scare ya, man." The voice is right beside him, a hand rests on the pew next to Egon's briefcase. The man is young, thin, his hair a greasy blond. In the dim light of the church he appears pale, his eyes nervous and bold at the same time. He wears a black shirt and stained jeans. When did he arrive? Egon wants to shift his brief case to the other side but doesn't move.

"Peaceful, hnh?" Wary eyes are fixed on Egon, holding him.

Egon nods, annoyed. He can't turn away or close his eyes and repeat, *I want, I want*, or *the Lord is my shepherd*, he must keep alert. The young man's hand has come to rest on Egon's briefcase.

"I'd appreciate a little something. Let's say the price of a coffee?"

Egon is furious. He'd like to punch this young vagrant, send him flying into the aisle. No smell of alcohol. Drugs?

"Make it a hamburger." The whisper is louder now, as if the speaker has forgotten he is in a church.

The bloody nerve, Egon thinks, to threaten him, harass him in this place. Making his blunt demands as if he's ordering at Wendy's. The gospel advice that if someone asks for your jacket, you should give him your overcoat too, flashes through his mind. How completely without logic; in this situation it surely doesn't apply. The young man is watching him. Egon moves his briefcase to the floor, clamps it between his legs and slides along the pew until he has put distance between himself and the intruder; stubbornly he closes his eyes. *I want, I want, I want.*

All morning, father and daughter have been casting in the waters around the islands in Big Whiteshell Lake, but so far they have caught nothing. When Rachelle suggests moving to another spot, Egon starts the motor. They do not comment on rock formations as they pass them, nor on the flight of cormorants and pelicans wheeling above them. A mother duck rallies her six young in among the reeds. There are no loons, though they've looked. The peaceful waterscape reminds Egon of watercolour paintings he has seen in galleries. Gazing at the beauty all around him he is overcome with a rush not so much of happiness, but of gratitude.

The rocky grandeur of the islands, the lure of the unseen loon and the rippling waters have a calming effect, and although the fish elude them, Egon accepts the direction the day is taking. The calm grey water suddenly offers the perfect setting for conversation. What if Josh were sitting in the boat with him instead of Rachelle? His heart lurches at the thought – what would he say to his son?

He remembers his own father talking constantly; he never lacked for words of advice or reprimand. *An idle mind is the devil's workshop*, he'd say. Or, *Don't slouch like that, Egon. Don't you know your posture gives you away? Straighten your shoulders.*

It wouldn't do to simply blurt out to Rachelle, So, how's school? Egon knows that much at least. Instead he says, "Does your class ever read anything by Saul Bellow?"

"Saul who?"

"Never mind," Egon says. "Dumb question." The wind is teasing his daughter's sun-bleached hair, flinging it this way and that. Now and then she tilts her head back to catch the sun in her face. Its warm rays have brought out freckles and her arms are beginning to tan. Rachelle is slender and not tall for her age, but to Egon she looks strong. There is another long silence before he tries again. "It's about this guy, this American who travels to Africa. He's on a kind of quest."

"For what?"

"Well, maybe to find out what he wants." Egon is beyond his depth, and he knows it. He remembers little of the story, less of its meaning. Only the protagonist's plaintive outcry, *I want, I want, I want*, has stayed with him, a plea that will not let him go.

Again silence, broken this time by Rachelle. "Dad, when you were a kid, what did you like doing most?"

Egon, embarrassed to be asked about his youth, pretends to be intrigued by the gulls circling and circling above them, then plummeting for food. A white gull, its graceful wings outspread, reminds him of the dove at St. Joseph's. "I kind of liked to draw." He feels sheepish.

Rachelle looks surprised. "I wonder what Josh likes. I mean, besides trouble." She looks up at the gulls too. "It's like something's always bugging him."

Egon suspects she's recalling their last visit to the Youth Centre, all four of them together in the drab visiting room with its lumpy sofas, Egon wire-tight in his son's presence, a caseworker bustling in and out, sharp-eyed and obvious.

"Can we bring you anything?" Karla asked Josh, trying to be casual, trying to mask her breathlessness, her unbearable concern for him. "Next time we come?"

"How about a gun? A crowbar to break open the window?" Josh said and Egon cringed at his attempt at cockiness.

"Easy, Josh," he warned, but Karla was already up and stumbling toward the door, her shoulders heaving.

A sign at the entrance to the visiting room announced: No Photos. As if anyone would want to record life's lowest points. Life's total failures. No, the 'total' wasn't fair, not with Josh only sixteen. A few pictures decorated the walls, paintings made by the detainees, youths who dreaded or anticipated afternoon visits in this room with nervous parents or embarrassed, noisy friends. Egon thought the room must house an accumulated weight of disappointment, shame, anger, accusation and blame. He studied the paintings of eagles and eagle feathers, tree-bordered streams that disappeared off the edges of drawings. Faces. A lean wolf.

A small water colour caught his attention: a bird's eye view into an enclosure formed by four grey walls, the space inside them empty, and above them a glaring orange sun. Egon admired the stark simplicity of the composition, its strong lines, contrasting colours, odd perspective, but he found the emptiness inside the grey enclosure chilling. Josh saw him staring at it. "It's mine," he said.

Rachelle had said little at first. She'd pulled a beat-up candy bar from her pocket and tossed it to Josh. "Guess who asked about you yesterday?" Her voice was mischievous as if she intended to keep him waiting.

Josh caught the candy and entered into her game, guessing the mayor, Mr. Hindley the school principal, and a string of the most exemplary students in his class.

"Get real," Rachelle laughed. "It was Thomas. Wants to know when you're coming to help him fly his kite."

Bravado vanished from Josh's face. He looked uncomfortable, then helpless as he stared down at his track shoes and Egon was sure his son was remembering the years when he'd been Thomas's baby sitter.

"Tommy," Josh said when he had gathered himself. "Is he...like...growing?" His voice was guarded, carefully gruff.

"No one calls him Tommy any more."

"Tell him I'll teach him to play soccer."

"Sure. And when shall I say that will be?" Rachelle turned her gaze on her brother and kept it there.

"Just bring me that crowbar." Josh averted his eyes, but not before Egon caught a glimpse of the hurt in them. Or was it fear?

Small ripples on the surface of the water sparkle in the afternoon sun. Above them the cloudless sky spreads its blue roof, a haven beyond reach. A vastness that calls for attention. Egon is on the verge of suggesting they head for the island where they found strawberries last year, when, at last there really is a nibble on Rachelle's line, a lake trout she pulls in easily, her movements confident.

"Our luck's changing." The small success animates her, she unhooks the fish, drops it in the plastic bucket, casts again. After a time of silence and waiting that seems long to Egon, he says, "Let's move on," thinking of the strawberry island.

"No, not yet Dad." Rachelle keeps on casting. Egon watches his daughter, intrigued by her determination. Her patience. She has about her a quiet air of expectation, as if she knows there will be another bite. She's not like me, he muses. Not a bit. She is only thirteen and already growing away from him. He wants her to speak to him, longs to say something of significance back. Not advice, he's not qualified for that.

"Dad, Dad!" Rachelle shrieks as if she's caught a trophy fish, but this one proves to be only slightly larger than the first. She brings it in without help, drops it beside the first one, baits her line again and casts. This time she has hardly settled in to wait when once again she is lucky. And jubilant. Egon too is glad for the three fish that have redeemed the day.

The sun is lower in the sky when Egon points the boat to shore. They pass a few paddlers and when Rachelle spots a loon not far away, he cuts the motor so they can watch it dive and surface and for a while nothing breaks the warm silence.

"How come it's always Wednesdays you work overtime, Dad?" Rachelle asks later at the gutting table. "Just Wednesdays. How come?"

Egon, scaling and gutting beside her, searches for a good answer, and because there is no better explanation, he tells her the truth.

"St. Joseph's has become a habit," he explains, trying not to sound apologetic. "Well, not exactly a habit. It's more like missing it would be unthinkable."

"What do you do, just sit there?"

"Yeah, we sit there. It's not like there's some sort of agenda. You can just think about your day if you want to, or read one of their pamphlets. Or pray." He pauses, as if to recall what else one could do at Adoration. "Or you can just wait," he finishes lamely.

"And think about Josh, right?"

About you too, Egon wants to say, but that wouldn't be true. Really it's himself he thinks about.

"Josh would hate this," Rachelle says when Egon doesn't answer her. She's clearing off the gutting area, cleaning the knives. "Fishing with his sister – he'd think that's so uncool."

And fishing with his dad even worse, Egon thinks and tries to picture Josh in the boat with him and Rachel.

"I should have told you and Mom about Wednesdays," he says, and adds, "I'm sorry," like a small boy caught red-handed.

"It doesn't matter."

It does, Egon thinks. It matters. He is chagrined to think that his daughter's questions about Adoration Wednesday have left him feeling impotent. It matters that he has nothing to show for weeks of Adoration. He doesn't tell her about the hand on his briefcase or the footsteps of the thin young man in the black shirt following him out of the church.

It's a rainy Wednesday when Karla calls Egon at work to say Josh's hearing has been set for next week Thursday and the lawyer is hopeful he can make a good case. Egon foregoes Adoration for the first time, not without reluctance, and comes straight home. He is greeted by a savoury aroma from the kitchen where Rachelle flutters over a pot of tomato sauce. "Dad, you're home early," she says, and Karla, surprised too, asks, "Does this mean no more late Wednesdays?" A swatch of brown hair has fallen across her forehead. There's grey mixed in with the dark. But her face is lit with expectation, her body alive with it. She is beautiful, Egon thinks, taking note of the fact that Rachelle has not told her mother about Adoration Wednesday. Instead of answering Karla's question he puts his arms around her, as if to protect her against sorrow.

The news about Josh has left them agitated, has loosened their tongues, they have not chattered so light-heartedly for a long time, but the conversation quickly veers away from Josh. Egon tells Karla about his golf game last night with Ed Barnes, and she reminds him that they'll need a new lawnmower before the summer is over. Rachelle asks if she can go to volleyball camp, her friends are going. Hope has animated them, but Egon knows the hope remains tenuously balanced against uncertainty and fear.

"So you don't have to work late any more?" They have finished eating when Karla repeats her question. Rachelle gets up, carries her plate to the kitchen. Egon, afraid that they are running out of things to say and anxious to prolong the celebrative mood, spills out everything: the soothing stillness at St. Joseph's, the white dove above the martyred Jesus, the flickering candles, light coming through the coloured window. Everything is so vivid in his mind he could draw it. He adds the scent of lilacs to his story.

"Once a guy off the street came in," he says, amazed that he is telling her this. "Sat right beside me. His hand kept moving toward my briefcase. Makes you wonder what life's been like for him."

"Think he was maybe a thief, Dad?" Rachelle has returned from the kitchen and stands facing her parents.

"I think so," Egon says. "I could be wrong."

Karla, puzzled by her husband's description of St. Joseph's, says nothing. Egon looks away from her, from the hurt his deceit has caused. He's ashamed of his foolish Wednesday alibi. He and Karla have been married twenty years this summer and still there is so much about her he doesn't know.

"You'll soon have Josh home," he says, but without conviction.

"And this time we'll *keep* him home," Karla says, rallying. "Keep him *safe*."

"Mom, who said anything about coming home?" Rachelle says. "Just because there's a hearing. You can't assume. And anyway, Josh has to *want* to be safe."

"Rachelle!" The word is a sharp and frantic plea. "I don't want us to go wrong this time," Karla says. "With Josh."

"Mom, it's not just about Josh, it's about us too. Don't take it all on yourself." Rachelle's voice is firm, her eyes flash. "Maybe he should have to deserve to get out."

Egon knows that for Rachelle life is easier without Josh. And if he's honest, for himself too. But her severity disturbs him. More than anything he wants to reassure Karla, wants the outcome of the hearing to fulfill her desires. What can he say that is grounded in possibility? He wishes he could speak to his wife and his daughter with assurance, and if not assurance, wisdom. Even more than stout-heartedness, he lacks wisdom. He knows that.

Egon's mind turns to the young man who had brought his need to St. Joseph's, once only, and never returned. That day the footsteps of the young man followed him down the church aisle to the door. Although he was resentful and anxious to get away, Egon looked up, from habit, at the dying Jesus on the balcony balustrade. He didn't for a minute imagine that his young pursuer might be looking up too. He imagined his eyes glaring with hate, envy, who knows what? A malevolent gaze targeting him, boring holes through his body. Egon clamped his briefcase tightly under his arm. When he walked down the steps of the church he increased his speed, holding his free hand up to shield his eyes against the late afternoon sun. The footsteps behind him kept pace. His heart thumped faster. What might the young man attempt? As if he could attempt anything in broad daylight, rush hour traffic, sidewalks filled with witnesses.

Egon didn't look up when he reached the car. He unlocked it, got in quickly. When he had locked the door again and started the motor, he turned to the side window and found himself looking into the face of the young man who had bent down to see in. His eyes were the eyes of a child, filled with a naked and absurd hope, as if in a minute he would get whatever he asked for.

Egon turned away and, moving automatically, manoeuvered his car into the street. He was sure he felt – or heard – a thud, as if someone had delivered a swift kick against a metal panel or banged a fist down somewhere on the body of the car. It may have been simply his own body shuddering or the beating of his heart.

After the incident, he wanted to stay away from Adoration but he couldn't, and every Wednesday he looked around for the thin, dark-clad vagrant. At first he worried the kid would actually show up, then his uneasiness gave way to expectation and now he scans the pews eagerly at each visit, planning what he will say. Sometimes he sits with his hands together, sometimes open and stretched out. And every week he's left the church disappointed.

Rachelle clears the table; Karla remains in her place, her gaze fixed on a point beyond them all.

Egon thinks that if the young man should ever return, that would be all he ever wanted.

One late summer Wednesday, the air-conditioning in Egon's office fails; all day he longs for the natural coolness of St. Joseph's. He hasn't been there since the hearing, when Josh was not released after all and the shock of it cut like a knife through Karla's hopes. And his. Adoration was dropped from his schedule.

After work, Egon enters St. Joseph's, stumbling from the sun's glare into the dim sanctuary. He finds a place in the soothing coolness. Without his briefcase – he left it in the trunk of his car – he feels unencumbered. He sees the candles burning, and resolves to light several before he leaves. At first the church seems empty. As Egon's eyes become accustomed to the gloom, he notices that today's flowers are zinnias, a cheerful bunch, coral and pink and gold. Looking around he spots several shadowy heads two or three rows up.

Relieved that he's not alone, he closes his eyes and finds himself in the stark room where Josh's hearing was held. The magistrate sits behind an ominous wooden table. A lawyer comes in, looks around until he sees Josh, then nods toward Egon and Karla, takes out a notepad and pulls a chair up to confer with the magistrate. Both men wear black; their faces lack expression. Josh wears a clean T-shirt that matches his blue eyes, deepening their colour. He looks younger than sixteen, his thin bravado no camouflage for his fear. Maybe the caseworker has persuaded him to be contrite. Egon lets the scene spread before him, every familiar, vivid detail. He knows the ending. But today he tries to blank it out so the magistrate can't speak the words that returned Josh to his room in the Youth Centre. A delinquent teenager given a cruel verdict: wait.

Egon rouses himself. He stares at the shadowy figures in front of him. He notices that one of them is blond, hair newly trimmed, the ears pale shells on either side of the head. In spite of the groomed look, it is surely his young vagrant. He half-rises, reaches across the distance as if to tap the man on the shoulder, but at the last moment draws back and sits down again. He makes no pretence of keeping his head bowed. The blond presence is a sign. A reprieve. A second chance.

When the elation abates, he closes his eyes, expecting Josh, but instead, Karla is there in the dimness behind his eyelids, her back turned to him. She is at the sink, where she stood this morning filling the kettle. Egon watches Karla stoop over the kitchen counter, her hands on the kettle. He wants her to turn around, but her facing away from him is deliberate and that shocks him. He wants to reach out and touch her hair, wet from the shower.

"Karla," he says.

And then his eyes fly open. His head snaps up. There is a movement in the pew ahead, the blond man rises, moves past the other shadows in the pew, turns and comes down the aisle to his right. Egon gets up to follow, but when he reaches the aisle he realizes this man is older and heavier. It is not his vagrant after all. Disappointed, Egon continues walking and catches up with the stranger who has stopped at the door as if unwilling to face the heat. Egon takes another look at the man who says "Hi," and smiles.

"First time?" Egon asks.

"Oh no, I've been coming for a few weeks." He pauses. "But I haven't seen you before."

"Oh, I'm a regular too." Egon smiles back at the stranger who nods and moves on, leaving him oddly bereft.

It isn't until he's started his car that he remembers the candles. He turns off the motor, gets out and returns to the church where his eyes must adjust once again to the dim light. The candles are a tan colour, the wax feels dusty in his hand. He isn't sure why people light them. The first one flares alarmingly and Egon thinks of Karla, her fear for Josh. He has lit this candle for her, he decides, and this pleases him. The next one will be for Rachelle. It sputters comically before it settles into a steady light. He wants to make a wish for his daughter, but she already has so much.

This is like lighting candles on a birthday cake he thinks and chuckles, but the chuckle is short-lived when he remembers a birthday – his eleventh. A decorated cake with candles was set before him. "Make a wish," his mother said, but his mind had gone blank, he didn't know what he wanted. His hesitation made his mother anxious, his father impatient, then visibly displeased. "Don't just stand there like a stupid dummy, Egon," he said. "Can't you even make a wish?"

Josh's candle flickers and goes out. Egon is tense as he tries again, and when he sees that this time the flame is steady, he quickly lights a fourth to complete the family. What he wants to do next is pull a wish from the ocean of his wanting, a wish so precise that no one can accuse him of indecision, a wish wide enough to embrace not only his desires but Karla's too, and Rachelle's and Josh's.

It's impossible, of course. He isn't up to something so vast. It will be best to give it more thought. Perhaps next time, when he is more composed.

Deliberately, as if to redeem the hour of Adoration, Egon lights another candle, the fifth, for the vagrant. As he hurries down the aisle, his eyes sweep the scattered worshippers, glance up to the painting, the outspread wings of the dove a benediction. He will come again, but right now he is anxious to be home.

Thursday at Agape Table

On her first day Isobel was assigned to peeling vegetables, two buckets of red potatoes and one of carrots gone slightly limp. She had counted on this kind of work, had said she would do whatever was needed at Agape Table. A whole month now since she had formed the Resolve, time enough to consider whether all this was possible. Yes, she had concluded. It was. Still, the quantity of vegetables to be peeled appeared daunting and the low-ceilinged church basement, stifling. She found rubber gloves in a drawer, "Next time bring your own." Beside her a grey-haired man sliced onions. "That's his job," someone said, loudly, as if he wasn't there. As if she, Isobel, was a child unable to grasp the obvious. Her willing fingers gripped the vegetable peeler.

On the large stove against the far wall a cauldron bubbled. Broth for the soup. A small woman, her jeans and T-shirt covered by a splashed and stained white apron, presided over the cauldron. She had tied a blue kerchief over her thin, red-blonde hair. Whenever she removed the lid to look inside a cloud of steam swelled out and she leaned away from it. "They start coming at eleven-thirty," she called over to Isobel, waving empress-like in the direction of the long tables.

Eunice presided over the whole business, not just the cauldron, Isobel soon discovered. "Gotta hustle, guys," she ordered now. "Time to set out bowls and spoons. And count them."

From her place among the vegetables, Isobel could see aproned volunteers hurry into action at each command. A young red-faced woman who had stood uncertainly before an open cupboard now grabbed salt shakers and carried them with a sense of importance to the tables. Two men bringing extra chairs kept passing each other. One carried three each trip, the other four. A straight-backed woman with snow white, shoulder-length hair had positioned herself next to the coffee urns. She began wiping them with a rag, first one, then the next. She did not hurry. Every movement of her hands was graceful, as precise as if choreographed. The peeler in Isobel's hand almost came to a halt as she stared at the woman whose elegance seemed out of place. What had brought these volunteers to Agape Table?

Before Hank left for work this morning he had asked Isobel once more, "You sure you want to do this?"

She'd been holding threadbare jeans in one hand, a brand new pair in the other, unsure which to choose for her debut at Agape Table.

"Because, you know, you could work at one of those Global Gift Shops. I bet they need volunteers."

There was a Global Gift Shop close to where they lived, a renovated space artistically decorated and filled with exotica from around the world. Carved elephants and giraffes from Africa. Onyx candle holders from India. There were batik scarves and table cloths. Shelves stacked with fair-trade coffee. Handcrafted cards. Whenever she browsed there Isobel felt as if she was in a foreign country where discriminating shoppers made careful selections and paid for their purchases with credit cards.

"Yes, I'm sure," she said. A Global Gift Shop would not do.

Isobel had experienced a conversion. She was reborn, and her next door neighbour Ruth, of all people, the midwife. Ruth had persuaded Hank and Isobel to come along to the refurbished Walker Theatre where Dean Whitwell, an American, was lecturing three consecutive evenings on three vital topics: Pacifism, World Peace, and Poverty. With the September 11 devastation still so fresh in his mind, Hank had agreed, and Isobel needed no persuasion. They chose to attend the second lecture, Peace, but after supper Hank had stomach cramps so severe he claimed he couldn't move. That left Poverty.

Dean Whitwell, from Washington DC, had illustrated his lecture with stories of destitute people, mostly black, living, so to speak, in the shadow of the Whitehouse. They lacked possessions, dignity. Were homeless. He described the appalling abyss that separated the privileged from the destitute, like the gulf between poor Lazarus and the rich man in the gospels.

"Consider the truly great people of the world," he said. "The ones who have sided with the marginalized and taken up the cause of the disenfranchised. Who have not been afraid to look into the gaunt face of poverty. Who have visited the sick and imprisoned. Martin Luther King, Ghandi, Jesus. Mother Teresa. Consider Jean Vanier." His voice lowered dramatically. "Vanier. A Canadian, educated, refined. He gave up comfort and success to live with the poorest of the poor. The unlovely."

The list of the truly great did not include anyone from Winnipeg, Isobel noticed. Was that because Dean Whitwell knew no one from Winnipeg, or had no Winnipegger so far achieved true greatness?

On the way home Hank had explained *charisma*. "Some people have it," he said. "Eloquence. Personal charm. Charisma gives them influence. And authority. These people are popular." The way he said it made those qualities somehow suspect. Made it seem as if she needed to be warned against the eloquent lecturer, casual in dark slacks and a smart, multi-coloured sweater. His authoritative presence behind the lectern had put her in mind of a captain at the helm of his ship, and her attention had remained riveted on the thatch of white hair crowning his broad, tanned forehead. His eyes, from that distance, could easily be imagined bright as burning coals. As he strode across the stage, his voice, amplified by a mike fastened to his sweater, had the resonance of water rushing through a verdant landscape. Not that the timbre of his voice mattered, of course. Nor his appearance.

"I've decided I want to side with the disadvantaged," she had told Hank when they got home. She had not been able to say *poor*; the word was too naked. She wondered if her voice conveyed her seriousness. This was not a passing whim.

"Doesn't mean you're moving out, does it?"

Hank was teasing, but also, Isobel thought, alarmed. She was alarmed too.

"I really want to do this," she said. "I'm Resolved." That was a word Dean Whitwell had used throughout his lecture. "Good intentions require muscle. There has to be Resolve." His emphasis capitalized the word for her.

That night Hank had lain silent and awkward on his side of the bed and she knew she'd have to move first. When she turned toward him in the dark, his gratitude and relief seasoned their lovemaking. Afterwards Isobel had slept, satisfied, and woke in the morning, exhilarated. Fresh in her mind were the names of those who had sided with the poor. Had they all, each and every one, possessed charisma? She'd wondered about it while she poured water into the coffeemaker and retrieved bowls and plates from the dishwasher. She grabbed the dictionary and discovered that the definition of *charisma* included the phrase 'a quality of extraordinary spiritual power.' She wondered who possessed that. Dean Whitwell? She knew that *she* could make no claim to it.

While she was at it, she'd run her finger down to *charity*, a word quite out of favour, as far as she could tell. There were several definitions, one of them, "goodwill to the poor and suffering." What was so bad about that?

It wasn't as though Isobel knew nothing about poverty. She had not thought about her childhood for a long time, but now, peeling potatoes at Agape Table, she returned to those lean years. Potatoes were usually plentiful in the rural landscape where her inexperienced immigrant father had tried to farm. Bags of potatoes were hauled into the cellar each fall. Her mother, the resourceful parent, canned beans and peas from her large garden, scoured the bush for wild plums and saskatoons. Rows of fruit-filled jars marched down the pantry shelves. Her father bought a sack of flour in preparation for winter. Two cows, the old blue one and the black and white, and a shed full of chickens provided most of what else they needed.

"Sugar, raisins and kerosene," the storekeeper would recite whenever she and her father had entered the country store filled with musty odours of food and fuel. There were only ever three regular items on the family's shopping list. Was this poverty?

Everyone was poor then, she thought, though she couldn't remember going to bed hungry. Or cold. She *did* remember her mother teaching her how to cross-stitch pansies on bleached sugar sacks.

Isobel scraped the last of the flaccid carrots.

"They'll have to be cut up quick. The soup's underway." Eunice indicated the section of the counter where Isobel could work. She was brisk. Imperious. Isobel, cowed by the woman's efficiency, wondered if that counted as charisma.

By eleven-thirty the savoury aroma of soup permeated the austere basement. Isobel was not prepared for the hunger that took possession of her. And now she could smell coffee too. The onion man, his job done, was dispatched to monitor the stairway leading down from the side door of the church and to keep an eye on the poor as the first of them began dribbling in from the damp November street. Isobel stood at the kitchen door and watched an elderly couple enter, the man frail, shuffling, the woman clinging to the railing. A young mother came with three children in tow. They were aboriginal, the children decked out in decent snowsuits, and all but one wore mitts. A disheveled woman in a thin sweater came in, arms folded so she could warm her hands under her armpits. She marched directly to the table, picked up a bowl, and was first at the soup cauldron. Three self-consciously noisy teenagers with heavy boots made their way toward a spot removed from the others, where they could sit in a pack. They should be in school, Isobel thought. Or did they come here on their lunch break?

A burly man in a grey unzippered parka brought with him an icy draft.

"Close that door," Eunice yelled in the direction of the onion man. The unzippered guest headed for the food line. A new contingent came down the stairs accompanied by more winter air.

"Where's Maggie?" Eunice asked, her voice too loud. When someone said Maggie, who always filled the baskets with bread and rolls, was taking a bathroom break, she grumbled, "What's wrong with letting me know?"

While watching the dinner guests – Isobel had decided to think of them as guests – she turned over in her mind the prospect of working with Eunice Thursday after Thursday. A firm voice interrupted her speculation. "Isobel, you'll take charge of the bread."

She wished it was fresh from the oven and that she could cut wide slices, or better, break off generous chunks, warm and crusty. But it was day-old bread, white, sliced, donated by a local bakery that also donated bags of stale doughnuts stuffed into plastic bags and stuck together in gooey lumps. She looked at the bread with distaste, reluctant to begin, until she sensed she was being watched.

"We take what we get," Eunice said.

Isobel had filled the baskets with sliced bread and was spelling off the soup server when the last cluster of latecomers clumped down the stairs. Trailing at the end with a barely noticeable limp was a black-maned man in a blue and green plaid jacket.

She paused, soup ladle in hand, and surveyed the assembled company with curiosity and a feeling she could not define, though it had to do with warmth and communion. Where did these people live? How did they navigate the days and seasons? Where had they slept? She scanned the long rows of heads bent over bowls, spoons conveying the cooling soup to open mouths. A diffusion of noise rose from the tables. Not the noise of conversation, but the noise of eating, of bodies shifting, the scrape of a spoon against a bowl, and, accompanying everything, the incessant hum of the furnace fan. A small child interrupted the general noise with her specific, miserable wail. A boy yelled out "I hate this stuff. It's yucky." The sweater woman hoisted herself up from the table and brought her bowl to the cauldron for a refill.

The largest meal Isobel could remember preparing was Hank's fortieth birthday dinner. His brothers and their wives had come, his mother, several buddies from the company where he still worked, and Ruth from next door. Eighteen people. Bea and Dylan were teenagers then, and not much interested in helping her prepare. She hadn't insisted. Hank was essentially a meat and potatoes eater, so she bought a good-sized roast and gravy mix, just in case, as she was never good at gravy. The most experimental item on the menu was the pear and red onion salad with a clove-and-vinegar dressing. Most of it was left untouched, the pears turning dark in spite of the vinegar. She had never tried it again. The best thing at the dinner was not the birthday cake she had decorated with candles and curls of shaved chocolate, but the poem Dylan had written for Hank. Something about having the greatest Dad in the universe. Afterwards Bea had helped clean up.

"Isobel, you go ahead, eat," Eunice said in her brusque way. "There's soup left."

But Isobel's hunger had passed. "They said we should, you know, mingle with the people..." She looked at Eunice, uncertainly.

"Oh, sure. Go ahead, go ahead." A wave of Eunice's hand.

"We don't just feed bodies," the director who interviewed Isobel had insisted. "We also consider the individuals, the persons in those bodies. It's possible they need attention. Encouragement. A listening ear." Isobel had wondered why an interview was necessary for a non-paying job; nevertheless, she'd lapped up the director's words and resolved to take the time to listen.

Several volunteers were already mingling with the guests. The onion man had squeezed in with the burly teenagers who eyed him briefly, then continued eating. She would have to put one foot in front of the other and approach someone, since no one was likely to wave her over, the newest volunteer. A stranger. She would have to choose, and by choosing to give her attention to one particular face of poverty, leave others out. Would she make the right choice?

The plaid jacket caught her eye. The dark-haired man in it was seated at a half-filled table, chewing on a slice of bread. She could not tell how old he was, forty or close to sixty. When she sat down opposite him, he did not look up. His bowl was almost empty.

"Could I get you a refill? Coffee?" She remembered too late Eunice's insistence that everyone had to help themselves, unless they were disabled. This man was not disabled, though he had limped down the stairs. He looked up now without raising his head, and it seemed to Isobel that his eyes contained a measure of cunning. He moved his tongue over his yellowed teeth and did not speak. His shoulders were broad, his lean face weathered by wind and sun. There was an assurance in his manner, as if he knew all about soup kitchens, this one and others.

"Colder today," she tried, thinking that his jacket was not very thick.

"Got a cig?" the man asked.

"You can't smoke in here."

"I *know* that." He waved his hand toward the door.

"No," Isobel said. "I don't. Have cigarettes."

The man looked as if he disbelieved her. He picked up his misshapen doughnut, scrutinized it, put it down, looked up again at Isobel. "Got some spare loonies?"

Isobel shook her head. "Never give them money," the director had said. "We offer only meals, and addresses of agencies we can refer them to." Very likely this man knew the rules better than she did.

They sat silent. The man continued to chew his bread. Isobel studied the frayed cuffs of his plaid jacket, the toughness of his large hands. When he hoisted himself abruptly from his chair and walked away, she felt as if he had slapped her hard in the face. She felt deflated. But he was not heading for the stairs, just getting coffee. Two steaming mugs, one for her.

"Rick," he said, extending a hefty hand across the table. His grip was firm. Beefy. Confident.

He's been here before, she thought.

"Me, I'm here every day," he said, as if reading her mind. "Ever since I got to Winnipeg. The hostel just off Main."

"Job hunting?" Was this a good question? What did it imply? Isobel did not want to talk about the weather.

He shrugged. "Haven't seen you here before," he said.

"My first time. I peeled the vegetables."

"Did a good job." Rick grinned, revealing dark gaps between stained teeth.

Isobel couldn't decide whether the grin was sly or just scornful. Or was it a challenge? "I'll be coming every Thursday," she said.

They sat in silence until Rick had finished his coffee.

"See you next Thursday then." He stood, unsmiling, and buttoned his jacket. No cap or gloves. Before he left, he let his eyes move over her in careful, unhurried scrutiny, as if committing her to memory. The boldness of his gaze left her uneasy. She wanted to turn away.

"Your hands will be cold," she said.

Rick ignored that and started for the door. Isobel wanted to call after him, tell him he could help himself to extra doughnuts, but he probably knew that too, and the after-lunch blur of conversation would have drowned out her timid voice. She began gathering up bowls.

When the last guests had left the church and the main lights were turned off, a mingled odour of perspiration, musty clothing and soup pervaded the basement. While stowing plastic containers of leftovers into the fridge, Isobel felt suddenly as if she were being watched, possibly by Eunice. When she looked up a man was standing halfway down the stairs, rubbing his hands. She thought it was the guest in the plaid jacket, returned for the warmth of the church basement, but in the dim light she couldn't be sure. When she next looked up, the stairway was empty. She scraped food scraps into garbage bags, amazed that even here there was so much waste. After the dishes were washed, the tables wiped, she was satisfied that she had made a good start in translating her Resolve into action. She had counted sixty guests – sixty guests served on her first Thursday at Agape Table.

The wind had picked up, Isobel noticed, as she headed for the bus stop. Low clouds released a scattering of powdery snow and already a thin layer covered the dirty sidewalk while swirls of it filled the air. The street was becoming opaque. Eerie. She pulled her hood down over her forehead and strode resolutely into the wind. When she next looked up she spotted a figure, back turned to her, hands stuffed into pockets, standing near a spiky hedge that paralleled the sidewalk near the bus stop. The capless figure wore a blue and green plaid jacket. She slowed her steps, considered going back to the church, or crossing the street to a three-story house converted into a travel agency. Economy Tours. Or should she keep her head low, eyes averted, walk quickly by and wait at the next stop? There was little traffic and no bus in sight. The afternoon was melting into evening. The waiting figure turned.

"Well, whaddaya know." Rick's voice was flat.

Isobel was unable to speak and her silence made a space between them in the murky afternoon. Rick was in no hurry to fill that space, as if he knew that here, on neutral ground, he held an advantage, and that advantage grew with the silence.

"Maybe this is a good time for them loonies, eh?" he said, finally, his voice still flat but edged now with steely sarcasm "No stupid rules here. I really could use a smoke."

Isobel tried to gauge the smile that hung on Rick's face. It was rueful, she thought, as if he regretted what he was saying but had to say it. He took a limping step toward her. She edged back, afraid.

"Whatsa matter? You look kinda nervous." Rick stepped closer still, pulling his hands out of his pockets as if to use them. Such large hands. Had he been waiting all this time? Had he calculated when she would finish her shift at Agape Table? The possibility of deliberate intention, of premeditation, unnerved Isobel more than anything. His shoulders loomed in the dim light. His leathery face seemed to float above the street and his enormous hands frightened her. She couldn't stop her own from creeping down to feel the bulge of her wallet in her jeans pocket.

"Don't carry a purse, it's too obvious," Hank had said that morning.

"Just a couple of loonies." Rick's wheedling tone implied that she was making a mountain out of his molehill request. He stepped even closer. She avoided his gaze, avoided the authority his eyes held. But she did not want to flee, not without speaking.

"I have to go," she said.

"Nobody's stopping you." His voice was soft now. Mocking. It caught her off guard and she tried to gauge the intention in his eyes, peering out from behind dark strands of wind-whipped hair. The eyes of an animal, she thought as she backed away. A caged and vicious fox. Or the gaze of poverty, a poverty she knew nothing about. His hand moved and she shrank further back. It moved to his chest pocket, pulled out a pack of cigarettes, removed one and stuck it in his mouth that was now twisted into a leering grin. She turned from it.

A red neon sign in the window at Economy Tours shone luridly in the growing dark. "Affordable Get-

Away Packages," it announced. "Escape the Snow." Isobel's eyes clung to it. Still no bus, but a sudden cluster of cars swooshed by, released from the traffic light a few blocks back. For Isobel, a source of comfort. And strength. When the street was clear again, she stepped off the curb and walked across.

"See you next Thursday," Rick called after her. It sounded like a joke. But also like a command.

Isobel opened the door to Economy Tours and stepped inside.

"Can I help you?" The woman behind the computer wore black-rimmed glasses and spoke with the raspy voice of a smoker.

"Just warming up," Isobel said. "Until the bus gets here." She stamped snow from her boots. Through the agency window she could see Rick's solitary figure, a murky silhouette in the snow-swirled street. She would simply wait here. She would call Hank to come and pick her up after work. He would not let her return to Agape Table. Not next Thursday; not ever again. This assurance enabled her to find a chair away from the window.

The woman turned to her keyboard and made a show of ignoring Isobel who was neither client nor friend, but an intruder. Aware of the woman at the desk, Isobel scanned the enticement of gaudy posters that surrounded her. Copacabana Beach. The Eiffel Tower. A cruise boat on the blue Caribbean. Castles on the Rhine. The splendid ruins of Macchu Piccu. The woman at the desk looked up from her work, her eyes beaming disapproval in Isobel's direction. Embarrassment flooded Isobel, who felt suddenly like a tourist who'd been caught shoplifting in hostile territory, and could produce no passport, no ID of any kind, and no money. Disoriented by the abundance of rich colours that danced and spun around her, promising excitement and adventure, she could not escape the dearth that lay uncovered inside her. She was empty of courage. Empty of confidence and spirit. She had dared to bring her emptiness to Agape Table. It was no wonder Eunice had so easily cowed her. And here, every glance and movement of the woman at the desk informed her she was treading on ground she was unfit for.

"It's coming. The bus." The glasses gestured in the direction of the window. "If you step out quick, you can make it."

Isobel turned to the window. She could see the bus, large and orange in the monochrome street. It seemed to skid slightly as it slowed and came to a halt. Against the surrounding gloom its lit interior appeared bright, the passengers plainly visible. She could see the plaid jacket enter. The man paused beside the driver, fumbled with his fare, then made his limping way down the aisle toward the back where he lowered himself heavily into a seat, his slumped body isolated in the mostly empty bus that swerved slightly as it began to move, slowly, like a ship heading out to sea. The sidewalk was left empty.

"There won't be another for twenty minutes." The woman's words rang with accusation. Worse, judgement.

The glance Isobel offered the woman was abject. Overcome with shame, and mustering what was left of resolution she pulled her hood back up before she made her way across the street to the bus stop.

"I peeled vegetables,' Isobel said at supper.

Hank looked up from his beef stew and potatoes, his face gone blank. Isobel guessed that her Resolve lay buried in his mind and had to be extricated from a tangle of the day's obligations. He had come home late, delayed by a meeting that had dragged on and obviously still preoccupied him.

"Agape Table," she reminded him.

He bestirred himself, spoke with a guilty heartiness: "Oh yeah. So how did it go?"

"Not bad. One of the regulars waited at the bus stop with me." Isobel paused for a response.

Hank, unsure what was expected of him, continued with the stew for which Isobel had cut up a lot of carrots and onions. She had added a large bay leaf, a bunch of fresh parsley, basil and a dash of nutmeg. She watched her husband empty his plate.

"Good stew," he said, reaching for more bread.

And then, since she had no desire to eat, she could have offered him the details of her initiation at Agape Table. The gathering of the poor. The aroma of soup she had helped make. She could have built up to the incident at the bus stop. Rick's large hands. The shape-shifting smile on his leathery face. Her fear. She could have told him how poverty surrounded her in the dark street. How it lived inside her too, a scary presence that swelled to occupy all available space. Where others – like the American who had spoken on greatness and Resolve – had charisma, she had nothing.

"Will you go again?" Hank pushed his plate aside, ready for dessert and coffee. The tablecloth showed a scattering of crumbs and a few gravy spots. "You don't *have* to, you know."

Isobel didn't say yes or no, but she felt an unexpected rush of annoyance at Hank for letting her off the hook. For offering an easy out when she had counted on his reassurance, had expected a little praise. The annoyance swelled and became indignation. Anger. At the man in the plaid jacket who had made her afraid, and the woman at Economy Tours who had shamed her. At Eunice, who ordered everyone around. At herself most of all. Anger filled her up, fuelled her as if she'd wolfed down a huge meal. She cleared the table without speaking, holding her head erect, controlling every movement. She made several trips to the kitchen. Hank followed, to start the coffee.

Before cutting the lemon pie, Isobel found a pencil and strode to the calendar that hung above the purple gloxynia. Mid-November and it was blooming lavishly. Gripping the pencil to steady her fingers she circled the remaining Thursdays in the month of November. Her knuckles were white and the pencil marks dark on the page as she flipped to December and continued.

Saved

Masha is telling me how her father was saved. His salvation was engineered by her mother who had just given birth to Masha when the order came for the men of the town to prepare for duty on the clean up crews. With a pregnancy and a birth so recently accomplished, Masha's mother refused to let her husband leave her alone in Dergazhi. How was she to care for the helpless little creature? Several years ago she had given birth to a boy who died within weeks. Did her husband's brain have no idea how scared she was for this newborn? But no matter how his wife badgered him, Masha's father had failed to muster sufficient gumption to plead with the manager of the collective whose headache it was to round up men for the job.

Obviously the manager had no choice. Action was required at Chernobyl. Orders had been issued. People were falling ill as clouds of poison wafted westward intent on circling the globe. The world watched and prophecies of evil still to come multiplied. The disaster had upstaged growing hopes of Peristroika.

It was her mother, Masha tells me, who confronted the manager, her arms squeezing her baby girl tight, as if she held a weapon. Terror blazed in her eyes. The man relented; Masha's father was saved.

"The men who go to Chernobyl," Masha says, "they get sick. So many die, Kevin, you don't know. So many funerals in Dergazhi."

Last weekend Masha took me to Dergazhi, her home town. She introduced me to her parents, Lena who works in a bakery and Pavel who built the family home. After a lunch of cabbage soup and bread we walked along the gravelled street past the vocational school with its broken glass and neglected grounds, past shuttered houses surrounded with dusty hedges, chickens, pigs, past the statue of Lenin and a bust of Nikolai Gogol. She showed me the elementary school she had entered at age six and will enter again this fall as a teacher of English. In front of the school a WWII fighter plane mounted at an angle appeared ready for take-off. This is the town her father had been saved for. I was relieved to return to Kharkiv at the end of the day. Masha walked with me to the bus stop, and I waved goodbye to her from my window seat, remembering that other farewell, when I'd said goodbye to Laura. Although the memory left me dispirited, I clung to it all the way to Kharkiv.

English is being spoken at the table next to ours. The man speaking it is middle-aged, beefy. His hair has begun to grey. He speaks slowly, distinctly, leaning across a giant ice cream sundae he is sharing with the woman facing him. She is younger, but also nearing middle age, pretty in her low-cut floral blouse, her dyed blonde hair. Occasionally I get a snatch of the man's words: *I'm not giving up*, *I'll try again*, and *Don't worry, you shouldn't worry so much*. I'm pretty sure I hear him say *Canada*. He enunciates carefully for her benefit.

I lean across my espresso to Masha. "How much do you want to bet that couple met on the internet?" I gesture with my head and her head follows. When our glances meet again she is smiling, but her smile is grave. She traces the rim of her coffee cup with a slender finger. Her skin is tanned porcelain.

I have come to Kharkiv from Canada to teach at the English Summer Institute. Because of my experience I've been given the best class – all of my students have taken English since elementary school and all of them are determined to speak it as if they were born in North America. Masha is not the best in the class, but she's fairly good, except when she's nervous. Every morning she boards a bus in Dergazhi for the slow ride to Kharkiv where she connects with the Metro. She is always the first of my class to arrive.

This small café on Sumskaya Street is Masha's idea. We've been here before, after classes, just the two of us. My other students plan group excursions to museums, galleries, parks, and their favourite, the zoo. But Masha wants me to herself. She is serious, and wants more than a chance to practise English. She keeps her dark, lustrous eyes fixed on me. Tired after three one-hour classes, I find little to say as I sip espresso.

The Summer Institute is organized by the Abundant Life Church of Canada. Every day there's a thirty-minute chapel right after the first class. Students come to it directly from their lessons, but since chapel attendance isn't mandatory, some of them spend the time over coffee instead. Or a smoke.

I was not required to sign a confession of faith or declare loyalty to Abundant Life, but it was mutually understood I'd go with the program even though I'm not affiliated with the church. I didn't mention my reservations about the religious jargon. The 'getting saved', 'encounter with Christ' and terms like 'justification' and 'atonement.' What does a word like 'redemption' mean to Ukrainian students a decade after the 1991 coup? I have no objections to the chapel, I always show up, but I wonder if the rest of the team thinks I lack conviction. I'm sure Don, my roommate, thinks so.

Masha never skips chapel. Today over espresso I ask her what she likes about it. She hesitates, as she often does before speaking, to clarify her thoughts or marshall the correct English words. "They make it, I think, too easy," she says finally. "It is all so very…so…." she move her open hand back and forth parallel to the table top with its red cloth.

"On the surface, you mean?"

"Maybe like that. On the surface." She accepts the offered word and keeps moving her beautiful hand, but now it's become an impatient gesture as if she's shooing away a pesky fly. "They leave out something important.

Something like..." The words she wants won't come and I can't help her. She lets it go, turns to me and says, "God is living in Ukraine. He is a long time living with us here."

"So what do you get out of chapel?" I'm not trying to play the devil's advocate; I just want to know.

"Every time I learn new vocabulary," she says. "I write the songs in my book. And words the chaplain says. To look up in the dictionary." She pulls a notebook from her bag, riffles through it. "Here," pointing to an open page. I take the book from her and recognize the song from that morning's chapel:

God our protector, keep us in mind
Always give strength to your people.
For if we could be with you, one day in time
It is better than a thousand without you.

There isn't a single word Masha didn't already know.

"It is good," she says. "Beautiful. I like it."

I begin to see that Masha has learned to take what she needs from the chunks and fragments a given day offers.

We finish our espresso and I pay the server. As we get up to go, the beefy man whom I suspect of browsing the internet with intent rises too, turns and offers his hand. "I'm Bruce," he says. "From Canada. Couldn't help hear you guys speaking English."

I tell him my name and Masha's and he introduces the blonde woman. "Tanya. We just got married."

My eyes seek Masha's but she's studying Tanya who scoops a spoonful of the ice cream sundae she's been sharing with Bruce before she too rises. She turns to Masha, addressing her in Ukrainian. Bruce tells me he's trying to get permission for Tanya to come to Canada, but the Canadian Embassy won't budge, not even for a visit. Not even now that they're married. "This is my third trip to Ukraine," he complains. "They're so stupid. So goddamn unreasonable."

He pauses, as if he's said too much. "What brings *you* here?" he asks, his eyes shifting to Masha, calculating our connection.

I tell him about the Summer Institute and when he hears the fees are minimal he wants to enrol Tanya whom he's set up with a pricey English language tutor. I tell him the Institute is full, and, anyway, soon to conclude.

"How did you meet Tanya, if you don't mind my asking? Was it the internet?"

"Actually, yeah. I picked her from a bunch of photos posted on this website. We started writing. And I came here to check her out, twice before. This time I thought if I marry her it should be easy to get her to Canada. But it's not. Nothing's easy about it. Everything's so bloody slow. And it's costing me."

Bruce's words have become an irritating whine. It's on the tip of my tongue to ask how come a Canadian male obviously not completely without means would choose to find a wife in a foreign country? Why does he want to marry a stranger who can't speak his language and he can't speak hers? Has he been married before? He bears the weathered, dejected look of a failed prairie beef producer.

Tanya is unsmiling and fidgety as she talks with Masha. It turns out she's scared, that's what Masha tells me when we leave the café and step into Sumskaya Street where the afternoon has turned muggy. "Tanya asks me, do I know a Canadian lawyer? She says how can she know what this man thinks in his head."

"What do *you* think he thinks?" I ask.

She shrugs. "He say to Tanya he is divorced. But she can not be very sure about him."

We walk slowly. The humidity is oppressive, leeching me of any remnant of energy, but Masha looks cool. Her narrow, high-heeled shoes keep pace with my walking boots.

"My friend, she wants to marry an American," Masha says, several blocks later. "She wants to find one. It's for her too hard to make a living. She has a baby."

"Where's the father?"

"She didn't want him. Not to marry."

"And she thinks she'd like to find a total stranger and go to America?'

"It's her only – how you say? Solution, yes? Her only solution."

Masha stops in the street and faces me as if she is about to tell me something so important she needs my full attention. "In my country it is like this between the girl and her boyfriend: After a while a baby comes. Then they live together. With parents. Then a wedding." She pauses. "Then, it happens very often, they can not any more – how you say? – stand each other. The husband goes. And the girl, she is now alone. Of course with the baby. And my friend anyway did not want to marry this boy."

I'm not sure what Masha expects of me. Or how we got on this topic. "What about contraceptives?" I blurt. "Don't girls get medical advice? A doctor or someone?"

"We not like visit doctors. Or hospitals. We not trust them. It's for the boy to bring the, you know, that thing." She motions nervously with her hand. "But he doesn't always. He doesn't want to use that." And after a pause, "But I think anyway a girl likes a baby. She is so glad for it. Very glad."

"I hope your friend will be happy," I respond lamely.

"Happy?" Tanya laughs as she looks up at me with something like pity.

We continue down Sumskaya. The leaden sky has gathered to rain and when it comes, it's an explosion, sudden and hard. Both of us are soaked when we reach the nearest Metro entrance, running, Masha graceful even on those ridiculous heels. We join the dripping crowd in the covered stairway waiting out the deluge. Again and again lightning splits the afternoon darkness and cracks of thunder follow, overriding the rain's drumming. Conversation is impossible.

Don is caught in the storm too. When I get to the dormitory his soggy clothes are heaped beside his bed. He's down the hall singing "God our protector, keep us in mind." His petition rises above the noise of the one cold shower that serves all fifteen of the teaching team.

"You were with Masha again," he says, stepping towel-draped into the room we share.

"Do you think getting saved is easy?' I ask, side-stepping his comment.

"Easy? Yeah, it's easy. It's pure and simple, Kevin. Like a present someone hands you. It doesn't cost you – you just got to take it."

"Like amazing grace?"

"Yeah, yeah. Like that." Don misses the cynicism. He possesses none himself and can't recognize it in others. Instead, he has enthusiasm. "That's the good news," he says "That's why we're here."

"I don't know about you," I say, "but I was recruited to teach English." And they must have been desperate to take you, I think. You can't even speak properly.

"It's not about teaching English." Don is becoming zealous. I grab my towel and head for the door.

"It's not *just* about teaching English," he says and I sense a backing down, a crack in his confidence. "It's about sharing good news."

His face has become transparent as a child's. I feel mean as I shut the door behind me and run for the shower. A gush of water drowns out his words, but now I hear another voice. A voice impossible to silence. Laura's.

I have to do this, Kevin. Does that sound crazy? How can I put it. It's like I've been given so much, it wouldn't be right not to offer help where it's needed. Well, health care's needed in Guatemala. I feel almost like...like I'm being told to go, or maybe not told, but invited. As if this is what I'm meant to be doing. As if this is the biggest opportunity I'll ever get in my whole life.

Laura accepted the invitation, packed her toothbrush and her nursing degree and flew to Guatemala. She left a good job as an OR nurse for the biggest opportunity of her life. Left her friends, her family, her country. Left me.

"We saw you go into that café. With Masha," Don picks up the topic when we are both dry, our wet clothes left hanging in the common laundry room.

"So?" I want to say, but stop myself because it would sound defensive, as if there's something to explain.

"Is she a believer?" he asks.

"You mean is she born again? Is she saved? Is she baptized? Has she joined the church?"

My barrage is too sharp; Don looks up at me, a mix of hurt and caution in his eyes. Ashamed of my rudeness, I watch him turn to open the journal he's always writing in. My guess is that after he's finished summarizing the details of the morning and copying the scriptures read in today's chapel, our conversation too will be recorded in his book.

Don was not given his own class; he's an assistant, and a big hit with the students. When classes are over they corral him for sight-seeing or swimming with a picnic afterwards. They end up in some Soviet flat where he's fed *borschtch* and *pelmenyi*. He returns well past midnight, often waking me, and I see him writing in his journal.

Don probably wonders why I'm still single at twenty-eight. He's told me he is considering missionary work. He's praying for the right person to share his life with. She'd have to be someone who feels called to follow the Holy Spirit, maybe to a foreign country. He speaks of this with an earnestness that strikes me as curiously unworldly. To ward off further conversation with my roommate, I rummage in the closet for my backpack that contains in a zippered pocket an email printout. I carry it to my narrow bed and unfold it.

Dear Kevin:

This morning the OR *was humming. We started with an amputation. The infection in the patient's foot was an ugly mess and so advanced we couldn't save the foot. He was an old man, emaciated and pretty scared. Then we had a little girl who'd lost most of her jaw to cancer. She's had massive chemo and two reconstructive surgeries already, and who knows how many more to go. Her eyes, just before the anaesthetic, were so pathetically trusting, I had to look away and force myself to concentrate on instruments and procedures. I won't bore you with a litany of today's surgeries. Most of them were critical. Not all past hope, but I wouldn't guarantee the eventual outcome of any.*

Kevin, you ask if I'm happy here. I don't know about happy. Not always, I guess. But I think I'm meant to be here. Don't get me wrong – I'm not being self-righteous. At least I'm trying not to be. I can't save the world, I know that. But I have this opportunity to help. And it doesn't mean I don't think about you. But not every minute, you can imagine how that would play out in the OR. *But sometimes, Kevin, I want you so much it hurts, and then I replay the mental videos I carry around with me, of the times we were together.*

There's a fantastic beach on the Pacific near this hospital and I'm heading for it right after I click 'send.' Picture me floating on the wide and watery expanse of the Pacific Ocean. Out there it'll be quite safe to think of you. Laura

I fold up the email, Laura's last, and once more picture her running across the burning white sand and flinging herself into the water, offering her body to the rise and dip of the waves. I hear her call out and watch her flail, aggressively at first, then frantically, then feebly, then not at all. Her body vanishes like a bit of ocean flotsam, reappears for a moment, and then is gone. A malevolent and arbitrary riptide biding its time beneath the water's surface has been roused. The locals name this force The Snake. The Snake has hauled her in and the ocean closes around her leaving only rough water where a moment ago her living body was welcomed by waves that will eventually wash her back up on the beach. The scene fades. The turbulence replaced by an unearthly silence.

On the last Friday of classes Masha insists I must come to Dergazhi one more time. I must stay till Saturday. Till Sunday, *please.* The team leaves Monday early, by train, for Kiev. Everyone has weekend plans, last minute sight-seeing, goodbye parties with students. Masha's invitation doesn't thrill me, but neither do I relish the prospect of a dull weekend in the drab dormitory. Her father meets our bus and her mother has prepared salads, roast pork, fresh pastry pockets with cherries inside. She's exhausted herself. Pavel pours wine he's made with apples picked from a tree in the backyard. The few Kharkiv students I've visited live in crowded flats in Soviet style buildings, but in Dergazhi small houses line the streets. This one is plain and still unfinished.

Both Pavel and Lena are so thin they look haggard. They eat slowly and not very much. I am ravenous. Masha sits beside me, her arm brushing mine as she offers me platters of food while she nibbles at cucumber slices. When coffee is served, Pavel lights a cigarette and Lena rallies, as if refuelled by the little she has eaten. Questions erupt as though the lid has blown off a reservoir. She directs them at me and Masha translates. What kind of house do I live in, in Canada? Do I live with my parents? Are they in good health? Are they educated? Do I drive a car? What kind? Do I get a good salary? Does anyone in Canada speak Ukrainian? Is it true every kitchen in America has a dishwasher?

She stops to let Masha ply me with more food. When I shake my head, no, no more, she continues. What do I think of Kharkiv? Do I get paid at the Summer Institute? Am I married? Am I a missionary? Do my students speak English fluently? Does Masha? What are the opportunities for young people in my country? Young people like her daughter, for instance, who speak English? Will I come back next year?

Pavel takes no part in the grilling. Masha lets the questions, and my answers, flow through her as through a conduit. But eventually she becomes impatient. She turns to Lena and speaks quickly in Ukrainian. The questions stop. Supper is over. I want to help with the dishes but Lena, assuming the authority of a stage manager, shoos me and Masha out the door.

Twilight is settling on Dergazhi as we wind our way along a street that takes us to the outskirts of the town. I think of the men sent from Dergazhi to Chernobyl. From life to death. We follow a path up a small hill covered in some kind of short forage crop. I know little about farming, but Masha tells me it's the second growth. She sits down to remove her shoes, the ones she always wears, and motions me to sit beside her. The ground is cool.

"I come here for the stars," she says. "It's the best place. Here you can see how close they are. How mysterious."

But the sky tonight is overcast as it so often is this summer. At supper Pavel had spoken about the possibility of more rain. It's good for growing, he'd said, bad for harvest. The rains started in spring, long before I came to Ukraine, and they haven't stopped.

I ask her if this is where she brings her boyfriends and she says who is there in Dergazhi to bring? She is old at twenty-one. In her country it's a problem, she says. Sons or daughters, although adults, have no choice but to live with their parents. Then she admits that in early summer she came here every night with the son of the mayor, a nice young man, the only one in Dergazhi she knows of who has ever attended a symphony concert in Kharkiv.

"What's his name?"

"Sergey."

I grin in the darkness. Sergey is easily the most common name for boys here. There were at least four Sergeys among my students.

Masha asks me if I like Russian literature and I tell her I have read *Anna Karenina* and *The Brothers Karamazov*. Do I know the work of Nikolai Gogol? No? She begins telling me one of his long stories. She has moved closer and her scent mingles with the fragrance of damp hay. The story is about a man who schemes to acquire status by becoming a land owner, at least on paper, and he begins by buying the names of deceased, but still-registered, peasants. Masha hesitates often in the telling, searching for the right words until the story becomes tedious. "It's called *Dead Souls*," she says, "and it's very famous."

"Buying souls, that's a pretty ghoulish business, don't you think?" I ask, to show I've been listening. I expect her to ask "What is that, *ghoulish*?" Instead she laughs and says. "Oh you are so very serious, Kevin. Don't be tonight so serious." She reaches for me with her warm, slender arms. "Lie down." She leans her head against my chest and pushes playfully against it.

"You never say me about Canada," she says when she has me beside her. "Is in Canada a girl waiting for you?"

"No. No girl's waiting for me." I try to sound carefree, not bitter.

Before Laura left me, we walked in the park one Sunday morning after a snowfall so heavy the evergreens were loaded down with it. Children struggled through the snow or fell backwards into it and made snow angels. "Isn't it just so beautiful it hurts your gut?" Laura said.

"Say me please about Canada," Masha says, summoning me back to her.

"It's just so beautiful it hurts your gut," I say.

Masha doesn't ask for more about Canada. We lie uncomfortably together staring into the darkness until she says, as if she is my mother, "Come. You must come home."

When we reach the house it is dark. A bed has been made for me on the sectional living room furniture every Soviet home boasts, but Masha takes me by the hand and leads me through the darkness past the room where her father and mother are sleeping and up the stairs. When we get to her room she doesn't turn on the light, but a faint glow from a light somewhere outside the open window mitigates the darkness. We slip out of our clothes and into the narrow bed. Into each other.

When I wake and grope in the darkness for my clothes, Masha rouses too. I ask her should I go to the bed prepared for me, but she only laughs and moves toward me.

In the morning I'm alone in the bed. I can hear Masha talking to Lena in the kitchen. They are rattling plates and laughing. When she comes up the stairs calling me, asking if I'm hungry, she finds me studying the words printed on a small card she's stuck to her mirror.

You God are my firmament
Roof for my head, shelter from storm
Nourishing bread, tender and warm.
I will give thanks, I will sing praise,
With all of my heart, all of my days.

Masha steps up behind me, places her hands on my shoulders, her face against mine. She is barefoot and surprisingly small. She begins singing the words from the card into my ear, her voice high and oddly free of vibrato.

Lena has made cottage cheese pancakes, a steaming plateful set in the middle of the table, flanked by slabs of sausage and cheese. There's a loaf of bread from the bakery where she works. I want only coffee, but the others are hungry and I'm expected to do my part. The mood around the table is changed from last night. Lena is charged with expectation. Masha can't stop smiling, as if we are celebrating. Pavel is unaffected, attentive only to the pancakes. Lena glances at the clock, and with mock horror, rises and hurries out, declaring she is late for work. I help Masha with the dishes.

At the Kharkiv railway station we huddle around our luggage. It is still August and if there will be sun today the mist that now shrouds everything will be burnt away. Three or four students have come to say goodbye to Don. Too recently roused from sleep, they have nothing to say. They stand with him, silent and as lacking in vitality as Gogol's dead souls. I envy him his circle of new friends. Watching my colleagues standing in groups, coming slowly to life, laughing, chatting, I feel miserable with no one near me, no one holding on to my arm. I imagine myself lying under the open sky with Masha, listening as she tells me stories.

"Shall I come to Kharkiv?" Masha had asked me after the dishes were done. "To the station, on

Monday?" Her eyes were guarded. We hadn't spoken much and I could tell that the morning's joy was giving way to another mood, not sadness, but a kind of calm. When I said, no, better not, I could sense a brief stiffening, but she didn't argue, as if she had expected a negative answer. But when I said I wouldn't stay till Sunday she argued so vehemently that I had to give in, even though I became suddenly aware of my strangeness in this place. In this house and in the town of Dergazhi.

On Sunday, Lena insisted that Pavel should drive me to Kharkiv. Masha sat in the back, translating my sparse conversation with her father, who drove too fast. We passed the school with its war plane caught in take-off. We passed an orthodox church, newly restored like so many of Ukraine's churches. I turned to Masha and asked if she'd ever been inside. Yes, she had. Often. She would go tonight, she said, because in the sanctuary she felt she was in the presence of God and it was a great…a great – she couldn't say it. I guessed *peace*, but it turned out *mystery*, was the word she wanted. I had learned that in an orthodox church there are no pews, so I asked how long she would have to stand.

"Maybe not stand," she said, and smiled as if I were a child asking a foolish question. "I will maybe kneel down."

I didn't ask if she would go to confession. Nothing about her that morning, or now, suggested penitence; she appeared composed and at peace.

At the dormitory I shook hands with Pavel who had been saved by his wife who now held hope of saving her daughter too. I kissed Masha on the cheek and would have held her, but she seemed suddenly distant and so self-contained it would have been a violation. Although she wore flat shoes instead of the usual high heels, she seemed tall and confident. I felt stupid, not knowing what to say. I hoped the summer had brought her what she desired. Or needed.

"Here, is for you." She handed me a package that I guessed contained a book.

I watched as she and Pavel drove off.

The train arrives, gliding out of the mist and into the Kharkiv station. We jostle into action, boarding and stowing our bags. I take my knapsack with me to an empty compartment. The excitement that marks the beginning of any journey stirs inside me; I'm glad to be leaving Kharkiv. Don lingers with his students. On his way to the compartment where I'm sitting he waves from every window. "See you next summer," he calls. He settles in beside me, takes his journal and begins writing. The train shudders into motion and makes its slow progress through the bleakest section of Karkhiv as if reluctant to leave the city, but eventually we are in the countryside travelling past farms and fields emerging from the mist.

Don nudges my arm with his journal, open at an empty page. "Write your email address here, Kevin." And I do, grateful to him for wanting it. The opposite page is filled with email addresses and messages from his students: *Thank you, Don, for coming here. You bring us such good news. Please come next year again. Thank you for friendship from Canada. Thank you for you tell us about Jesus.*

I flip back a page. More addresses and flowery messages for Don to carry home with him. As I write my address on the page he's opened for me, I fight back a stab of jealousy. I return the journal to Don and open the book Masha gave me. It's a worn English translation of Gogol's *Dead Souls.* As I flip through the pages I find a note inside: *Thank you for coming to Derghazi,* in Masha's neat writing.

A yellow ocean of sunflowers moves past our window. I picture Masha alone on the path we walked together on Friday and again on Saturday. I see her kneeling in the candle-lit interior of the orthodox church. By now her parents will have risen from their beds in the unfinished house in Dergazhi to begin another day of work.

I wonder if Bruce will succeed in getting Tanya to Canada and whether she will regret it.

The train's rhythm is relaxing. Beside me, Don is humming as he writes: *You God are my firmament*. He is happy. "I think the Summer Institute was a pretty cool idea, don't you?" he says, stowing his journal in his luggage. "I mean we made a start, didn't we? And that's all we can do, right?"

I flinch, and remember what Masha said about God living in Ukraine. I also notice he said 'we' as if including me.

"You coming back?" he asks when I don't answer.

It's the question all the teachers were asked on the last day, except that it was phrased as an appeal: *Come, please, next year*. Or a prediction: *I think you will be next year in Kharkiv*. They brought cakes and champagne, turning the final class into a celebration. When I told them, no, I didn't think I would be back, they smiled as if they already knew. Or as if they knew better.

"*Are* you?" Don prods. I ward him off, saying I might. It's not impossible. He nods and after a while he says, "I'm not really a teacher, well obviously you can tell. I wasn't all that effective, I guess. I mean my grammar's not up to scratch. And that's one reason I've got to come back. To make up for it." He continues, telling me he'd like to be a teacher, but he doesn't know if he'd make a good one. He asks me what I think.

I am unfit for the role of counsellor. Unworthy. "You made friends," I say. "That's good."

After a long silence he asks, "Any plans to get married, Kevin?"

I turn away so he won't see me grimace at this change in direction. We are passing a village and I catch a glimpse of a farmyard where a man and woman struggle with a horse. A simple scene from a hard life.

I turn back to Don who has watched the scene with me. And then, as if I owe it to him, I begin telling him about Laura. That I loved her. That she left and where she went. My voice is perfectly steady when I tell him how she drowned. He gives me his complete attention, and when I'm done he doesn't speak.

Because I can see the wet in his eyes, I get up and walk out of the compartment to the window where I can study the landscape on the other side, the small shimmering bushes dotting fields of green or brown. I am thinking of Masha who has not pressured me to come back to her. Who told me my first Gogol story. After a while Don joins me and we stand together a long while.

"Aren't we heading in the direction of Chernobyl?" he asks when we're almost at Kiev.

"We won't come anywhere near it."

The
Carpathians

A dark-skinned boy from the street darts up the steps to the patio cafe and edges noiselessly toward the elegant, straw-hatted woman waiting with her two younger companions to be served tea and the parfait glasses of fruit and ice cream tourists crave on a hot day. All morning they strolled in the old centre of Lviv, keeping to the shade, pausing at statues of poets, at a ruined synagogue overgrown with wild flowers, a partially restored fortress, the ancient city hall. By chance they stumbled across an open-air market where they navigated a maze of embroidered shawls and aprons, ceramic bells in all sizes, oil paintings of ships tossed on rough seas, key chains and antique silver teaspoons available in distracting abundance.

The woman, who does not notice the child creeping up to her elbow, removes her straw hat. "I had a feeling you were going to buy that white bell with the heavy clapper," she says to the young woman who has shifted her chair so her bare, tanned shoulders catch the sun. All morning the young man's attention has been fixed on her shoulders, on her, and now he bends to tell her something. The older woman smiles in their direction, but the smile is stiff.

Only a few tables in the patio cafe are occupied. Languor has taken hold of the afternoon, a droning absence of energy. The waiters are slow.

"Please, Senora, dollar. Please." The dark boy speaks with the exaggerated rhythm of practiced pleading. The younger woman smiles at the way he says "Senora" The older woman's head turns sharply toward the voice, but her body hunches away from it, as if from a buzzing bee.

The waiter, balancing a tray of tea and ice cream parfaits in one hand, moves menacingly toward the boy, flicking a white napkin at him. The boy dodges the napkin, takes refuge behind an empty table, circles it, advances defiantly. The waiter sets down the tray and flicks the napkin again. Again the boy retreats, hovers out of range, darts forward and is rebuffed once more. His face is hard, his eyes wary, unwavering and bright as nails. He continues to play this game until the waiter grabs him by the shoulders, drags him past the tables and sends him running into the street to join six or seven other dark-skinned children grouped in the shade of a chestnut tree.

One of the girls in the group, the oldest, sits on the ground, her back against the tree's broad trunk, one knee bent to her chin. She holds a bundle in her arms. A doll wrapped in rags. Or could it be a sleeping child?

The children's chatter is animated, contentious until the girl unfolds her tall body and straightens her skirt. It is her turn, ready or not. She shifts the grey bundle from one arm to the other and after a decent interval strides with an actor's grace along the pavement and up the steps to the almost empty patio.

At the edge of the red and white umbrellas she stops and lets her gaze rove. Choosing. When her eyes come to rest, they are staring straight at the bare-shouldered woman with the sun-streaked hair. Holding her bundle close, she approaches.

"Please, Americano," she whispers. "A dollar." She rocks the bundle casually.

The young woman, not American but Canadian, looks into the dark, bold eyes and her face breaks into an amused smile. Her hands want to reach for the child – there really is a baby in those grey rags – but instead they reach for her bag, open it. The older woman sets down her teacup, places a firm hand on the younger woman's tanned wrist. She shakes her head. The young woman's smile vanishes. The young man spears fruit from his parfait, pretending not to have noticed. His white polo shirt is dark with sweat.

"A dollar, a dollar," the girl insists, laying her free hand importunately on the young woman's other wrist. "Give me. Please."

The young man, irritated, looks around for the waiter, but he has joined two others at a far table, their backs turned to the besieged trio.

"No," the older woman says. "Go. Go away." She makes broad, shooing motions with both hands.

But the girl won't go. Won't take her ragged grey bundle back to the chestnut tree. Won't take her bold eyes from the young woman she has chosen. "Americano," she repeats. "Give me. Please."

The young woman is undecided, troubled, her hand moves again toward her bag – a black leather that matches her low-heeled, good quality walking shoes – but she knows better than to open it. The older woman's eyes are on her. But so are the dark eyes of the girl. She turns to her male companion who shrugs as if to say, "What do you expect of me? What can I do?"

"*Now*, lady. Give me *now*." The girl no longer says "please." She has sensed a momentary advantage and ceases to be a beggar. She knows the women are mother and daughter and at any minute the mother might clinch her control. "*Now*," she repeats, her voice hard and demanding.

The waiter hurries toward them with his tray to clear the table. He barks harsh, foreign words at the dark girl. He gestures. The girl's face turns sullen. She refuses to budge. There is a movement in the grey rags, a stirring of small limbs. Any moment a child's wail might rise from the bundle. The waiter lunges toward the intruder, as if he will throw himself at her. His voice rises until he is shouting. He raises an arm to strike.

The younger woman stiffens, alarmed, and a small cry gathers in her throat. To her relief the waiter does not strike. She wants to do more than give money to this girl who can't be much younger than she is. She wants to ask, is it your child? Will you show me its face? Where do you live? How?

But the heat is intense, the older woman – her mother, of course – sits alarmingly upright in her chair, the beggar's language is foreign, and the parfait glasses still half full.

The dark-eyed girl – young woman, really – turns unwillingly and carries her bundle slowly from the patio to the chestnut tree, where a much younger girl gets nonchalantly to her feet because now it is her turn. As if to gain time she stoops to tie her shoelaces, runs her fingers through her hair.

The trio on the patio lingers in silence a long while before the older woman, looking first at her daughter, then at the young man, says, "I'll be glad to get to the Carpathians."

There is no response.

"Tomorrow," she says. "The Carpathian Mountains." The words are meant for the man in the damp polo shirt who must return to Kiev and will not be going to the Carpathians. He takes money from his wallet to pay the bill. There is a generous tip for the waiter who has been helpful.

The three foreigners rise from the table and leave the pleasant cafe. The little girl under the chestnut tree has taken a few steps in their direction, but then, as if her target is moving beyond her jurisdiction, she turns back to the other children.

On a hot day in Lviv it is the quiet coolness of the sanctuary that draws travelers to St. Mikolay's, more than the attraction of art and architecture, music and history, certainly more than the authority of religion. Not that devotion and faith are absent, but they are not the main impetus behind the constant opening and closing of the heavy door.

The three western tourists enter, leaving behind the blazing street. They remove their shades. When their eyes have adjusted to the dim interior with its scattering of visitors, all three turn to the icon wall that at first appears to be an expanse of darkness broken here and there with glints of light. Gradually the outlines of saints become discernible.

The older woman walks toward them, leaving the young couple alone near the door. Close up she studies the elongated, ascetic byzantine faces and bodies of the saints. They stare steadfastly into the sanctuary with their all-seeing, ageless eyes that do not require, as hers do, the aid of glasses. The woman straightens her shoulders glad for the soothing coolness, a foretaste of the Carpathian Mountains. She looks around for a pew where she might sit down for a few minutes, but St. Mikolay's is orthodox; the faithful worship on their feet. Or knees. The relief of slipping off her shoes and putting her feet up is unavailable. Her joints ache. She has had to walk several long blocks to see this church, the oldest in Lviv. Her daughter had her heart set on it.

At the back of the church the daughter is whispering into her friend's ear. "We should sing," she says. "This place is built for singing. The sound would be so..." The word "holy" is on her lips, she can think of no better word to describe what the sound would be like. But instead she says "awesome" and regrets at once the outworn word.

The young man puts his arm around her tanned shoulders, and she does not pull away. Perhaps she has suddenly remembered that bare shoulders are an offence in an orthodox church, and lets him cover them.

"We should sing," she repeats.

"What? What would you sing?"

The young woman has no idea what a visitor might sing in such a place, only that there should be some response to that sombre cloud of witnesses staring at her from the icon wall. The painted murals too, and all the flickering candles, call for conversation.

To one side, a kerchiefed woman leans forward to kiss the sarcophagus of a saint. She holds a child, a boy, in her arms and as she bends, he bends down with her. His tiny arm brushes the top of the stone. The young woman sees this and smiles.

"*Jesu joy of man's desiring*." She has put her mouth close to her friend's ear to whisper it, surprised that this almost forgotten piece from her piano lesson days has leapt to mind. She hums a few bars.

The young man buries his face in her hot, moist neck and shoulder, overwhelmed with sudden gratitude. His arm around her shoulder tightens. He thinks he adores this young woman whom he met only last week in Kiev where she was sightseeing with her mother. "I'll meet you in Lviv," he had insisted, taking her smile for invitation. The mother did not smile when her daughter named the hotel in Lviv where they would stay. She did not say anything, but her face and body stiffened noticeably and grew icy.

"I've got a better idea," the young man says now. "How about..." And then it is his turn to hesitate, because what he has in mind has little to do with the spirit, more with the flesh. He pulls the young woman behind a pillar, draws her warm body close again, his hands move to her breasts in an outburst of worship. He is convinced that on this day he can only become happier.

She pulls away.

From somewhere above them a stream of sound is released, a surprise that comes to them like a single beam of light through a small window. A soprano voice is singing *Pie Jesu*, spinning the melody like pure silver. When she has finished, a choir takes up the anthem; music fans out and floats on opulent minor harmonies, filling the sanctuary to its dampest corners with adoration and longing that transcend the gloom of the church.

At the icon wall the mother turns as if to discover where the song is coming from, the song that rises above the day's annoyances and the restlessness that plagues all humans. She is no exception. Her hand flies to her throat as the high notes float and swirl around her, weaving a comforting net from which she has no desire to be extricated.

The daughter walks forward to stand beside her mother. For a moment their hands meet in an unplanned touch.

Near the entrance, where the door opens and closes constantly, the young man, forsaken, leans against a pillar.

Beyond the door of the cool church, the street children wait for the travelers. They are too superstitious, or too conscious of unworthiness, to confront the saints. Or maybe they know that money given in this place is dropped through small slits into locked boxes. In any case, sooner or later the heavy door will open and the three foreigners, refreshed, will step once more into the street where the worst heat will be over.

Evening arrives unobtrusively on Svoboda Prospekt, dropping long shadows on the hot pavement. The benches lining both sides of the boulevard are occupied; it is the time for chess. Each bench hosts two men – their faces mostly lined, their heads greying – bent over a chessboard. Around them a small audience assembles, squatting or standing, some waiting their turn, others withholding advice, suppressing approval or disapproval. This is not the time for words. It is the time and place for silently-mustered strategy, for shrewd calculation, offensive and defensive. Queens and pawns wait to be moved. To be taken. It is time for checkmate and stalemate.

Pedestrians making their way between the two rows of benches pause in their conversation as they pass the chess players, sometimes stopping to watch, or simply out of respect. The street children, sent out begging by their parents, know better than to approach any of the benches. It would be useless. They dart keen- or sullen-eyed from the sidewalk cafes beyond the boulevard and attach themselves to anyone who seems foreign, like the young couple over there, hand-in-hand. And, somewhat apart, an older woman swinging her straw picture hat lightly at her side. The tourists ignores the beggars, though the young woman cannot resist an occasional glance in their direction. It is enough to keep them converging on her like a flock of pesky sparrows.

The man, who has walked farther today than he wanted to, is cheered by the sight of the chess games. He slows his pace. The women with him slow down too. At college he competed at chess and often won. He would like to join these men. It would be a reprieve from the relentless architecture of Lviv. The burden of antiquity. His flagging energy is renewed as he imagines the young woman's blue-grey eyes watching his moves. A victory at chess would redeem the long and inconclusive day. He longs to be tested and proved worthy. Approaching a bench he notices that each player puts down a *gryvne*, a small investment, a deposit betokening expectation. He scoops a handful of *gryvne* from his pocket and holds out the coins. The men nod, and one of them raises his hand, signalling that he must wait his turn.

The two women stand aside, as if resigned to wait too, but then the older one links her arm into her daughter's and pulls her away. The two resume walking until they reach the opera theatre, an ornate building that dominates the end of Svoboda Prospekt. Allegorical sculptures representing life and death flank the main entrance and the entire facade is lavishly decorated. The women gaze without speaking. Even the younger one has exhausted her store of enthusiasm and spontaneity.

"Imagine coming here for *Tosca*," the older woman says, finally. "Or *Aida*." But it is not opera season and in any case the evening air is irresistible. Who would want to sit indoors?

People are gathering in the square in front of the opera theatre and soon there is a sizable crowd, its attention focused on a group of young people, some of them in mime costumes and make-up, some of them struggling to set up a sound system, others talking to the bystanders. Their leader announces in English – and someone translates it into Ukrainian – that this group has come to bring good news. *Awesome* news, he says. A choir of young people in their late teens and early twenties begins singing to taped accompaniment that is much too loud. Someone fiddles with the volume and the sound sputters, fails, rises again, fails, rises and settles into its former loudness. A few of the spectators join the singing, but most listen and watch, their faces emptied of expression. Dark-skinned children, scurrying through the crowd to find what they can find, ignore the music.

The leader – American, the older woman tells her daughter, disparagingly – rallies his troupe for a mime performance. There are two main characters, one dressed in white, the other in black. The action begins with languorous, vague movements that gradually lose their dreaminess and gain tempo as the conflict intensifies, grows ominous, then almost violent. The limbs and body of the black figure bend and contort and reach aggressively for the cowering white one. The black hands are always about to grasp or strike. The rest of the troupe forms an undulating wave that circles the protagonists with threatening movements, then pulls away, and again threatens and pulls away. Tension animates the silent crowd. Their eyes move with the actors; their faces gain expression. Suddenly the white figure rises like an unfolding lily and with gestures of conciliation that are both amateur and poignant reaches out to the black figure, causing the opponent to retreat and then to shrink and shrink, collapsing finally on the pavement.

After that the performance stumbles to a close. A shower of applause scatters through the evening. On Svoboda Prospekt the shadows deepen.

"It's never that simple," the older woman says. She smiles wryly and glances at her wristwatch. The younger one, entranced by the passion of the mime, would like to stay, but her mother has begun moving away from the crowd.

"Your hat, Mother," the daughter says, when they have left the show behind.. "Where's your hat?"

The mother stops. Her face alters, the lines deepen. "Damn gypsies." She turns to retrace her steps, drawing her daughter with her, but there is no sign of the pretty hat purchased with the Carpathian Mountains in mind.

When they return to the chess game they find their young man hunched over the board, his head bowed. There is a streak of sweat on his forehead. He is looking at the white queen, *his* queen, who is about to be taken. His grey-haired opponent is waiting for the foreigner's next move after which he will move and the game will be over. A feeling of rage has overtaken the Canadian. Rage against his skilful opponent; against himself for not anticipating the older man's moves; against this entire day.

The young woman knows nothing of chess, but she understands that her friend is defeated and leaving her mother she pushes through the observers to sit beside him on the chess bench. Her hand wants to wipe the gleam of moisture from his forehead, but it settles instead on his shoulder. He shrugs it away. She watches his hand move toward the chess piece, hesitate and finally grasp it. She thinks he will fling it, but he simply moves it on the board. And then the older hand moves. There is the briefest space of time when nothing moves and then the two male hands meet and grip each other before the younger man snatches his away.

The stream of pedestrians carries the trio along Svoboda Prospekt. No doubt the older woman is thinking of the Carpathian Mountains. Her daughter is half inclined to take the hand of her friend, but he strides on ahead, still angry. A ragged circling of street children closes in on them, crow-like. She pulls a change purse from her leather bag, snaps it open and flings its contents with a wide, arcing motion of her arm into the air. The children swoop silent as vultures on the shower of coins.

The Grand Hotel is a respectable establishment, its original elegance muted by encroaching shabbiness, the shabbiness somewhat mitigated by poor lighting.

The chairs in the room are covered in dark, velvety fabric, the pattern worn thin. A tray with coffees and liqueurs has been placed on a side table. China and crystal are the best the hotel has to offer. Very soon the older woman, the mother, will offer the tray to her daughter and to the young man who has been with them all day, an awkward burden. They will drink and make polite talk because the hostess believes every action, whether kind or cruel, should be accomplished with civility. And then at last the young man will return to *his* hotel, a more modest one, from where he will leave in the morning for Kiev.

Right now the mother is describing the Carpathian Mountains, the real reason she has come to this country. The mountain air will be fresh, the countryside pastoral, dotted here and there with healing waters springing from the ground, some beneficial to the liver, others to the lungs, spleen, joints, heart. She repeats what she has been told by her travel agent and by friends who have been there and come home healed. She embellishes the description here and there, hoping her daughter will speak and reinforce her praise of the Carpathians. She wants the young man to hope for an invitation, or at least some sign that his company would be welcome. Naturally no invitation will be given. In any case, he is obliged to return to Kiev. Let him go with the knowledge that he is superfluous.

She knows the young man is bored with her words, bored and restless. Possibly he is becoming frantic. Time is running out. Good, she thinks. If only she could count on her daughter who is also bored.

The daughter listens politely to her mother. Her limbs are free of pain, her joints do not ache. After a night's sleep she will be free of all weariness and once more ready for anything. For climbing tourist trails in the Carpathian Mountains.

The young man is trying various scenarios: When it's time for him to go, the girl will fabricate some excuse to accompany him. No, she will not make excuses, why should she? She will take his hand and with a polite "Good-bye, Mother," walk with him to his hotel. Even better, she will defy her unbending parent, "You go on to the Carpathians, Mother. I'm going back to Kiev. No, don't try to persuade me. I've made up my mind."

None of his imagined scenarios will come to pass. The mother has made plans; the daughter will accompany her.

He looks helplessly around the room. *His* hotel room is not as fine, and there is no table for liqueurs. His bed is not as luxurious as the two he can see through the open doors to the adjoining bedroom. Suddenly this is as unbearable as his inevitable return to Kiev, alone. He wants the woman he adores to resist the Carpathians. He wants her to choose him. To find him worthy. To forget that he lost at chess on Svoboda Prospekt.

The mother moves toward the table, picks up the tray, sets it down because it is heavy and her wrists ache. Her daughter comes to her aid. She takes the tray and holds it for her mother who takes a cup of coffee in her thin hand before she sits down. Then the young woman offers the tray to the young man who grasps it as if to take it from her, but she doesn't let go. They are face to face in a way they haven't been all day. The young woman is startled by the fire in his eyes. It reminds her of the dark eyes of the young mother at the outdoor cafe this morning.

She lets go of the tray and the man is left holding it.

In the cool Carpathian Mountains, mother and daughter walk along a shaded path that leads to a spring. The older woman fills a cup from that spring and drinks. The lines of her unsmiling face ease a little as she listens to the carolling of a bird in a branch above her: a simple melody, the notes incredibly clear. She allows herself the faint hope that tonight she will sleep, unburdened. Dreamless. And without pain.

The daughter, who has been persuaded to taste the water too, neither likes nor dislikes the taste. Because she is free of pain she expects nothing from the spring. That night, she believes she can see the shadowy forms of vagrant children dancing under a chestnut tree, lurking at the doors of St. Mikolay's, and chasing each other around patio tables. A baby held by the oldest child opens its eyes. They are deep brown and alert. In the moments before sleep she recalls vividly the enraged eyes of the young man she does not expect to see again.

Beyond the Border

It was mid-afternoon when the half-empty bus stopped at the border post and the driver got out. The passengers, most of whom spoke only English, opened windows and stuck their heads out to watch him negotiate with the border patrols, three bulky fellows with indifferent posture and bland faces. The conversation was not friendly; the watchers at the window feared the bus would be turned back.

The journey, begun somewhere between breakfast and lunch, had been unremarkable, the road winding through towns and villages, past fields of grain, past huge storks' nests and meadows. Poppies bloomed everywhere, small speckles of blood kept in constant motion by a dry wind that bent the slender stems. The same dry wind had whipped the hair of the travellers as they stepped from the bus when the sun was well past its zenith. The driver had turned down a gravelled side road and stopped where a row of lime trees cast shade on a clearing. An ideal spot for a late lunch that would have to sustain them until they arrived at their destination. Out came bread rolls. Slices of cold meat. Cheese. Cucumbers. Everyone contributed leftovers they had gathered up after breakfast at the hotel that morning. George had taken the last of the boiled eggs from the bowl in the centre of the table and wrapped them in plastic. There were beverages too, bottles of cola and mineral water bought from vendors along the street in front of the hotel. The drinks were warm, the sun having shone down on the bus and its contents for hours though it hadn't seemed that long.

That morning after breakfast, George, the leader of this small band of travellers, had announced that the bus hired to transport them out of this country and across the border to the next needed further maintenance and they would not be leaving right away as they had been told, but everyone should be ready to board at eleven o'clock. Quick calculations, hasty glances at the map assured everyone that they could still arrive before nightfall, and so the altered schedule was a bonus, they told themselves. It would have been a shame not to stroll along the streets of the city, observe its inhabitants, buy pop and water to take on the bus. After stashing the salvaged food in the baggage room the desk clerk had reserved for them, they set off.

The bustle of people going to work or school or to some government office had filled the wide street flanked on either side by solid grey buildings. The day was still cool. The foreigners tried to decipher the signs along the street, but had to content themselves with clues offered by an occasional English word. Or pictures. They exchanged small amounts of money to spend at the kiosks where snack foods were sold, along with bus tickets, occasionally film and novelties such as the wooden nesting dolls common to this part of the world. Four or five such nesting figures were bargained for and purchased by members of the group, wrapped and stuffed into handbags. Since a party of twenty couldn't move comfortably together, groups of two, three or four broke off and ventured into side streets and alleys to see what could be seen.

Well before eleven o'clock, the passengers had begun arriving back at the hotel. Repairs had been completed; the bus stood ready. George wore a frown as if the delay had begun to worry him. Although his profession was academic – he was a professor of psychology – he had organized the tour, planned every detail of the itinerary. He had taken care of travel arrangements and made sure everyone was supplied with the correct documents. He was somewhat surprised, even disappointed, when except in the case of one doctor, interest in the tour did not come from the kind of people he had expected. Those who signed up, and paid up, were ordinary folk. But decent, he assured himself.

Naturally he couldn't have foreseen the delay caused by engine failure, a problem that he, lacking all mechanical talent, couldn't fully understand. When the bus was ready to leave he counted his troupe and found that two were missing. At first no one seemed to know who these might be; no one remembered them exactly. Where had they sat at breakfast? Had they slept on the second or third floor? What were they wearing?

By the time someone figured out the missing people must be the woman who always wore the beige raincoat and her balding husband, someone else spotted the pair hurrying along the street, breathless. After retrieving their bags from the hotel they boarded the bus and made their way sheepishly to the back, fully aware that no one was amused by this further delay. In a vehicle built for forty passengers, they had no trouble finding a place where they could sit side by side.

And so the bus trip had begun, and now here they were at the anticipated border and apparently they were being turned back. The travellers' faces registered not so much alarm as bafflement. The maps they consulted assured them the route they had followed to this crossing was the shortest one to their destination, and they could see no reason why they should have any difficulty getting across – hadn't they checked and rechecked their documents before they left home, as George had instructed them?

The group had, of course, obtained the services of a translator; George had seen to that. But the translator was showing herself to be phlegmatic, almost reluctant to speak, as if each request for her services was an imposition. Then too, she was dressed too flamboyantly for a woman whose duty it was to serve them. The shawl she draped in various ways across her shoulders was a brilliant shade of red that matched perfectly her nail polish and lipstick. She moved with a studied languor. At breakfast the group had surreptitiously dubbed her the Duchess. Her real name was Larissa. At the moment the Duchess was asleep in the seat beside George, unaware that they had come to the border. Unaware that they must turn back.

It was Larissa through whom George had been informed during breakfast that the engine of the bus had behaved sluggishly when the driver started it and certain repairs would need to be made if they wished to travel safely. Of course everyone did. Eager to see the city, no one thought to ask questions about the engine, or wonder why the maintenance work had not been taken care of earlier. When George had asked the translator if she was familiar with the route they were taking, she had either nodded perfunctorily or tossed her head, he couldn't remember which. Now, as he shook her awake, he wondered, as the passengers were beginning to, at what hour they would arrive at their destination.

Larissa, scarcely awake, climbed out of the bus and joined the driver and the border guards. George followed. To the observers at the bus windows the discussion appeared to lose its animation, become desultory. Some saw it as sombre. Larissa translated for George the guards' insistence that at this border crossing tour buses were not permitted to pass, only private vehicles and registered lorries. She explained that when she'd asked if this wasn't rather discriminatory, the official had shrugged, a shrug that she replicated perfectly for George's benefit. He had not been in this part of the world long enough to know how adamant officialdom could be, she insisted. Here it was expected that those in authority would dig in their heels.

Ask him to make an exception, George urged. His hand slid into his breast pocket to make sure the wad of American dollars he had been advised to take for just such an emergency was in its place, but she saw the move and with a deprecating smile waved his intentions away. We turn back, she said matter-of-factly and began mounting the steps of the bus. At this George slipped a few of the bills out of his pocket and showed them to the officials who hesitated briefly, then laughed mirthlessly. The driver took George by the elbow and steered him back onto the bus.

There is a border post where any vehicle can cross, but it's much further south, the driver told Larissa who then told George.

Why for godsake didn't the driver head that way in the first place? George demanded but Larissa refused to translate the question. She settled back into her seat.

The driver turned the bus around and the journey to the correct crossing began. The passengers fell silent, pondering this unexpected change of direction. Maps were passed back and forth and soon everyone knew they would be required to retrace most of the distance already travelled.

Like unravelling a sweater you've just about finished, a woman muttered. She wore a blue jacket and a face habitually shrouded in gloom.

Everyone became uneasy and some were hungry because now it was several hours since lunch.

But it's also several hours before the sun will set, George reminded them. We are lucky to be travelling on one of the longest summer days. His hopeful words drew no response.

At the back of the bus the couple last to board showed no interest in the change of direction. The man turned to his wife: I was wondering just now what I might be doing if I was home. I can't figure out, have I left for work or am I still sleeping? This time difference, it's got me mixed up. Anya?

But Anya had as little sense as her husband of what time it might be in the country they called home. The country they'd left behind. She gazed steadfastly into the passing landscape, even while she was thinking of her kitchen. The temperamental coffeemaker on the counter. The lace curtains she'd intended to launder before they left – she'd have to attend to them when she returned. The fridge might be humming at this very moment, she thought with a kind of wonder. It was only by visualizing details of the kitchen, then of the other rooms – the living room, two bed rooms, there was no dining room, meals were taken in the kitchen – only in this way could she bring herself gradually back to the life lived inside that house.

Jakob, she said after a while. Look. She pointed to a stork's nest perched on top of a dead tree. It was empty.

George had been enthusiastic from the start about this trip that would bring him and his fellow travellers to a landscape different from the one they were accustomed to, yet linked significantly to each one of them. His wife had refused to come. I'm perfectly happy right here where I am, she'd said. Why would I trade in my comfortable bed for who knows what kind of lumpy mattresses? Or our van – it was quite new – for buses that will most likely break down. And someone will get sick, you'll see. What will you do then? And it'll rain a lot, you can bet on it. She disliked damp weather. Besides, she'd said, what good is all this? Think you can turn back the clock? Time moves on. What's wrong with enjoying the here and now? While we've got it. She was planning to fly to Toronto during her husband's absence for a week of shopping.

George wondered now whether his wife had been right, whether all this was the result of wrong-headedness, but he did not allow himself to worry. He had initiated this venture, undertaken to lead it, and he would see it through. He would *have* to see it through. There was no way but ahead.

Near the front of the bus the passengers were expressing their displeasure. The morning's delay was now a contentious issue. The engine's malfunction should have been detected earlier; the repairs not left to the last minute. The time spent on the streets of the city was now seen clearly as wasted time, and the tardiness of the couple seated near the back, simply unforgivable. And what about the Duchess, asleep again? And George – how reliable was this man who had hired her?

When it became necessary to refuel the bus, the driver communicated this fact loudly to George, gesturing at the dials. He didn't bother with the translator, but Larissa, wakened by his voice, spotted the petrol station before he did. The driver pulled in behind a long line of cars, lorries and buses waiting for the one pump. The line appeared to be at a standstill. One of the passengers needed a washroom and George announced they might as well all redeem this time of waiting, so out they piled, some of them stiff from hours of sitting still. They joined a queue that stretched back from an uninviting outbuilding and moved at a snail's pace. They tried to converse with the local drivers and travellers, the few who spoke a halting English. Are you crossing at the border? they asked, searching for simple words and gestures. Have you been there before? What should we expect?

Whether or not the person asked had previous border experience, the answer always prophesied a daunting obstacle ahead. You will wait all day, one person said, shaking her head. Two days, another. You must at the border be prepared.

George feared his party would not be easily resigned to the prospect of a long wait; their purpose was to arrive. And food – what they had brought from the hotel was gone and they had only a few candy bars purchased at kiosks and partially filled bottles of water. They had passed no stores or cafes worth stopping for. He couldn't help noticing that the sun had fallen closer to the horizon. And they were still far from the border.

Our tardy couple timidly took their places in the washroom line. Although they had been assured they could safely leave their hand baggage on the bus, the woman held hers close. Inside was the reason she and her husband had been late that morning.

They had left the main party, attracted by a group of people clustered around a street vendor selling roses, carnations, chrysanthemums and gerbera daisies in huge bunches. Anya would have liked to buy an armful of carnations, but they would only wilt in the warm bus. They strolled on, choosing a side street, then another. A display of small metal pendants, figures of saints with severe faces, caught Anya's attention. She took one in her hand, upon which a man rose up from behind the display, angry, speaking loudly, words she couldn't understand. Passers-by too began scolding and pointing at her, adding to her confusion. When she backed away, they became more vociferous and some took a step or two toward her. She looked to her husband for guidance, but he too was baffled. Finally she placed the saint – there was no chain with the pendant – back on the display, but that only caused more indignation.

Just pay for it, her husband said, just pay for it. He gave her a handful of the local coins he had exchanged for dollars and she offered them to the vendor who took the saint from the display, turned the pendant over and pointed to numbers so faint neither she nor Jacob could be sure of the amount. A man in the growing crowd began to open and close his splayed hands very quickly several times to signal the price of the item. Confused, Jacob produced more coins from his pocket, but they only generated more anger. It wasn't until he reached cautiously for his wallet and drew from it several American bills that the vendor was finally placated, the situation resolved. The couple moved away quickly, the saint in Anya's handbag, Jacob's hand in his pocket guarding his wallet. Soon they were running, retracing their steps back to the main street, back to the hotel to board the bus. Which way? Anya gasped. But Jakob wasn't sure, he simply kept running down one street then another. They were close to the hotel, but they were lost. They'll be waiting, Jakob thought and ran faster, Anya trying to keep up. She was panting like a dog when Jacob finally spotted the hotel and in front of it, their bus.

Neither the line-up at the petrol pump nor the one at the outhouse were stationary after all. Eventually the purpose of each was accomplished, despite jostling, haggling and unpleasant smells. The journey resumed, the passengers free to contemplate the imminent border crossing.

Halfway up the aisle sat the oldest man in the tour group. The others treated him with deference, perhaps because of his age, perhaps because he claimed to have been born in that village toward which this journey was taking them. A village where their ancestors too had been born, though none of the other travellers had ever seen it. The old man, whose family had emigrated when he was two years old, said he could remember the village his family had left behind, even the house they had lived in.

Well, that's like saying you can remember when you were born, the blue-jacketed woman scoffed. Her talent for displeasure had begun to irritate the others.

But that *is* possible, the doctor said, and because he was the most educated person in the group next to George, the others did not argue but turned expectantly toward him.

I once had a patient, the doctor continued, a boy of…oh…maybe ten, who told me he could remember his birth. He remembered coming out of the darkness. How the light was so strong, it hurt his eyes. And he was cold. All he wanted was to turn around and go back.

I can't believe that, the red headed girl across the aisle from the doctor said. That's wa-a-ay too weird.

Ssh..ssh, her mother cautioned. Don't be rude.

The boy became a loner, the doctor continued, directing his attention now to the girl. He became a homebody who stayed mostly in his room. Didn't like to go out. His mother worried because he didn't have friends.

A homebody, the redhead said scornfully. That's just, like, too depressing. She was eleven and couldn't believe that anyone would choose to withdraw from the world. She missed her friends who would be at volleyball or swimming camps while she was stuck in a bus in the middle of a boring nowhere.

Yes, he *was* depressed, the doctor said, as if the girl had made a correct diagnosis and he was confirming it.

The girl, by far the youngest in the group, was travelling with her parents and her sixteen-year-old brother who was even less enthusiastic than she was about the trip. He had demanded to stay back, surely he could be trusted to be on his own for a few weeks, but the mother wouldn't hear of it. We all of us go, or nobody goes, she had told her husband, who thereupon calculated the cost of visas, transportation and accommodation for four and had been compelled to take out a loan.

Candy bars broken into chunks were passed around by those who still had some and everyone took one or two pieces, grateful for the small sustenance. The bustle that greeted this refreshment was followed by silence settling on the munching travellers. Then dusk and eventually, darkness. The couple at the back peered out into it. The oldest man closed his eyes and allowed details of the village he was sure he remembered to appear before his eyes. The Duchess soon slept again and so eventually did the red head and her brother though their parents did not. Neither did George, who tried not to picture the long line of vehicles ahead of them at the border.

It was not so much a line-up as a chaos that greeted them – cars, motorcycles and vans parked or idling randomly in the clearing in front of a ramshackle building. There were even a few horse-drawn carts. Officials, carrying their authority like gold badges, came from or went into the building clutching clipboards. Drivers were attempting to inch forward. Some found ways of edging out of their spots at any opportunity to cut in front of the vehicles ahead. The slightest success on their part received a response of angry horns and curses from cheated drivers.

The bus driver had anticipated this game – later the passengers would be convinced he had previous experience of it and knew its perverse rules. Seeing the confusion he had turned off the highway onto a dirt road so rough that all sleepers were shaken awake. The road curved through a stand of trees and emerged near the front of the waiting vehicles. The driver nudged the bus toward a small space a negligent motorist had left between his car and the one ahead. The motorist got out, fists balled, and roared like a demented cow at the bus driver who stared ahead ignoring the nuisance. The passengers leaned out the windows to watch the man beat his fists against the bus and kick at the tires. His angry words, incomprehensible to them, were curses, they knew, and snail-like they drew their heads back into the bus.

Jumping the queue, the teenager, awake now, said. Right on, man. You gotta kick ass, or you're stuck. It was the most enthusiasm he'd shown since leaving home.

Sh-sh, his mother said.

The pale lights at the customs building added to the lights of idling vehicles kept the darkness at a distance. Above, a black sky bristled with millions of stars that no one noticed. Whenever there was the slightest movement up ahead, every driver prepared to press forward. The angry man delivered one more blow to the bus before he returned to his car and gripped the wheel.

Several packages of cigarettes had appeared on the dashboard in front of the bus driver, clearly visible to the passengers furthest forward who passed the information back along the bus though it never reached Anya and Jacob. The packages had flown across the ocean in George's hand luggage, and now he had placed them before the driver who nodded with approval at the potential strength they added to the wad of dollars nestled in George's chest pocket. George had discovered that he could communicate well enough with the driver and he regretted the money spent hiring a translator who wanted to do nothing but sleep. He hadn't noticed that Larissa was no longer asleep.

The mother of the teenagers sat praying quietly for everything to be well, while the woman in the blue jacket announced in the kind of voice one would expect from a doomsday prophet, We're gonna be turned back. Again. You mark my words. All that money we paid? Might as well we flushed it down the you-know-what.

Oh we'll get through all right, the doctor said soothingly. The unhappy woman glared at him.

The father of the two youngest travellers, a railroad worker, wondered what they would find in the country they were headed for, provided of course that they would be allowed in. It was his wife's father who had first shown them advertisements for the heritage tour. Go, he had begged. I would if I could. But he couldn't, he was in the last stages of terminal cancer. The railroad worker's wife had sat with her dying father, besieging him with questions he would gladly have answered years ago if only they had been asked. Now he lacked the energy. After the old man was buried, his daughter became convinced it was their duty to join such a tour; it had become a kind of sacred pilgrimage. The railroad worker had learned that it was best to take his wife's sentimental inclinations into account, but those inclinations had never before involved heading into the unknown. Nor had they required a bank loan.

The couple at the rear of the bus had no opinions one way or the other about the prospect of getting across the border. They were not the kind to take initiative or to question authority. Anya took out her little saint, held him in her hand. She had never before possessed a saint and felt slightly foolish about the purchase. She wondered if she should feel guilty as well since as far as she knew her kind of people held no commerce with saints but addressed their petitions directly to God. Was it all right for me to buy it? she asked her husband.

No harm in it, Jacob said.

Anya returned the pendant to her handbag which she held close to her chest.

In spite of the driver's short-cut it was two AM and pitch dark when the driver was directed to edge the bus forward until it straddled a metal grill positioned over an excavation deep enough for surly officials in greasy jackets to walk beneath the vehicle and scrutinize its underbelly. Meanwhile their equally surly but senior colleague, uniformed, boarded the bus and made his way slowly down the aisle shining his flashlight in each face as he passed. For a few moments each passenger endured the scrutiny of sullen eyes that read each face, finding in it evidence of weariness, fear, hope or silent petition. When he arrived at the last couple the official stopped, studied their faces closely and spoke to them, his voice brusque, demanding. Anya became flustered and blurted something unintelligible. Jacob said, What, what do you want? Neither of them thought of the obvious – passport and visa. In the quiet bus their anxious voices carried to the front where the translator, before George could nudge her, rose and teetering on her high heels walked grandly toward the back where the couple cowered in the flashlight's glare. Anya appeared to shrink as if she wished to disappear inside her husband. The official repeated his words, towering over the couple with the formidable patience of one prepared to shine his light into their alarmed eyes until the rising of the sun.

The other passengers half-turned in their seats, craning to see and straining to hear. They no longer pressed their faces to the windows; the focus of all action had entered the bus and was right here. Why's she scared? someone asked. What've they got to hide? Their words drifted back to Anya who became more frightened.

He wants only your passport, Larissa said. You must show it. And your visa he wants to see.

Well there it is, the blue-jacketed woman grumbled. Now they've gone and lost their IDs. Somebody always spoils the soup. Now we'll never get across.

Hostility toward the pair who had been late that morning swelled, spreading to every corner of the bus, or so it seemed to Anya as she fumbled in her handbag and pulled out the leather case containing the necessary documents. The saint came along too, caught on her finger. The official took everything into his hand, studied the documents at length and returned them. He shone his flashlight on the small saint that had slipped into his hand and delivered a rapid flow of words meant for Larissa who took the pendant and returned it to Anya. St. Christopher, she said. When Anya did not respond she repeated, St. Christopher. He is for travellers the patron saint. Larissa knew that St. Christopher was also the saint of thieves but she saw no reason to tell that to Anya.

When the official left the bus there were no cigarettes to be seen and George's wad of bills had become considerably thinner. The driver revved the motor, the bus lurched forward, they crossed the border. No one cheered; instead there was a hush as all eyes turned once more to the windows. At one the side of the road a circle of people huddled around a large blaze, leaning toward it. Perhaps for warmth. Or they may have been cooking something over the fire. These people were travellers too, wanderers with no land of their own, no ancestral villages to return to. Their blood pulsed with an urge to keep moving, moving; their memories were unencumbered with scenes of permanence.

Wonder what they're eating? the teenager said. He was starved.

Those are gypsies, the doctor said. I'm pretty sure that's what they are.

The teenager thought of the bonfires he'd learned to build at boys' club, and those he and his friends had kept ablaze on beaches. He thought of hot dogs roasting until they split, dripping their juice into the crackling fire. Marshmallows, charred but sweet. Guitars and singing. Empty beer bottles littering the sand. The marvellous gift of drugs that inevitably appeared as if from nowhere. Here on the bus, with nothing at all for his hunger, he would have to try to sleep.

The bus reached its optimum speed and the driver settled back to cover the remaining distance to the village. Soon enough the sky would begin to lighten.

Larissa did not return to her seat up front, but sat across from Anya and Jacob who were wide awake, Anya still trembling in the darkness. She observed them for the better part of an hour before leaning across to whisper, Why in God's name are you here? For what did you come?

She had not intended her words to be theatrical, nor had she wished to startle the couple, who didn't at first reply.

You must to have a reason. Having slept off the weariness that had weighed her down at the outset of the journey, Larissa was alert, and curious about this tour group, especially this reticent couple.

Anya was first to gather her thoughts into an answer. When I was a child, she began, her voice too a whisper, my mother told me stories about this village. One story after another, as if she wanted to fill me up with them. Well, I couldn't contain them. They overflowed. I've forgotten most of them. But some things I can't forget – and here Anya leaned toward Larissa and her voice took on a new rhythm, as if she were reciting a well-rehearsed litany.

In this village are orchards, she said, with fruit-bearing trees of many kinds. Plum and pear trees flourish; apple and apricot trees. Cherry trees too. In spring, clouds of pink and white blossoms float above you as if you are in a dream. Evenings when the sun sets and the wind dies down to a soft breeze, O then you cannot imagine how pleasant it is, how lovely to walk among the apricot trees or sit beneath the spreading branches of an apple tree with someone you love. And who loves you too. It's a small sample of heaven. You believe then that the whole world is young and perfect, and you are full of hope. You are so lucky to be alive.

Anya stopped, blinked her eyes and shook herself as if waking from a trance. Well, you will see for yourself how it is, she whispered. And then you will understand why I, why we – she motioned toward Jacob – we all – now she included the whole bus – why we have to come. We have to see for ourselves what it was like. How beautiful it was, this place that we lost.

Anya's voice was melodious, almost like singing, and so youthful, Larissa thought, leaning back into her own space. She imagined Anya's eyes shining in the dark bus, not with tears but with a kind of ecstasy. She didn't think the village they were travelling toward would be anything as charming or romantic as Anya had described it. She knew about orchards in this part of the world. Mostly they were overgrown, the trees left unpruned, the farmers hard pressed to make a living from them. Her husband, before he left her, had held the job of supervisor in a large apple orchard. He had despised his work and complained every fall that the pickers were slow and deliberately careless. She had got the impression he was trying to drive them the way a teamster would drive horses to go faster. Always faster. His leaving may have had nothing to do with the orchard. And nothing to do with her inability to have a child. He had been a restless man who hated apples. She had loved him. Mourned him still. After he left, she moved back to the city and took a job as tour escort for an employer unwilling to give his employees time off.

Larissa leaned across the aisle once again toward Anya. My family has lost too, she whispered. My grand-parents lived in a ghetto in the city where you had breakfast this morning. She drew back to watch Anya's reaction.

Anya heard the words as an accusation, as if there was inherent wrong in eating breakfast in such a place.

That was before they were murdered, Larissa whispered, then paused again for reaction and when she sensed none, leaned closer. I am a Jew, she said, and was gratified when she sensed the tremor vibrating through Anya's body. The two women faced each other.

Anya didn't know that somewhere near the orchard she had re-imagined for the translator, Jews lay buried in a mass grave. She did not know that among her ancestors were those who had hated Jews and were implicated in their disappearance from that landscape. And she had given no more thought than the rest of the travellers to what less-worthy legacy her people might have left behind besides houses and orchards and farms.

Anya could not have explained why she reached across the aisle until her hand touched the hand of the translator. For several moments the two women were joined in the darkness.

It was still early when the sun slipped from the horizon and quickly gained height, rising above the trees and shining its benevolence down on the moving bus, intent on bringing its occupants to life. When the bus finally came to a stop, Larissa, wide awake and more animated than the group had seen her, bustled along the aisle rousing the sleepers. Outside the bus sunlight filtered through leafy trees causing shadow-patterns to shimmer and dance in the dusty street. The doctor peered out into the anticipated landscape and saw a sprawling village, grey and unremarkable. He experienced a jolt of disappointment, a stab of regret that made him want to turn from the ordinariness, the spreading dullness of the place. But he was able to overcome the feeling by fixing his gaze on the fantastically shaped white clouds that inhabited the blue sky above the cluster of grey buildings.

I'm starved. The teenager sat up, straight as a tree.

Shut up, his sister snarled, keeping her eyes closed against the light. I wanna sleep. She shifted her body and returned to the warm darkness of sleep.

Anya discovered that when she'd finally slept, it was with the saint clenched in her fingers. She opened her hand to show Jacob, who smiled and opened his so she could place St. Christopher in it. The metal was warm to his touch. Jacob decided that before they returned home – already he longed to be home – he would buy a chain for the pendant so Anya could wear it properly around her neck.

After the border crossing George had finally been able to let go of the fear that his cigarettes and dollars would not be sufficient, that the officials searching his bus and his people – he thought of them as *his* – would be unreasonable. Keeping his face serene and his words optimistic for the benefit of the others had proved tiring. When they had crossed safely he allowed himself the luxury of anticipating the arrival. He pictured himself standing in a place he had never seen but long considered hallowed. A place about which he had gathered information, maps, old photographs, historical records and stories. His university colleagues had sometimes joked about his painstaking attention to details. They had teased him about his preoccupation with the past. Obsession, some called it. Others, brooding. George did not think of it as brooding; he thought of it as offering respect. He wanted no detail of the past, no experience of the ancestors, to go to waste. Did the others want this too? he wondered, looking around at the waking passengers. He realized that he didn't know what they were actually expecting to see. They might be disappointed. Even angry.

George stood up, pulled from his pocket a folded page of notes and, turning his back to the village outside the bus window, faced his people, who seemed not to have fully grasped the reality of their arrival. The sixteen-year-old, sensing the coming speech, groaned. The doctor who had half-risen, sat down again. The oldest man looked puzzled. Larissa stood at the back near Jacob and Anya, listening. Sunlight shone full on her red shawl brightening the bus aisle.

We are an unusual gathering, George began. Most of us were strangers before we started out, but strangers with a unique link to each other and to the village you see before you.

What village, Mum? the red-head, finally awake, asked.

Ssh, her mother said.

Let's cut the speeches, the doctor thought.

The usual thundercloud overshadowed the face of the woman in the blue jacket.

Our ancestors owned land here, George continued. They lived and worked together, planting and harvesting, thriving and suffering, growing old and ill. And then they were driven out by war and disease and famine. And brutal terror. They vanished and *the place knows them no more*. He paused to see if anyone would react to the quotation. No one did, so he went on, his voice assuming a new urgency as if this was a matter of life and death. Our people are forgotten here, he said. Then, as if to underscore the magnitude of such forgetfulness: The villagers living in the houses of our people have forgotten the story. *Our* story.

The oldest man, his eyes alert, straightened himself and raised his hand, like a school boy: I want to say a story. Before George could give or withhold permission he began. In this village my grandfather was robbed. The bandits came at midnight. They wanted grain. Horses. Money. Grandfather, he was scared to go out so they came after him, dragged him into the yard. They cut him down with a sabre. He lived, but his blood soaked the ground. *This* ground. He gestured toward the street. All eyes turned as if to acknowledge, or verify, the reality of the village.

They came into the house, the old man continued, and took my uncle. Hung him from a tree like Jesus. And my mother…my mother…. The old man's voice, risen to a high pitch, faltered and seemed to choke on the words. He lifted his clenched hands shakily, his face was livid, he couldn't finish speaking.

George rushed to his side, fearing a stroke. Some wondered whether the old man actually remembered the fateful night he had described; others believed that horror can easily etch a deep groove in a child's brain.

This is where we're from, the mother whispered to her children, a hint of wonder in her tremulous voice.

We come from *here?* Her red-headed daughter turned to the window, puzzled.

After alighting from the bus the travellers, forgetting their hunger, wandered the main street of the village and down the many side roads and lanes. The village was surprisingly large. It was on the verge of becoming a town, George explained. It was prosperous once. Before the desolation.

Everyone studied sketchy maps and faded pictures they had brought from home. Larissa wondered if some of the documents the travelers held had been part of the baggage belonging to people headed away from this village, bent on moving from death to life, if she was to believe their stories.

The school was next to a pond, one said.

No, no, the school stood between my grandfather's house and the mayor's. Look at this map.

My uncle fell from the roof of the neighbour's barn, the biggest in the village and broke both legs. I think this must be the place.

On Sundays the church was packed and the singing flowed out through the windows and across the grain fields, maybe to the next village.

The travellers looked around. There was no church visible anywhere.

And they sang in harmony, George said. Always in harmony.

My uncle's neighbour had a store – food and dry goods, somewhere on this street.

They were planning to build a school for girls, the woman in the blue jacket said. They left it too late, if you ask me.

Curtains in the modest village houses were pulled slightly back and faces appeared at the windows. Curious children playing near a flowerbed paused to stare. Chickens stopped and raised their heads before resuming their morning dust baths.

It was George who discovered that a house not unlike the others was really a store, and with Larissa translating, learned that the woman in charge was willing to sell them black bread and coffee and, if the travellers so wished, she would make cottage cheese blyni. After the long night, everyone was hungry except the red headed girl who turned up her nose.

Replenished, they continued their search, arguing, comparing. Nothing was what they expected. The old man was unable to identify the house he was born in. George's painstaking research could not help him find a trace of the flour mill his family had owned. The doctor believed he recognized the remains of a hospital his great-grandfather had helped found. The building was a near-ruin, but traces of an earlier architectural style were discernible. Anya found in this desolate village no orchard to match the one that flourished in her mind, but she and Jacob were overjoyed to come upon a stork's nest with four half-grown storks in it.

The sun stood high above them, its heat merciless, when the travellers stood on a hill overlooking the valley in which nestled their ancestral village. To someone passing by it may have looked as if they were scouting out the best picnic spot. The gloomy woman had spread her jacket on the ground and was sitting in the shade of a shrub, wiping tears from her face.

The hill was spangled with the same red poppies they had seen yesterday. They bloomed around ancient gravestones that populated the summit. Most of the stones were half-sunken into the earth or leaning tiredly and some had obviously been vandalized. Only a few stood upright. George told the doctor it had been the custom to locate villages in pleasant valleys with streams running through them, but for a burial ground a location closer to the sun was considered proper.

Of course the travellers wanted to read the names carved into these ancient stones, but the stones were weathered, the words eroded by time and the wind, impossible to read except for an occasional letter.

Look, part of your name! Anya called Jacob over. The J was clear and now she wanted to find an A also, and succeeded, but it was on a different stone. In spite of this they were both pleased.

The oldest man, no trace of anger left, stumbled across the neglected cemetery with the help of a cane, searching unsuccessfully for names that were slipping from his memory. Larissa had found a hat for him to wear, Or else you'll get sunstroke. When he reached the crest of the hill he stopped before a large grey stone and moved his hand over the line of text, then repeated the motion, not so much tracing the letters as caressing them. George, concerned because of the heat, came up beside him. Larissa followed. She took the old man's arm.

The sixteen-year-old came too. Can you read that? he asked the old man The letters appeared less worn than those on the other stones.

The old man bent closer, studying the text with his eyes now instead of with his hand. At first he shook his head, but then he began to read: *Unser… Leben… ist…ein… Schatten… auf… Erden.*

What does he say? Larissa asked. She understood the language of this area, but not the one a forgotten people had once spoken here.

It means, the old man said, our life is a shadow. On the earth. He felt shaky and had to cling to both Larissa and George.

Hey, that's like Shakespeare, the teenager said, springing alive as if two wires had been joined and sparked. It's like in Macbeth. He struck a pose, raising his hand and trumpeting into the air: *life's but a walking shadow, a poor player that struts and frets his hour upon the stage….*

His speech was interrupted by his mother who had also come close, and was embarrassed by the outburst. Don't be rude, she told him.

George urged the old man to try and read the names on the stone, but he could not.

Larissa was the only one who noticed an old woman making her way slowly up from the village to where the bus passengers were wandering among the graves.

Seeing the woman stop when she arrived at the top, Larissa approached her. What are you looking for, Granny?

The woman replied that she was not the one looking. From her window that morning she had observed the strangers alight from their bus and swarm through her village like a small army. She had heard them speak their foreign language and ogle the houses of the villagers as if they owned them. The villagers were saying these people had come to reclaim property they believed belonged once to their forefathers. Houses and fields, they had come to take everything for themselves, as if it was now theirs. They came armed with government documents. Is it true? she asked.

Not true, Larissa said, a bit too rudely. Whoever put such garbage in your heads?

The old woman – Larissa estimated that she was not as old as the oldest man on the bus in spite of her wizened face – was not convinced.

The village belongs to us she said, raising her thin, hoarse voice to a higher pitch. Nobody needs to think they can drive out the real owners. We aren't planning to leave this place. We are not like the people who lived here once long ago and then snuck away like thieves in the night.

Those landowners hadn't exactly been saints, she continued. They had taken the peasants for servants and treated them badly. Had looked out only for each other, but not for their servants or peasant neighbours. Ask anyone in the village, she said, and they could tell you stories of how a grandfather or father was beaten by his well-off employer. There was fire in the old woman's eyes. And fear. Her thin body was tense, her hands balled into fists ready to be raised in defiance of an invading force. Her mouth opened to scream out, Thieves, but what began as an outcry ended as a pathetic whimper.

No Granny, Larissa said, more gently. Nobody will take anything. Tell your silly neighbours they should right now stop this worrying.

The old woman stared at Larissa as if to determine whether she could be trusted.

What does she want? George had seen the two women in conversation.

She thinks you have come to take over the village, Larissa said.

George laughed.

The teenager too had overheard and immediately began imagining how he would tell his soccer team that he had become heir to land in a foreign country. He wouldn't tell them that the property he would inherit was located in some kind of rural slum. He would call it an estate.

Tell them what I told you, the old woman whispered to Larissa. About the cruelty. Tell the truth.

The truth has many faces, Larissa thought. She decided at once that she would not relay this woman's version of it, a version that might not be groundless, might be a mix of accuracy and exaggeration equal to George's version. Or Anya's. But it was not the kind of truth the travelers had come to hear. Watching their incursion into the village that morning, she had understood their enormous expectations, how they had interpreted what they saw in terms of those expectations. They had not given way to disappointment, but convinced themselves that they had arrived at the paradise they'd been told about or read about. Hadn't she been barraged by their rhapsody over the village which they declared beautiful beyond words, well worth the effort to get here? It was all rather foolish. She had figured out that some could not even afford this trip, and some did not deserve it. But who was she to confront them with possible flaws – theirs or their forefathers'?

In the valley below, the bus stood parked in the shade of willow trees lining the banks of a small stream that flowed through the village. Stretched out along the back seat, the exhausted driver closed his eyes. He reckoned his passengers would spend a long time on that sun-baked hill. Well, let them take as long as they wished. They had him to thank for getting them here. He was the one who had haggled with the officials at the border. He had doled out the cigarettes pack by pack and then started on George's wad of bills, stopping before it was completely gone. He was proud of that. He was the one who had driven all night while they slept.

He found it convenient to forget that he had been drinking with his bus driver buddies on the day when he should have been attending to the roadworthiness of the bus. And he preferred not to remember the embarrassment of being turned back at the first border post. It shouldn't have happened, but did, and not because he had neglected to inform himself about border protocol, but because he had deliberately, perhaps perversely, taken the wrong road, believing that he could find a way to cross any border, forbidden or not. Everything turned out well, thanks God, as Larissa had said, after telling him of the saint that had accompanied them.

The translator, he thought, was not the best sort, but not the worst either. He was pretty certain she was a Jew, but he liked her all the same

His passengers were not a bad lot either, all things considered. There wasn't one that had particularly impressed him, but no one had caused trouble. He couldn't for the life of him figure out why they would want to spend their vacation and their money in such a shabby village. Just because their grandparents were born here. Just because they had pictures and stories. He wished he could have taken them on a better journey, to a better place.

Still Life

Halfway through the class Adam still has not arrived. I keep turning toward the door, expecting his lanky form, that diagonal slash of oatmeal hair across a wide forehead. Eyes the colour of a November sky.

At the first of Pierre's art lessons I noticed a young man looking several times in my direction and when our eyes met he smiled. At the break I took my coffee and peanuts from the vending machine over to his table.

"You don't recognize me," he said.

"Should I?"

"Adam Blye."

Of course. The skinny kid who kept a hamster up his sleeve. He would let it slip down onto his desk and play with it, feed it, hold it against his cheek until his classmates snickered. Annoyed, the teacher would send him to the principal's office. From there he would get rerouted to Guidance where I had to listen to his explanation. Eustacia couldn't be left at home. She got nervous if he didn't hold her a lot. His hands reassured her. Eustacia needed that.

That was…what?..ten, twelve years ago. Now in Pierre's art class Adam looks twenty-something. The naked insecurity that once marked his face is gone. Gone too that nervous gaze that kept asking: Can you hear what I'm saying? Do you believe me? Can I trust you? Some kids have masks securely fixed over their doubts by the time they reach junior high. Everything's okay. No problem. Adam was not one of these. But his face has lost its former transparency and his movements are easy.

In the centre of the still-life arrangement Pierre has set up there's an oval lamp base of marbled milky glass with a yellow metal frame for the missing shade. Next to it, a round wicker basket sits on its side, the whorl of woven straw at the bottom facing me. I concentrate on the pattern of the straw, squinting as we have been taught to do, becoming familiar with the way light from the two spotlights interacts with the pattern. A red and yellow child's wheeled toy, a rusted watering can, a blue, open umbrella and a length of gold and green floral fabric draped over an empty packing crate complete the arrangement. We have placed our wooden donkeys and drawing boards in a ragged circle around it. Margot, a year of design studies under her belt, sits beside me, still as the objects before her, sketchbook clamped to the drawing board.

"We'll start with pastels," Pierre said at the start of tonight's class. While we work he prowls like a cat behind our backs, stopping at one, then the next. "Work on colour. And tone. Intensity brings objects closer. Sketch in lightly, then bear down. Don't be afraid to be bold. If you need to tone down, use cool colours. To lighten up, try yellow."

At our first class the arrangement was simpler – a square box, a paper cone and several cylinders clustered on a small table, their shapes overlapping. "No colour, just pencil today," Pierre said, instructing us to measure distances with a pencil held in one hand, arm extended. "Look at what's closest to you. See how the light strikes the side of the cone? Use at least three different pencils. For highlights, leave the paper white. Don't forget the shadows."

My being here in this drawing class has nothing to do with becoming an artist. That is not my intention. I have come because drawing absorbs me completely, directs me to focus on simple things. Ordinary, concrete details. Over the past weeks I've begun to learn about distance and how to achieve it. How to overcome flatness. Problems that technique can solve. The act of drawing will position me in the clearly defined, neutral realm of objects. Inanimate objects endowed with form and outline. A solid world.

Amy keeps telling me I live too much in my own head. She is new to Guidance. Not yet jaded, she believes solutions are not only possible but also probable. Help is always available. Each student, rebellious, indifferent or withdrawn into a shell, embodies potential. Everything will turn out in the end and whatever decision I make about Jennifer will be the right one.

Jennifer lies in her hospital bed day in, day out, a breathing still-life attached by tubes and wires to machines whose muted hum alternates with silence. At first the machines buzzed out sharp warnings and triggered frantic beeps on monitors. This does not happen much now that Jennifer is stabilized. She will not wake.

Beside me, Margot has adjusted her sketchbook, ready to begin. If she were to set up her drawing board beside Jennifer, she would get every detail just right. Volume and depth, angles and subtle shades of light would be meticulously reproduced on her sketch pad.

Adam would go at it differently. He would not worry about the details. Breathing evenly, he would stare, alert and intense, at the arrangement, then lean forward as if to embrace the project with his whole body. He would finish the drawing quickly, bringing to paper not the exact angle of the chin, curve of the forehead, shape of a shoulder, but the poignancy, the hopelessness he'd gleaned by observing my Jennifer.

Sometimes I wonder how my daughter, who as a child loved drawing, would draw herself.

On a cold December morning, a dozen years ago, Adam arrived in my office before school. Voluntarily, this time; not sent by the principal and not with a message from his mother. He carried a package wrapped in red fabric and tied with a grungy scrap of ribbon. "It's for you," he said, "A Christmas present. Open it."

I hesitated, worried that Eustacia would emerge from his sleeve. Impatient, he tore away the wrapping himself, exposing a cardboard box that he handed to me. I opened it: a half dozen marbles and as many clothes pegs.

"Know what it's for?"

I shook my head.

"It's a bowling set." He let me absorb the information and then repeated, "It's for you." His eyes shone alarmingly.

"Adam, does your mother know you took her clothes pegs?"

He looked even more anxious then and his eyes shifted away from me as if he sensed he was on shaky ground. "I wanted to give you a present."

Adam's parents belonged to a religious group bound by peculiar rules. During 'O Canada' he stood outside the closed classroom door, separate from his classmates. As early as October his mother had called, requesting me to inform Adam's teachers that if they planned on singing Christmas carols or staging pageants or seasonal concerts, Adam could not participate. It was forbidden by their religion. And no gift exchange. She needn't have worried; this wasn't elementary school. Junior high teachers have no time for carol singing and any students not in choir wouldn't tolerate it in any case. Adam was not in choir.

"I didn't have nothing else to give you," he said.

"*Anything* else." I said. "You could have made a picture." I regretted the rebuke right away, but Adam was already at the door, his hand cupping Eustacia, his gift left on my desk. I shoved it into a drawer.

At the Health Sciences Centre there's a shortage of beds. The doctors and nurses, overworked and overwrought, are waiting for my decision. They see it as a simple one; why don't I just tell them, yes, it's time. They see Jennifer as an object, clearly defined. Out there, at arm's length, so to speak. A problem for which a solution is available. Solutions are not always available, though my students expect them when they barge into my office with their anxieties about everything from homework and mean teachers to shoplifting and contraceptives. And difficult parents and difficult love. Each new problem a matter of life and death.

Every day after school I visit Jennifer. Some days it feels like a visit to a museum or a sculpture gallery. Sometimes I deliberately sit near the window, a distance from the bed, and focus on the external Jennifer, the outline of her life-supported body under hospital sheets. I consider the compositional relationships between the occupied bed, the electronic gadgetry, the table, the charts above her head registering vital signs, recording intake and output. Other times I come as near as I can. I sit on her bed, place a hand on hers, bring my eyes up close to study the finely shaped nose, the definite chin, the pale, lifeless hair, those thin hands inert on the sheet. I speak, but she doesn't hear.

"What if…?" That's Pierre's way of getting us to see things differently, to discover that the umbrella is not a monochromatic blue but streaked with red and green and orange. "Observe the way light strikes the surface of a drapery. It alters the pattern."

Jennifer's window faces north. The light is subdued. I watch the slight rise and fall of the sheets, the evidence of breathing. Assisted breathing. The tangle of tubes casts tangled shadows. I imagine a stick of charcoal in my hand and an empty page in front of me.

Over the months I have memorized the details of her features. Her face is there when I come home. A companion at supper. A presence in my dreams. Perhaps eventually I will know her completely. By heart.

"It's up to you," the doctor says. "You are the mother."

And how does a mother remove a daughter from life? From *her* life? There would have to be a sign, surely. Something clear and obvious, an arrow pointing in the right direction, at the right time.

"If you like, choose a small section of the arrangement," Pierre says before he resumes prowling. "One element. Focus on that. Pay attention to it. Look at it."

Margot is still serenely motionless except that she has picked up a beige pastel. We do not speak much to each other while drawing. Etiquette. I think Margot will draw the whole of Pierre's still life.

At first it bothered me that a teacher would say so little to his students about their work. No praise or censure. The most he will say is, "Look at the angle of the basket, the distance between the lamp and the wheel of the toy." Or: "You might consider standing back to look at your drawing. Squint at each section of the umbrella."

Should I draw the umbrella? A corner of the green and gold draped fabric? Or the milky lamp base? The whorls of weaving on the basket? While I try to make up my mind something in the room shifts. I look up and there is Adam setting up his drawing board with assured movements. He scans the circle, spots me and grins. Then he takes a pastel, and keeping his eyes on the arrangement, begins drawing.

At break, I leave my still-blank paper clamped to the board and follow the others on a tour of the drawings. A sort of peer review in which either criticism or compliments would be equally presumptuous. And not necessary, Pierre says. On Adam's paper, a section of the milky lamp base, enlarged and articulated in bold strokes of purple, green and ochre, spills over the edges of his paper.

"What did you decide?" he asks over coffee, his hands cradling the paper cup. They are the hands of an artist.

"The basket. I like the pattern," I say, with fabricated calm. I know he is referring to Jennifer.

We have fallen into the habit of sitting together for coffee, and last week he told me about his business – lawns and gardens. I told him about Jennifer who for six months has lain motionless. I did not say the words "brain dead."

"They want me to decide," I told him.

"So she would have been a little kid back then," he mused, calculating." You never said you had a daughter."

"Teachers lead several lives," I replied, miffed that he had missed the seriousness of my dilemma. The raw question of life or death.

"And how many do you think students have?" If there was censure in his words and voice, it was slight.

I said nothing then, and tonight too I want to let him talk, but I remember that bowling gift and ask him if he remembers it. "You gave it to me for Christmas," I say.

"That pathetic bowling set?" Adam laughs, self-consciously. I wish I hadn't mentioned the incident.

"You told me I should have given you a picture instead. Well, actually I made one during science class. I drew my hand, open" – he holds out his left hand to show me – "with Eustacia sort of curled inside it" – he makes a tight ball with his right hand and places it inside the left, curling long fingers around the fist. "It was tricky, one hand busy with the hamster and only one for drawing with." His hands fly apart to demonstrate, "But it occurred to me that some artists are one-handed. And there are those mouth-and-foot painters." Adam stops as if to make room for me to speak.

"I don't remember you giving it to me."

"Actually I didn't. It was pretty good, though." He says this almost defensively, like a declaration and then, abruptly rewords his earlier question, "What are you going to do about Jennifer?"

No one, not my sister who emails daily from Toronto, not Amy or anyone else at school is this direct with me. They skirt around the question of Jennifer. They keep their distance. Jennifer's father, long lost in space and time, is farthest of all. If he had anything at all to say about Jennifer, about the state of her mind and body, her steadfastly closed eyes, I would listen. But there is nothing except silence from that direction.

The others are moving back into the studio, and we follow them, Adam's question unanswered. After the break we always take our drawing boards to a different location, turn to a clean page in our sketchbooks, and start over. "So you get to see the objects from a different vantage point," Pierre says. From my new spot the lamp base is hidden by the open umbrella and instead of the bottom of the basket, I have a full view of its shadowed interior where the pattern is unclear. The depth would be hard to achieve, I think, and consider drawing the umbrella.

Adam has taken up a position directly across from me; he is almost hidden by the arranged objects. It happens that Margot is once again next to me and, on the other side, a woman I've never spoken to. She has several pastels in one hand from which she keeps selecting with the other. She brings a colour close to the paper, pulls it back and takes a different one. She is fidgety and mutters something about her red pastel being nearly finished. Pierre stands a while behind her saying nothing, then moves in my direction. Faced with my blank page I know I must not fail again.

I hand my red pastel to the woman who says, "Oh thanks. "I'm Linda.'

I choose a blue pastel and bring it to the clean page.

If Jennifer had been paralyzed in a traffic accident or while skiing, everything would be different. Then cause and effect would have about them a kind of neutrality. A clarity. An overdose is never simple. In Jennifer's case for instance, how can I know if it was deliberate? A perverse choice? An act of desperation? It could have been a miscalculation. Who knows what she intended, if she intended anything.

Jennifer stopped going to school halfway through the twelfth grade. "I can't believe that education happens in stuffy rooms, in fifty-minute slots," she'd say, coming off a migraine or a late-night party. She had allergies, too. "Everything's changing. Music changes, friends change, governments change, your feelings change, but school never does."

Her words implied that I was spending my life at something obsolete or hopelessly archaic and I tried to argue. "Well, if everything's changing isn't it good to have some structure? We all need structure and right now school gives you that." She paid less and less attention to me and gradually I stopped raging at her erratic arrivals and departures, a coming and going that no longer included school. And seldom me.

When I found her lying curled and cold in her room, it was too late for words. Action was called for. An ambulance sped my daughter and me along the shortest route to the hospital, sirens announcing our progress through the city. We had not been so close for a long time. I was afraid to look. Afraid to watch the paramedic who monitored her breathing.

Now Jennifer is incapable of intention. And so, it seems, am I.

A blue circle has appeared on my white paper, too small for an open umbrella, too small for the rim of a basket. I have not been bold. "How could you make use of it?" Pierre would say. Or, "What if this circle became part of something bigger?" He is standing across from me, bent over someone's drawing. He will not notice if I take a clean sheet and start over. Instead, I grab a handful of pastels and with erratic movements set to work filling the paper with colour. I need the red but Linda is still using it. Pierre is working his way around the circle back to me. Frantic, I bear down hard, grinding the pastel crayons down to stubs. The intensity of blues, greens and yellows becomes alarming.

"A holocaust," Adam says, seriously, when the class is over. Then he grins. He is looking directly at me, and I can see the concern in his eyes.

Linda is still fussing with paper and pastels when Adam and I pick up our bags and drawing boards and leave.

The city surrounds us with light as we walk to the parking lot. Tiers of windows blaze in office towers that stretch toward the sky. On the top levels of the parkade across the street isolated cars look like blackened teeth. Traffic rushes headlong, buildings throw shadows. We are caught in a vortex of light and darkness, of unrelenting movement. I feel dizzy. Adam takes my arm, a gesture of courtesy, and comfort.

"Look," he says, and we both look up to where the Golden Boy on top of the Legislative Buildings holds out his glowing torch.

"What happened, Adam?" I say, finally asking the question. "I mean you're…you're changed."

I pause and have to begin again. "In the staff room, everyone was concerned. They worried about you." I tried to laugh, to show I was never part of such absurdity. I don't mention the disdain with which the math teacher predicted Adam would turn out a basket case, nor the sarcasm with which the prediction was delivered, nor the jokes about Adam that spiced up our lunch hour. "Is he a few bricks short or what?"

Above a sporting goods store a neon sign blinks on-off, on-off although the store is closed.

"Well you guys didn't know everything, did you?" The words are blunt, but free of accusation. At the entrance to the parking lot, Adam stops and faces me. "By the time I hit high school, my parents split up." He is trying to be matter-of-fact, but I detect a trace of sorrow. "That church we belonged to? My Dad wanted out. So he left us. Mom got a full-time job."

I must have known that. Details of family break-ups regularly found their way to Guidance. What had I done with that information? Recorded it? Shoved it in a drawer?

"At lunch I avoided the multipurpose room. Too crowded, and mostly I didn't know who I'd sit with. So I'd usually head for the library and hide my sandwiches behind a propped-up book. At noon the library was pretty much empty. I had to be ready to pop Eustacia into my lunch bag on short notice." He laughs nervously and turns, as if to go.

"Wait," I say, reaching with my hand to bring him back to his story.

His eyes are shadowed but I know they are fixed on mine. "I always checked to see which teacher was on supervision," he says. "The eagle-eye kind or someone who got busy right away marking papers. Mr. Krentz liked to stroll around. 'Adam,' he'd whisper," – and Adam bends toward me mimicking Krentz – "'A rolling stone gathers no moss,' or 'Do unto others as you would have them do unto you.' He was odd; the kids made fun of him.

"His favourite quotation was that line, 'To be or not to be, that is the question.' I started laying bets with myself every time he was on duty, would this be a 'to be or not to be' day? I had no idea where that came from or what it meant but it sort of wore a groove in my brain. I'd repeat it to Eustacia. Then, in grade twelve I read Hamlet and there it was. 'To be or not to be.' Anyway, why am I telling you this? You're probably thinking something spectacular happened to make me normal. Something big and dramatic. How else could I look after myself, you're thinking. Take drawing lessons, even. Well, sorry, there was no epiphany, no conversion. My Mom slogged on. We managed. There came a time when I had to get a job. I guess I decided somewhere along the line it's better 'to be' than 'not to be.'" He chuckles wryly.

"You're doing well, Adam," I say, wanting to encourage him. I am ready now to leave, but he continues.

"Mr. Krentz taught science. I remember the caterpillars he brought in one fall. A couple of fat neon green things, with bright yellow rings and black dots. They were stretched along stems of dill he'd crammed into a jar. You could see them move, eating the dill. I used to draw them, like I drew everything those days, on any scrap of paper I had. We watched the caterpillars spin cocoons that Krentz said contained butterflies. Black Swallowtail. 'A miracle,' that's how Krentz described the whole cycle. He explained how the wings would be damp and fragile when the butterfly emerged, but in the end nothing could stop them from flying."

"Sounds cruel to put them in a jar." I could say this because I had never chased down insects or tried to contain them. I couldn't remember ever pointing out bugs or butterflies to Jennifer.

"Leaving them in the garden on a dill stalk is just as risky. Birds can get them, easy. Few survive, Krentz told us."

"So did his specimens ever fly?"

"Well, if they did, I wasn't there. Science class was chaotic, mostly."

"Did you bring Eustacia to science?" I can hardly imagine Adam without his hamster.

"Oh, Eustacia." He speaks the name with a tenderness that's usually reserved for a troublesome child. There is a long pause before he adds. "Yeah, I did. At first. Then she got lost in the science room. Or stolen. Whatever. She was just gone." He pauses then, out of respect or grief, and his voice is soft when he adds, shrugging, "It happens."

"You must come across green caterpillars when you do gardens." I say when we resume walking.

"Yeah. Lots. Late summer. In fall too. And I've seen a couple of Black Swallowtails. But never the cocoons. Except those in science class."

Adam escorts me right to my car the way he always does, then strides to his small truck with "Adam's Yard

Care" painted in bold letters on the door. I wave as I drive from the dark lot and turn into the brilliantly lit street.

I should not have hesitated after the coffee break. I should have started immediately to draw the dim interior of the basket, unafraid of its shape and its dark depth. I should have worked quickly, colouring in bright folds of the floral drapery around the basket. When I get home, I'll take a clean page and practise. I'll use every one of my pastel stubs except the red which Linda has not returned. I'll draw a fat green and yellow caterpillar, magnified to fill the page. I won't draw the dull cocoon, but I'll find a picture of a Black Swallowtail in the B volume of the World Book Encyclopaedia and draw it too. I'll work as precisely as Margot. And with understanding, like Adam.

By the time I arrive home and put on the kettle for tea, my good intentions have evaporated. Instead of unpacking my pastels and sketchbook while waiting for the water to boil, I simply think of Jennifer. Not the hospital Jennifer, but little Jennifer who loved to draw. She didn't need a still-life arrangement in front of her, nor someone to tell her what to draw, or show her how. She simply drew. Only rarely would she scrunch up her paper and announce, "I start over." She would sit at the table and fill page after page with stick children in all colours of the rainbow, big smiles on their cookie faces, tumbling off the edge of her paper. Or she'd draw a figure so large it occupied the entire page. Sometimes she'd push her picture toward me and say, "You draw the eyes, Mom."

Surprised

Erica's colleagues at North-East Life Assurance would be astonished to see her down on all fours in torn jeans, her streaked brown hair in disarray, fingernails dirty.

"That's not like Erica," they might say, and someone might add, facetiously, "Is she praying?"

Someone else would venture, "Need a hand up, Erica?"

Not one of her colleagues is anywhere near, of course. At five o'clock they tidied their desks, and on the elevator reminded each other of urgent messages to be sent first thing in the morning, potential contacts to be tracked down, sales to be clinched, deadlines to be met. Everything connected somehow with assuring life.

Sales and deadlines have been relegated to the periphery of Erica's mind, though her cell phone is jammed into her jeans pocket. Nor is she looking for a hand up. She is kneeling in her garden a few feet from the six tomato plants she set out last week and somewhat farther away from the tiger lilies already in the process of transformation from tight green buds to fiery blooms. Although her position might suggest humility and petition, Erica is not praying. She is running her slender, manicured fingers back and forth, back and forth through the black soil, looking for a cutworm.

Her bent knees flank a cucumber seedling limp on the sun-baked earth. Just yesterday – newly planted, fertilized, watered – it stood as upright and green as its three sister seedlings. Today Erica found it sheared off just below the surface of the soil, the leaves wilted and losing colour. When she finds the culprit responsible for this devastation she will kill it. Then she will return to the house, where her daughter has upped the volume on her CD player until the beat of the Backstreet Boys pounds in every room.

"Turn that down," she'll yell.

Diane, at eleven, has made sullenness a weapon that she hones through constant practice. Music provides the cover. She's playing the Backstreet Boys at a volume that annoys her mother, though it wasn't music they disagreed about today, but the movie *Drive*s. Diane's friends are going to see it after supper, why can't she?

"On a school night?" Erica said, outrage amplified. "Over my dead body." Diane shot back with: "It's your mind that's dead, Mom." She will not come out of her room or tone down the decibels until she is good and ready. She's no child. She knows a thing or two.

She is lying on her bed, staring at the ceiling, scanning the walls. Amidst posters of Hillary Duff, Brad Pitt, in-your-face slogans, her eyes come to rest on a modest incongruity, almost lost in the collage of colour and gloss and celebrity. A cross-stitched motto in a narrow frame announces: "I am the Resurrection and the Life." It was a birthday gift from her grandmother, five years ago. Not a gift she received with much enthusiasm then, nor one she particularly prizes now. Whenever Gigi or Aynsley or Judy enter the room Diane gets nervous and hopes they won't notice it. It would be so embarrassing. Once she removed the framed image, but returned it to its place afterwards, as if it had become impossible to go to bed at night or rise in the morning without it.

From her prone position she scrutinizes the exquisite stitching and the ornate cross superimposed on the "I." Her grandmother who made those perfect stitches with her own hands has become an old, helpless woman. Diane can't imagine ever being so motionless. She wonders whether her grandmother, who once quilted and made pickles and the best ginger cookies, was ever as unreasonable as her mother.

The Backstreet Boys blare into her ear. She shifts, restless. Bored.

Determined to find the cutworm, Erica searches for it with her fingers, the way her mother taught her. Later this evening she will visit her mother in Resthaven. She'll bring a bunch of tiger lilies, a guilt offering, she admits, for not coming oftener. The lilies are amazing. When it's the season for blooming, the long buds loosen and the petals unfold, creating a brilliance in the garden that draws her mornings and evenings to the kitchen window. At North-East Life Assurance everything depends on human effort; here in the garden, in spring, growth happens almost in spite of it. Nothing can stop the lilies from opening. Or noxious weeds from flourishing.

Erica experienced her first cutworm in her mother's garden, when she was younger than Diane is now. "Just move the earth around the fallen plant, gently," her mother instructed. "Likely the worm's overstuffed from chomping through the stem and can't move far." Sure enough, the worm was easily found and destroyed, though it was her mother, not Erica, who killed that first one, demonstrating how it was done – the worm dropped on the hard sidewalk and crushed with a stone. Gross, Diane would say.

Erica keeps looking.

Two nurses are bent over a thin old woman curled tight and small in her white hospital bed, hands motionless, eyes closed, her breathing almost imperceptible.

"You grab the top, I'll get the bottom," one of them says.

"Poor old thing," the other replies. They take hold of the woman's shoulders and buttocks, turning her cautiously onto her other side. They tug at the bedclothes and try to settle the stiff limbs.

"Pain, Granny?" They hover uncertainly over the bed.

The slight motion of the woman's head could be yes, could be no.

"Bye then, Sweetheart." They hurry off.

The fetal woman is not the oldest in the nursing home, but perhaps the most pathetic. Her muscles have atrophied; she needs help with everything. Every movement is painful and speaking has become a huge undertaking that she seldom attempts. Sometimes the staff assumes that there's as little activity in the mind as in the body.

"Just keep her comfortable," the charge nurse says.

The woman, cocooned in bed sheets and pain, might be imagining the world beyond this small white room. That world is hazy, as if someone has pulled a veil over it. Or as if it is receding, and she sees it from a distance. She is vaguely aware that it's spring, and the grey winter trees have taken on the pale green of the season.

She has long known, both in her mind and in her body, that she's no longer necessary. Spring will give way to summer without her. But her daughter will feel it. And her granddaughter. She pictures them in a field or park, surrounded by birdsong and the shimmer of flowering trees and shrubs. They breathe in the scent of linden blossoms. Wind riffles their hair; they lift their faces to the sun. Their movements are ephemeral. The old woman believes, or imagines, she can see their shadowy forms turning to each other, their shadowy faces smiling. Her own face too twists into a kind of smile.

And then the muted tones and shades give way to vivid colours: pink, scarlet, blue, purple. She hears music of startling clarity. Everything around and inside the old woman vibrates with light. And with anticipation. She feels, or imagines she feels, her limbs stirring as if they want to unfold. As if she is beginning to grow, not larger, but lighter. And free of pain. Any minute now she will rise like the fluffy seed of the cottonwood tree that in June floats on the air and is carried on a breath of wind to every corner of the city.

"Looked like she was smiling," one nurse will observe afterwards.

"Surprised," the other will think.

Just when Erica is ready to give up on the cutworm, there it is. An inch long and thick, the colour of earth. Gorged with chewed cucumber stems, it lies inert, stretched out to its full stubby length. There is no curling up for protection. No hint of resistance. Erica is caught off-guard, surprised by its utter helplessness and momentarily distracted. But she's not deterred from taking the creature to the sidewalk and stomping on it with the heel of her Reebok.

"They're tough," her mother used to say. "If you don't do a good job on them, they'll recover. They'll kill more of your plants. They'll go spin a cocoon and become a moth and come next spring – the whole business all over again."

Erica, if there were time, might ponder the evidence everywhere before her of the unstoppable urge to keep on being and growing. There's a right time for everything, she'd think, and spring is the season for newness, for growth. It's also the season when, while she's asleep or selling life insurance, rabbits graze her tulips and peas, slugs eat large holes into hollyhock leaves and cut-worms make a meal of tender cucumber seedlings. She knows she hasn't killed her garden's last predator, and she can't guarantee the survival of any of the bedding plants or perennials flourishing today before her eyes.

Before she returns to the house, to her adolescent daughter – Diane is growing too, she has gained one and a half inches in the last months – and the blaring music, she surveys with satisfaction, and hope, the six sturdy tomato plants and the three remaining cucumber seedlings. Then she strides purposefully toward the unbridled orange lilies.

Diane is considering whether her life will be worth living, or even possible, if she doesn't get to see *Drives*. What will she tell Gigi, Aynsley, Judy? So mortifying to have a dull, narrow-minded mother. The late afternoon sun pours into her room. She is bored and hungry. She reaches over to turn down the Backstreet Boys.

When she enters the kitchen, heading for the fridge, her mother is there in front of it, half-hidden by a shocking orange blaze.

"Oh my God," Diane gasps.

"I'm taking them to Granny's, right after supper," Erica says. "Want to come?"

The flowers in Erica's arm seem to fill the kitchen, demanding attention, crowding out lesser sensations.

Diane considers rejecting her mother's invitation because she's going to a movie, but she can't take her eyes from the lilies. From their brazen authority.

"Wow," she says, trying not to relinquish her cool, her practised condescension. Okay then, she'll come. "Granny is sure going to be surprised," she says, reaching for the flowers.

Erica is about to agree but her cell phone rings and with her free hand – a Life Assurance hand, a hand recently in contact with black soil, a worm's cold skin and fresh lily stems – she reaches for it.

A Perfect Location

Although it's early in the day, there's a line-up at Canada Customs at Fort Francis, and an RCMP vehicle parked near the building. Leila puts her car in neutral, clicks off the air conditioning, and rolls down the window. She reaches out as if to grab the wind. The two cars ahead of her are pulled over and uniformed officials have begun searching them. She wasn't expecting to be detained and wonders what this will do to the rest of the day. She turns off the ignition, gets out of the car.

"Wonder what they're looking for?" The motorist behind Leila has stuck his head out the window.

"Drugs," someone calls from a black Volvo. "They're after drugs."

Bad joke, Leila thinks.

Several customs officers poke around in the car trunks ahead, rummaging through clothing and personal possessions. They crawl into the vehicles, shine lights into small spaces. Two RCMP officers stand stolidly by.

Leila takes a notebook and pencil from her shoulder bag. She's a writer for whom the world in all its mundane or spectacular manifestations offers up raw material, sometimes in huge chunks, sometimes in fragments so unremarkable they are easily overlooked. She reaches for these offerings and sets about arranging and rearranging the imperfect, incomplete bits and pieces of life. She will add snippets of her modest knowledge, apply her imagination, hoping that facts and details can be transformed into fiction.

Leila likes to tell other writers that she published her first book when she was ten. Her teacher invited Old Bob Tanner, one of the oldest residents in the rural school district, to visit her class. Old Bob, bent and burly in a rumpled tweed jacket worn over farm overalls, emerged from the coat lobby at the back of the classroom and lumbered down the aisle leaning on his cane, supported by the neighbour who had chauffeured him in his truck. Leila crooked her elbow into the aisle as he passed by so his worn tweed jacket brushed against it. She squinted at Old Bob until he became a grotesque, fantastic blur.

"My first job was chasin' crows from a farmer's haystack," he told the class. "That was in England. Way back in ancient history. It's the kinda work don't get you nowhere."

The children, mesmerized, stared at this ancient, shaggy storyteller who had left the far country of his birth, left home and parents and crossed the ocean too long ago for their young minds to fathom. A boy of thirteen, he had come to the bleak bush country wedged between Manitoba's lakes to seek his fortune. Leila tried to imagine Old Bob at thirteen. Would he have been as foul-mouthed and rough as the grade eight boys sitting next to the windows?

"When the boat landed us out east, we got our first look at Canada. Big and grey. We got on a train, days and days on that train, seemed like, with nothin' but rocks out the window. A god-forsaken country, it looked like. And then we came here. Nothin' but bush and bush and more bush. And stones. Had to pick stones from the fields we cleared. Years I dreamed nothin' but stones."

Afterwards, the teacher handed out foolscap, showed the children how to cut and fold it into pages on which they wrote down the story of Old Bob's new beginning, choosing the best words they knew. Leila was happy. *Bob Tanner was born in England,* she began. *He never imagined he would come to live north of Winnipeg, in a grey bush and pick heavy stones from the fields.* She looked critically at what she had written, erased the words and began again: *Once upon a time in a far country a boy was born to a poor family.* She paused to consider what she might add to that sentence, how to extend the short line, how to stretch it to the horizon.

The teacher had let each child choose a sheet of coloured construction paper for a book cover. Leila chose blue, and wrote on it in black letters: THE STORY OF BRAVE BOB TANNER. When the teacher picked hers to send as a gift to the old storyteller, her cup overflowed.

The customs official who has begun searching Leila's car is called over to confer with the RCMP. The drivers of the waiting vehicles are restless. They have destinations in mind. Deadlines. More cars are lining up behind them. Waiting, Leila has discovered, doesn't have to be fruitless. She records, mentally and in her notebook, the official's grim expressions; the rumpled uniforms of the RCMP; the tense voice of the man behind her, the half-smoked cigarette between his fingers reflected in her rear view mirror. She notices the way the wind takes hold of the garish print skirt of the woman who has stepped out of the maroon Sunbird.

Leila's second book was published this past winter, a thriller. *Seared by Memory*. It has become successful, though not a best seller. The publisher, pleased, is pushing her to complete the next manuscript. She has recently come from a book promotion tour: Chicago – where she lives now, New York, Philadelphia. She has been quoted in culture pages of newspapers, interviewed on television. She has been short-listed for a crime fiction award, and is hopeful that with her next book she may become a winner. A small sweep of the limelight on her work, on herself, and Leila's appetite for celebrity status is whetted. She craves it, though she has not admitted to herself how much.

Her four friends whom she will meet in a few hours at Echo Bay are not having this kind of writing success. She will have to be careful not to let *Seared by Memory* take centre stage this weekend. The others, she senses, have moved away from writing, their earlier commitment to it worn thin by the weight of what life has handed them. It must be at least two years since Lis's daughter was shot dead in the lunchroom of her high school. Unbelievable. Senseless. Delores, apparently, has been teaching English in some East European country newly independent from the Soviet Union. Helen, she learned from Eleanor, has gone back to university.

She can't figure out what's happening to Eleanor. Eleanor was the beautiful one, the one who wrote with such passion, the one Leila envied most. The one from whom she expected to hear frequently when she left Winnipeg. For a while they wrote and phoned regularly. It was from Eleanor she first heard that the writing group no longer met. Now their exchange of letters is in danger of drying up. Eleanor agreed, with some prodding, to have the reunion at her cottage on Echo Bay. The location is perfect, a midway point.

The sun continues to shine on the line up of cars, the officers, drivers, passengers, the customs building. This check point has spawned a unique meeting that will never be replicated, Leila reflects. Sooner or later the detained cars will move on. *She* will move on. This tenuous configuration of people and words and light will undergo constant alteration as the day unfolds. Is this significant? Would that harried customs official be surprised if someone told him he was searching the car of a writer of thrillers? She adds to the jottings in her notebook – fragments of conversation, phrases she will shape until they are 'nicely turned.' Possible plots.

Leila never intended to become an author of thrillers. She had expected – no, assumed – she would write literary fiction. Short stories. Alice Munro was her model. And Mavis Gallant. She wanted to explore the hidden lives of women and men. Children too. Their inner landscapes would be her territory. She would write about the yearnings and struggles of the human spirit. But any stories she managed to complete were rejected more often than published.

"You seem to have reached a plateau," Professor Conway said seven years ago, at the end of the creative writing course Leila and the other four women had taken at the University of Manitoba. Stung, she was determined to prove him wrong, the arrogant prick. She would move her butt off that wretched plateau, clamber up to higher ground, if necessary on hands and knees. If necessary, bloodied. She would get better and better. In the writing group the five of them had formed, her work was admired.

"Where do you get those plots?" they cried.

"Your stories move. There's so much action."

The attention pleased Leila and for a while she squelched all misgivings about the reach of her imagination and believed her talent had no limits.

It isn't easy to lay to rest a long-held hope. But not impossible. One winter Leila decided simply to set aside her short fiction, the whole hopefully-begun manuscript, and write a story in the thriller genre. She was surprised how much fun it was, and how easily ideas came to her. True, the characters weren't given the kind of attention she liked to give. Inner landscape gave way to sleazy back rooms, deserted warehouse buildings, boardrooms and government offices rife with intrigue.

The manuscript was accepted and published and there had been a second and now, soon, a third.

"There's definitely a market for this," her publisher keeps saying.

Leila has already told the customs official where she is from, the purpose and duration of her visit to Canada. When he completes his inspection of her car, there is a form to fill out. When Leila signs and returns it to him she notices his shirt is sweaty and rumpled, a smudge has appeared on his left cheek. Truth to tell, he looks rather drained. What will this day offer him? Maybe he'll discover crack cocaine in the upholstery of an ordinary car, or hidden beneath the false bottom of a suitcase. Or cartons of illicit cigarettes and bottles of liquor stashed in the van of someone who insists there is nothing to declare. Pornography? A hand gun being smuggled across the border? He might open a trunk and find in it a stowaway, desperate and vicious. Or curled like a foetus and gasping for air.

"OK ma'am." The official waves her on.

Leila drives a short distance down the highway, but soon pulls off, stopping where she can still look back and see the activities at the customs building in her rear view mirror. The woman in the garish skirt returns to her car and drives it forward. Leila looks and writes, and in a short while has scrawled several pages of notes. Raw material. Snatches of life. A few tentative titles: *Crossing the Border. Contraband. Fatal Delays.*

It's possible this delay will keep Eleanor waiting at the Echo Bay boat landing. It can't be helped. Writing takes precedence over other things. It is a calling, at least that's what Leila believes most of the time. Tonight she will read to the others from her manuscript-in-progress and rekindle their passion for writing. The whole weekend, she believes, will offer riches for all of them.

She closes her notebook and resumes the journey.

Driving east on the Trans-Canada, Helen and Delores chatter about the Balkan War, the civil unrest in Sierra Leone, the coming elections. And of course they speculate about the weekend. Helen does most of the talking; Delores drives.

"I've got this feeling Eleanor isn't too crazy about the whole reunion thing," Helen says. "It's Leila who's pushing it."

"You think so?"

"Leila's quite the literary success, I hear," Helen continues. "Two thrillers. Imagine. One of us poised for fame. I'd never have guessed it would be Leila."

"Hmm." Delores is noncommittal.

"And then there's Lis. She's pretty much a basket case, Eleanor tells me."

"Poor Lis."

"Are you writing?" Helen asks, and turns toward Delores who has to keep her eyes on the highway. So far the subject of their own writing has not been mentioned.

"No. You?"

"Yes. Essays." They laugh.

Helen, at fifty, is half way through a master's program in history. She has become a student. For real, not just auditing. And that, she tells Delores more than once, is a life-transforming experience. When Delores asks if she doesn't feel like a mother hen with all those young students, Helen says, only a little defensively, that she's learned a lot from them. She admits, though, that she's relieved her own children have chosen anthropology and computer science. No danger of finding herself in the same class with them.

"What will you do?" Delores asks. "I mean, will you teach? Do research? Write a book?"

"I've still got a year before I graduate." It's clear Helen doesn't like the question. She may have asked it of herself too often. It is an odd time of life to be looking toward a different future. She's never had a real career. A brief stint at real estate proved that she wasn't meant to sell property.

"I guess this weekend will be a review of ancient history for us," Delores says. "Remember how we stuck together in Conway's class? How scared we were of him? How insecure we were?"

They had been the five older students surrounded by a dozen or so aspiring writers in their late teens and early twenties who were confident in their creative abilities and afraid of nothing.

"Scared of Conway? Insecure? You felt that? We were so damn serious. Do you remember how terribly important it all seemed?" Helen turns toward Delores, who allows herself a brief glance in her direction. There isn't much Helen can read in that glance; her companion's eyes appear blank. Dull.

Professor Conway's class met Tuesday evenings in a grey room in one of the old stone buildings of the university. Helen, the oldest of the five women, remembers it all as rather bizarre: Conway's annoying habit of munching lifesavers; the outpouring of violence that glutted the plots of the young man who looked fifteen; the anorexic teenager who sat across from her and never, as far as she could make out, wrote anything. Once, during coffee break, Helen confronted her. "You should eat. I'll buy you a doughnut." But the offer was refused and the anorexic girl never again appeared in class.

"History is what we remember," Helen says, settling into the topic. "It's not about facts. It's about shoring up your own convictions, what you believe. How you experienced things or how you think you experienced things. In the end, every history is a construct."

"You make it sound like something we invent, like fiction. Are you telling me history's not objective? Not really true?"

"Listen. When the storytelling begins at Eleanor's, we likely won't recall the same things. Our writing group? We'll all remember it differently. We'll remember each other differently."

Delores is silent, wondering how the others might remember her.

"You'll see," Helen says. "What happened in Conway's class, and later in our group, moved straight into memory. And that memory has been filtered through what's happened to us since. What you remember won't be what Leila remembers. She's the one who was insecure if you ask me. And God only knows what Lis will remember.

"Oh why don't you just tell me to shut up," she laughs now, embarrassed. "I'm lecturing. Here, I've brought the *Anonymous Four.*" She inserts the CD and the ethereal, unaccompanied chanting of the four vocalists fills the small interior of the car: *Kyria christifera.*

Delores, meanwhile, has entered, unwillingly, a memory of recent history that since her return from overseas hovers without mercy close to the surface. Night and day it will not let her go.

She has finished teaching her last class for the day – John Donne's poetry, simplified for twenty-six students whose first language is not English. They struggle and sometimes resist, but half a dozen of them are passionate about poetry in any language and their passion energizes the others. She leaves her students and walks toward a park a short distance from the school at the edge of the small port city on the Baltic Sea. Various thrill rides dot the park: a dilapidated ferris wheel, a circle of small cars intended to lift and whirl children up and up to safe but thrilling heights, a merry-go-round with paint peeling from the horses. The shadowy shapes of the rusted structures lurk half-concealed behind lime trees; they surprise you when you come upon them. The place is stagnant, although Delores has seen the ferris wheel in motion once or twice, but never the merry-go-round. The amusement machinery holds little interest for her. Choosing from several paths, she walks past the leaning, overgrown structures. Broken pavement gives way to gravel. Easy to stumble here. She is headed for a spruce forest that continues beyond the park, majestic trees whose branches control the amount of light that seeps through. An enchanted forest. She has been there before, but never alone. Everyone warns against coming alone, but the sun is still high and the air filled with the sound of traffic from the street beside the park. The mystery and coolness of the forest draw her. Surely there can be no malice on a such beautiful day. In such a lovely location. She will enter the shade and when she has walked safely through it, the sea will welcome her. Delores's destination is the white beach along the Baltic Sea.

She entered that spruce forest unreluctantly, but there will be no voluntary returning to it. The memory of that afternoon takes hold of her frequently, with a dreaded, inescapable clarity impossible to fend off. One minute she is sheltered in the magic of the trees, safe in their grandeur, the wind in their crowns moaning like the sea waves beyond them.

The next minute, footsteps behind her, a hardness clamped over her mouth, her body smashed viciously down on the gravel. Stones grind into her face, her limbs are bent into grotesque lines, all breath is sucked out of her, she is on the verge of implosion. Two enormous hands, purposeful and without mercy, move along her body. She prays they are looking only for her money, not for her, not for her life. She has a few bills in her jeans pocket and there is a lull when the hands find them. But she hears thick breathing and the breathing demands more. She shuts her eyes. An animal whimper of protest quivers in her throat, but a hand shoves it back. She will choke, she will be throttled. A fierce weight pushes down on her, crushing her, declaring dominance, demanding entrance into every part of her. Pain tears her open. Someone is screaming. The forest turns black.

The *Anonymous Four* are chanting: *Gloria, gloria.*

Delores starts and comes to, shocked that she has become oblivious to where she is, unaware of the setting – highway, traffic, trees, occasional buildings flying past. A monstrous rig is roaring toward her. Her hands grip the steering wheel as if it were a life raft and she on the edge of drowning. She clamps her tongue between her teeth.

At a Shell station Helen insists they stop for coffee and Delores is too shaken to remind her that Eleanor has promised brunch the minute they arrive. The chrome and vinyl tables and chairs in the cafe are classic, the coffee superb, the cinnamon roll they share has been toasted to brown perfection.

"You looked like you needed a break," Helen says, startled by her friend's pallor, the terror in her eyes. "You okay? I could drive for a bit."

Delores shakes her head. "No, no, I'm fine." Her voice is almost inaudible, her half of the cinnamon bun barely touched.

"You must have your head full of memories from teaching abroad," Helen says, and when she gets no answer, "Lots to write about, I should think."

The darkness of that forest, the fear, is not something Delores wants to give words to, ever, but as long as it is there, it will block out anything else she might want to write about. "Well, yes, of course," she says. "Living at the seaside is exciting, it's an adventure.

Especially if you come from the prairies. We walked on the beach whenever we could. The sand is so white. And endless. And the sky is endless too. And crammed with stars. At night." She stops, lost.

Helen waits for more, and after what seems a long pause Delores says: "The trees are what I remember most. They're magic. Really. The way they filter the light so it makes patterns on the forest floor." She pauses, aware that Helen is staring at her. The paper napkin is scrunched in her fist, her knuckles are white. She gets up and reaches for her car keys. "We better get moving. Don't want to keep Eleanor waiting."

Eleanor stands at the kitchen window looking out across the smooth, unwrinkled bay that shimmers with restrained exuberance. Soon the wind will begin riffling the birch leaves and stirring the water into ripples, but for the moment everything is still, and into the stillness floats a line from an almost forgotten poem: *There lives the dearest freshness deep down things*. Hopkins. She feels a small stirring of gratitude. And joy.

She has not slept well. Last night's dream was another anxiety dream – guests arriving at the cottage by boatloads even before she had time to pull on shorts and a T-shirt, let alone mix the waffle batter. The dream ended when she ran out to where the dream guests were clambering onto the dock. The few faces she caught a clear glimpse of were the faces of strangers.

The weekend guests Eleanor is expecting are neither dream women nor complete strangers. They are coming to mark the seventh anniversary of a friendship that began in an advanced writing class at the University of Manitoba. Leila was the one who phoned everyone, her adamant plans overruling any reluctance the other four harboured. Eleanor had not intended to volunteer the cottage, but Leila nudged her hard, and Leila was always a bit frightening.

As Eleanor watches the gulls swooping down on a rocky outcropping to feed their young, the squirrels racing up the maple trunk, a boat flying across the bay, she wants to walk out of the cottage and give herself over to the solitude of the woods and the warmth of the morning sun. She wants to walk out to the dock where the pull of the cool, clear water is irresistible this time of day. When they bought this cottage two years ago, she and David resolved to make it a retreat from the rush and frenzy that kept eroding their lives. A place for rest and meditation. At Echo Bay they would be made whole. Made new.

"Let's never invite guests," David said.

"What about Bill and Jana?"

"Well, of course the kids," David conceded. "And your mother."

"Let's never feel guilty about not sharing this cottage with anyone else," Eleanor said, recognizing at once the impossibility of such a resolution. She had already bragged about the utter charm of this location to friends.

There have always been guests, of course. Eleanor has met them at the landing and brought them to her dock, not without joy, but the joy always shadowed by a nagging desire for solitude, like longing for another country, or longing to keep time from whizzing past. Right now she would like to divest this day of everything except sun and air and water, the song of birds and the wind increasing in the trees.

But there is no time. She has to get across the bay to the east landing to pick up Helen and Delores. And Leila. Lis will come on her own, from Kenora. But first she has to prepare for the brunch she has promised her guests. It will be the first weekend meal the five friends will eat together. Friends, Eleanor thinks, may not be the right word. She, for instance, has settled for Christmas cards sent well after the season's rush, a hastily scrawled note if there's time. It used to be "My best for a new year of writing," but now she writes only, "Be well," or "Shalom." Leila still sends letters with her cards at Christmas and at birthdays, too, and these must be answered. Her telephone calls, spontaneous and unexpected, often at inconvenient times, are usually reports on her current work-in-progress. When Leila speaks, you listen.

Lis does not take any kind of initiative. When they last met – in early summer, shopping in Kenora – Lis seemed sad and more frightened than usual. Her sorrow stayed with Eleanor, another reminder of life's cruel underside.

Helen was the lively conversationalist, the one with ideas. Her writing was mature, substantial. Eleanor looks forward to seeing Helen.

Eleanor hasn't written for years. Not poems, not stories. She's even given up the journaling that once gave her such delight. The day's glad or troubling moments and encounters transformed by a newly awakened imagination. At one time all five of them kept journals. Once in a while they would read to each other from particularly poetic entries, though Eleanor doubts if any of them ever read aloud what they deeply believed. Or felt. For her part, she believed making public anything very personal encouraged voyeurism. Couldn't the practice of keeping a journal degenerate into exhibitionism?

Still, she's sorry she burnt her journals.

The burning happened five years ago, when her affair with Allan came to an end. The affair itself had generated the period of most faithful, most intense and necessarily the most secret journaling. Every page chronicled the intoxicating ecstasies of passion and the torment of guilt that now seem pale and slightly ridiculous. Eleanor remembers clearly how the words were reduced to grey ash in the flames. The final traces of longing and misery escaped through the fireplace chimney as smoke.

But fire could not erase all of the words.

"When a woman meets the man she can truly love, the man who can enter not just her body but her spirit, her essence, who can bring her to life, as if for the first time, then nothing else can matter. A gift has been given. It must be received."

"*How do I love thee; let me count the ways.*"

How silly, she thinks now. How juvenile.

Her stories became love stories, her poems love poems. When she showed them to the group just before it broke up, Leila said, "Good God, you're having a real break-through, aren't you?'

"Has David seen them?" Helen asked. "What does he say?"

"Definitely publishable," Lis said.

In spite of their enthusiasm and, yes, envy, she never sent any of her writings to one of those lit mags they read so avidly in those days. Eventually she stopped bringing work to the group, which was doomed to disintegrate when Leila moved to Chicago where her husband was transferred. She had been the driving force of the group, and soon after she left, their meetings became infrequent, then stopped.

Of course Eleanor hadn't shown her work to David. "I'm meeting the writing group," she'd say on the nights she was meeting Allan. David had not entered into her writing in any significant way; it seemed to puzzle him more than anything else.

When Allan left for Toronto, warning her he probably wouldn't call or write, since in his estimation their relationship had run its course, she was devastated. Disbelief and incomprehension were followed by anger, then mourning so intense it was all she could do to keep from screaming out her misery. How could such betrayal be contained or kept hidden? How could she have been so naïve?

"You all right, Ellie?" David would ask, coming up beside her, awkward as a boy, sometimes putting his arm clumsily around her.

Last weekend, she and David had walked out to the dock at midnight. She had told him her old group was getting together at Echo Bay for a reunion next week, would he mind staying in Winnipeg.

"I'll be fine," he said. "You have a good time with the old gang. You might start writing again, Ellie."

Above them the northern lights streaked wildly across the sky. Ribbons of light scrolling and unscrolling, fiery and at the same time cold. Their vivid greens and blues and pinks spread a canopy over Echo Bay. David held her against the chill, his warmth flowing generously into her. David knows, she thought. He's known all along. Two people living together know these things about each other. And knowing, how could he not accuse, or at least confront her? There were times she wanted him to.

The affair is encrusted now, as if a hard carapace has formed around it. It is a possession, a thing, a foreign body she carries with her like a splinter she can't get rid of.

Eleanor moves from the window to the kitchen counter. Flour, oil, milk, eggs. She takes out the electric mixer, the waffle iron. She sets the table. Washes the fruit.

Then she puts on running shoes, grabs the boat keys and heads for the dock. As the boat moves out into Echo Bay, she turns, as she always does, for a view of the cottage set high on the rocks. The windows of the second level are diamond-shaped. The reflection of trees and cottage is distorted by the modest wake her boat leaves in the tranquil water.

Eleanor turns her back to the shore. Increases the speed. She wants to arrive at the landing before her guests. She wants to be unhurried and welcoming. She thinks again of the poem that came to her earlier:

And for all this, nature is never spent;
There lives the dearest freshness deep down things;
And though the last lights off the black West went
Oh, morning at the brown brink eastward, springs –

A small motorboat is slapping briskly across Lake of the Woods heading for Echo Bay. The lone traveller, a woman, appears to be at home on this stretch of water, confident with the boat. The wind whips her shoulder-length brown hair, already showing streaks of summer blonde. Her skin is deeply tanned; she should be wearing a hat, at her age. Lis is headed for Eleanor Lund's cottage, where she's never been, but she knows Echo Bay and has directions.

"Look for the cottage high up on a rock with three windows on the second level," Eleanor said on the telephone. "If no one's around, just make yourself at home."

"At home" is exactly where Lis longs to be. Just ten minutes out of Kenora and the small allotment of energy that allowed her to get up, pack towels and bathing suit, fill the cooler with steaks and broccoli and cheese and wine, select books to take – all that energy is dissipating. She can do nothing to hang on to it. All week she's worked at anticipating good woman-talk, long carefree hours in the sun. A skyful of stars after dark. She has pictured herself returning after the weekend, buoyed and revitalized. Now, as the boat brings her closer to Echo Bay, a familiar heaviness flows like liquid lead sluggishly through her veins. Her body is weighted down, her head like stone, eyelids heavy. Her sadness is a rock that could sink the boat, sending it to the lake bottom. She shouldn't have come.

Eleanor, Delores, Leila, Helen. She recites the names like a mantra, as if repetition spells hope, though she's not sure what she's hoping for.

Lis doesn't often try to recall Professor Conway's writing class. Hard to believe she once wanted to write. Conway's attention was directed mainly at the younger students, but she never resented that. The wild leaps and daring omissions in their fragmented narratives, the blatant physicality of violence and sex in their stories fascinated her. One young man – Bob couldn't have been more than seventeen – came to class with story after story of brutal and bizarre drug deals that left her numb with shock.

"Anybody can write about violence," Delores had said, and her next story was built around a rape.

"Overwritten," Professor Conway said.

Lis's first poems were love poems. To her daughter.

On the whole, the five older women tended to be romantic, though it would have offended them to hear the class or Professor Conway say so. When they met later in their homes, every poem and sketch pouring from their minds onto the page left them giddy with wonder. They possessed the joyful hope of children. The eagerness of travellers before whom a new country has opened, its vistas limitless and astonishingly beautiful.

Back then, Lis's daughter was bringing home report cards that said: 'Brenda is a good learner; a pleasure to have in class.' Her progress was almost glittering in high school when a student, deranged or angry or simply confused, rushed into the lunchroom with a handgun. He fired at random, putting an end to her daughter's life.

Lis's marriage snapped the way these days the thread of her energy, strong one minute, breaks the next. Lis has lost her love of parties. She doubts if she is capable of friendship. Wherever she goes she is a stranger. The weekend will wear her out.

When Lis thinks of her daughter it's most often not the murder, but the day when Brenda, only three years old at the time, interrupted her headlong exploration of the world to stand still in front of the full-length mirror in the hallway, engrossed, as if she had never before seen herself. She touched her short brown hair, her cheeks, her ears, turned her little feet this way and that, peered into her own grey-green eyes. She seemed to be submitting every part of herself to critical scrutiny. She was absorbed in this deliberate self-examination for a surprisingly long time before she looked up at Lis and said, "I look nice, Mummy."

Lis hasn't seen any of the group except Eleanor for years. It seems a lifetime. The world is not the same. *She* is not the same. Will Helen have become even more the intellect? She remembers Leila as rather short, with heavy black hair piled up as if to increase her height.

A green curve of shore and the first cottages of Echo Bay appear. Lis cuts the power. Trees and rocks at the water's edge slow down almost to a point of standstill. A family of ducks swims by to her right, their brown-feathered bodies gliding effortlessly, as if an unseen force propels them along the surface. Lis thinks that if she could glide over the water like that with the wind in her face until the sun sets she would be content. She pictures herself at day's end steering toward some not-too-violent vortex that welcomes her into its swirling darkness.

Ahead of her, there's a new dock that matches Eleanor's description. And there, beyond the dock, the diamond windows. They peer out over the bay, three resolute eyes, watchful, serene. The cottage sits up on rocks sheltered by birch and spruce. A perfect location. Lis looks up. The clear sky triggers a gleam of joy that startles her. She brings the boat close to the dock, hoists up her bags and the cooler with the steaks, then scrambles up and secures the boat. She is the first one here.

The Seven Steps

Dorothy Dodd – Dody to her shrinking circle of friends – dropped her seniors' ticket into the receptacle and made her way to the back of the bus where she found an aisle seat near the rear door. As she lowered herself into the spot, she caught sight of a leaflet on the unoccupied seat ahead of her, a bright yellow rectangle covered with black text, the caption at the top announcing THE SEVEN STEPS TO SALVATION. The paragraphs that followed were too small, at that distance, for her aging eyes, but they seemed to be arranged as a list that she concluded must consist of seven items.

After several stops the seat ahead of her was still empty and she thought she might reach over for the leaflet. Something to occupy her on the long stretch to Polo Park besides noting the two spans of the Disraeli Bridge, watching for the usual vagrants on Main Street, or checking on progress of the winter-long demolition of the old Eaton's building on Portage Avenue where she'd worked for decades. Any kind of reading would better redeem the time. And she might have something to tell Elizabeth.

Before she could make up her mind, a group of five or six teenagers got on the bus and grabbed the remaining empty places, mostly the aisle seats. The boy who sat down in front of Dorothy had automatically picked up the leaflet and held it while he continued a conversation he'd started at the bus stop. His words were aimed at the entire group but his attention targeted the girl opposite him, a girl with flawless skin, cheeks bright as candy from the cold, and a halo of tightly curled hair, though Dorothy wondered if one could refer to black hair as a halo.

The boy leaned his long, parka-protected torso into the aisle and gestured with the leaflet as he spoke. The girl laughed in response but the others in the group were bored.

"Hey Mike, stop waving that bloody thing. Makes me nervous," someone yelled at him.

"Yah, Mike, what's your problem?"

"What's that you're shoving at us?" A hand reached out, grabbed the yellow leaflet. "What've we got here?'

"Propaganda."

"Something to sell."

"Sell? What? Sex?"

"Drugs, man, drugs."

"Some fuckin' religion." The boy who had grabbed the paper was reading it now.

"Hey, you stole that, Jason," Mike said. "I got it first, so give it here."

The boy they called Jason held the yellow page beyond Mike's reach and began reading aloud: "THE SEVEN STEPS TO SALVATION."

A chaos of laughter greeted his words.

"Well, that's what it says." Jason said, annoyed, "THE SEVEN STEPS TO SALVATION."

"What are they, the seven steps?" the girl with the flawless skin demanded.

Dorothy Dodd leaned forward.

Jason, nervous under everyone's attention, cleared his throat. "Okay, you guys, shut your yaps and listen up. Here's your wisdom for the day."

"Ooooh, wisdom for the day," someone mimicked.

"Cut the crap," someone else several rows forward complained. "Just read."

"Okay, okay. Number one: 'Admit that you are a sinner…'"

"All right. I'm a sinner. So?" The interrupting voice came from several rows forward. As if pulled to her feet by the group's hooting laughter, a thin girl stood up and stepped into the aisle clownishly waving both arms above her head. Her red jacket flared briefly before someone pushed her down into her seat.

Rudely, Dorothy thought, too roughly.

"Not me. I'm pure as the driven snow," someone said and the others hooted.

"Me either. I'm sure no sinner."

"Just read."

"Mike. Mike's the sinner."

"Yah, Mike. You're a sinner."

"I wasn't finished." Jason raised his voice. He continued: "Admit that you are a sinner and you need to be forgiven." He paused.

"I'll never forgive *you* if you don't get on with it," a voice said. "Read, already."

"Number two: 'The Bible says if we confess our sins God is faithful and just to forgive us our sins, and to clean – uh – clen-z – us from all un-right-uh-un-right-ee-us-ness.'"

Jason looked for reaction to his struggle with the words, but there was none, the words incomprehensible to his friends. It struck Dorothy as odd, hearing words like 'cleanse' and 'unrighteousness' coming from his mouth. Such words belonged to a different era. Hers. To these boys and girls they must be foreign.

Just then the bus pulled to a stop opposite the Centennial Concert Hall and the teenagers filled the aisle with buzz and bustle as they swarmed toward the exit.

Jason held the yellow paper with THE SEVEN STEPS until he was almost even with Dorothy, then he paused and dropped it on the seat where it had originally lain. Good, Dorothy thought, but when the thin girl hurried by she swooped it up. Dorothy noticed that her eyes seemed nervous and her face was scarred with acne. Her jacket was a crimson blob. As she moved along the sidewalk she folded the paper carefully before putting it in her pocket. Then she crossed at the lights with the others, trailing Mike and the black-haloed girl. Dorothy followed them with her eyes until the bus moved on. She wondered if they shouldn't be in school, marvelled at their energy. Impossible to tell who in that noisy group would one day be an eminent scientist, president of a corporation or a university, who would settle for a menial job, and who would be a total failure at life.

Dorothy was disappointed at having THE SEVEN STEPS snatched away, but she was used to disappointment. The longest part of her journey still lay ahead, time enough to figure out for herself what THE SEVEN STEPS might be. Propaganda was mostly predictable, it should be easy. She'd already heard the first two. What were they?

She was a sinner. She spoke the words, "I am a sinner," then looked around quickly, afraid she'd spoken aloud the way she sometimes did in grocery aisles or in bank line-ups. Or in her kitchen. *She lifts the baked potato from the oven. Places it on a blue plate. She's lucky – there's a half-full container of sour cream left in the fridge. A dollop of sour cream is the perfect topping for a baked potato. Nowadays she doesn't eat much meat.*

Dorothy wasn't sure now whether the words of the first step had really been "I am a sinner," or whether that was how she remembered them. In any case, she was pretty sure she was close. Unfortunately she couldn't find pencil or scratchpad in her handbag. "Always have a scrap of paper and something to write with," Elizabeth often cautioned her. "It's such a big help. At our age." Dorothy couldn't argue against that. Of course it was a good idea to recite or record information before it slipped away like the dreams she rarely remembered in the morning.

Last night she had dreamt of Eddie. In the dream he was still a child playing with a toy, a yellow transport truck perhaps or what might have been a train or a toy horse. His blond head shone and all his movements were strangely mesmerizing. She woke with the image of her haloed child crystal clear in her mind's eye and even now it lingered. Recently she had dreamt about Elizabeth, something unpleasant. The dream woke her with a jolt, and though all details of it faded immediately she had been unable to fall asleep again.

Dorothy hated the way Elizabeth said "at our age." And the way she doled out advice. Suddenly the word "forgive" surfaced through her musings. Yes, forgive, was definitely part of THE SEVEN STEPS. Forgive, Forgive, Forgive, she repeated until she was sure nothing could expunge it from her memory.

The bus passed a clock on a signboard: eleven-thirty. By the time she got to Polo Park, reached the shopping mall and found her way to the second floor food court Elizabeth would be waiting for her at one of the tables, her walker parked beside her. "You're late, Dody," she would say, and today she'd be right: Dorothy should have left earlier. Elizabeth would remove her coat from the seat she'd been saving. Then they would take turns, one going up to order food while the other guarded her place. Predictably, Elizabeth would go first, and come back with her usual cheeseburger and tea.

As the bus bumped along Portage Avenue, Dorothy imagined leaning across the table toward Elizabeth. "I learned something on the bus coming down. Want to hear it?" Of course she would say yes, she never could resist information of any kind. Dorothy wondered what Elizabeth might make of THE SEVEN STEPS.

The bus stopped at the downtown university campus and several students got on with their backpacks. One, a girl who looked no older than those boisterous high school students earlier, took the place in front of Dorothy and pulled out a text book, but though she strained to see, Dorothy could not make out the title.

How many years since she, Dorothy Dodd, had stepped off the bus or boarded it at this very place? She could never pass the university without remembering the small campus as it had been then, a far cry from its present clumsy sprawl. She and Elizabeth had met in Professor McFee's third-year Milton class. McFee had been a huge man who would stride into the classroom wearing a black gown, something most professors had given up even then, and glower down at them like a vulture from a mountainous height.

"Read Milton," he'd thunder, waving *Paradise Lost*. "Discover who you are."

She and Elizabeth had been a little afraid of him, although Elizabeth soon became preoccupied with Christopher, a history student. Wrapped up in love, she did not take the professor's pronouncements seriously, and the poetry of Milton mostly passed her by. It seemed to Dorothy that her friend, always eager to learn, had switched abruptly to another course. Neither she nor Elizabeth had earned a university degree.

She pulled herself together, letting the past recede into a far corner of her consciousness. I'm too easily distracted by memory, she thought, turning her attention to the street where pedestrians walked cautiously on packed snow. A sign in the window of The Fabric

Shoppe announced a closing out sale. At the soup kitchen a lunch line had formed. Dorothy returned to THE SEVEN STEPS. Number one: I am a sinner. Number two: something about forgiveness. Sin and forgiveness aren't much in the public domain, she thought. They're left largely to the individual. They are private matters and best left that way. What kind of person would leave information about sin and forgiveness in buses?

"Garbage," Elizabeth would probably say if Dorothy could actually show her the yellow tract. "Utter garbage. It's a kind of brainwashing, you know. You always were a bit gullible, Dorothy." And she would push the leaflet away without reading it, or crumple it up.

Dorothy had to admit she didn't much care for Elizabeth's strong opinions. But she didn't have many acquaintances who were still able to meet for lunch. At her age she couldn't afford to be choosy. But she wasn't naïve about THE SEVEN STEPS. Con artists lurked everywhere, and even the media conspired to manipulate the ordinary person such as herself.

Ordinary? The thought unsettled her. Was she, Dorothy Dodd, ordinary? She looked down at her beige parka with its drawstring waist, the shiny knees of her navy polyester pants, the worn leather handbag she'd carried for ages, the unfashionable boots. No one would say she cut an impressive figure, but they would be seeing only the surface, wouldn't they? They wouldn't see the long years of her life. The small whiffs of joy that had come her way from time to time. When Eddie finally spoke his first words. When he learned to tie his shoe laces. She had persevered, and didn't that amount to a kind of success?

Besides McFee's Milton course, she remembered taking one on the English novel. She and Elizabeth had both chosen an essay topic on character development in Thomas Hardy's fiction. She had chosen Tess Durbeyfield and her essay was given an A, with the comment "Your discussion is perceptive and insightful." Elizabeth had chosen Eustacia Vye and got a C with no comment. "Oh, well," Elizabeth had dismissed it as being of no consequence. She and Christopher were more deeply than ever absorbed in studying each other.

Dorothy didn't think it was her fault, Christopher suddenly switching his attention. It had happened quite innocently, she always believed. It was Elizabeth's idea that the three of them sign up for a skiing weekend at La Rivière. Dorothy knew from the start that she was expected to be, in the eyes of Elizabeth's mother, the chaperone and, in the eyes of Elizabeth, blind to what might transpire.

Actually nothing had happened, and for that Elizabeth held her responsible.

"You were always there, Dody. I think Christopher felt that."

"Well maybe you shouldn't have insisted I had to come." Dorothy said, thinking with guilty satisfaction, yes, Christopher knew I was there. Male attention had been scant in her life. Of course from her present vantage point it seemed a bit silly, her being so thrilled when Christopher said, while they munched ham sandwiches after a morning of skiing, "You have nice eyes,

Dorothy. Like flowers." He had never called her Dody.

She remembered the rest of the winter as a kind of ecstatic blur. By the time graduation occupied her classmates, a summer wedding was being planned – Christopher and Dorothy.

"What's the hurry, Dody?" her mother kept asking. She was nervous about Christopher, not yet accustomed to his constant presence – hanging around, Dorothy's father called it – and his enormous appetite. It was difficult to tell whether her mother was overcome by surprise or actually alarmed. Dorothy hoped she was secretly pleased. That would make everything easier.

A truce of sorts had been negotiated with Elizabeth. "I want you to be my bridesmaid, Elizabeth," Dorothy had said simply on an evening when her friend agreed to go for a walk with her down to the river. Elizabeth had dropped a Math course shortly after Dorothy dropped Sociology, and both had had to contend with baffled parents. They sat together on a large rock, talking as they hadn't done for weeks, staring into the opaque water until darkness fell. Then they turned their eyes up to where the night sky was alive with stars until Dorothy became dizzy and slightly nauseous.

Patterns in Royal Albert china and Lady Hamilton silver were carefully selected, a blue floral design for the dinnerware, plain lines for the cutlery. "A bride should think about laying a proper table," Dody's mother said. Following several showers, she counted two complete china settings, six more cups and saucers, three place settings of silver, a sugar shell and a serving spoon. She splurged on a catered trousseau tea.

"I'm a bride," Dody marvelled, a bit stunned by her changed circumstances. Never had she expected to be the first of her friends to marry. Christopher, looking perpetually abashed, followed her around like an eager puppy when he wasn't kept at the beck and call of her mother, who, having overcome her objection to the speed of things, was determined no formality and no ritual would be overlooked in planning the wedding of her only daughter who had missed the ceremony of convocation. She had purchased a book on wedding etiquette at Eaton's to help her navigate this unfamiliar ground.

Elizabeth's betrayal had come as a shock that spoiled the rehearsal dinner Dorothy's mother hosted. She had served poached salmon, basil-infused potatoes and asparagus tips. Cries of "Scrumptious!" "Have you ever tasted the likes!" and "Prima" left the hostess flushed. It was the casualness of Elizabeth's statement that stung, and the timing. She delivered it just after the crème caramel had been served. "You must be just so happy that you'll be a grandmother, Mrs. Hillis." Around the table spoons were dropped and eyes raised. To Dorothy. To her mother.

"How was I supposed to know you were keeping your mother in the dark?" Elizabeth whined, when Dorothy declared her words unforgivable. "I thought she'd have long caught on, with you throwing up every morning."

Dorothy had not thrown up all that often. Later she would remember how she had accepted the pregnancy as being part and parcel of her love for Chris. There had been scant discomfort throughout the nine months and no hint of what lay ahead.

The wedding, after the rehearsal fiasco, could not be the glittering occasion Dorothy's mother had envisioned, although she doubled her efforts to ensure that both the marriage service in Knox Church and reception at the Tennis Club would be tasteful and elegant. Guests were aloof. There were comments. Glances. And Elizabeth, after first performing as a model bridesmaid, drank herself into what Dody's father declared "a culpable state of inebriation."

The spotlight that had been turned on Dorothy at her engagement, and which deepened to an uncomfortable glare at her wedding, followed her throughout her pregnancy to the anticipated birth. A baby boy arrived, sporting a thick head of dark curly hair and Christopher's high forehead. They named him Edward, after Dorothy's father, who had said little during the pregnancy and stood stoically by through everything afterwards.

Dorothy watched as the student in front of her closed the textbook, shoved it into her backpack, rose, and made her way to the exit. She had a strong and serene face, and her gait on the moving bus suggested the natural balance and confidence of an athlete. The school yearbook might refer to her as someone *Sure to succeed.* Dorothy wanted to wish this young woman luck. For her studies. For her final exams. For her life. She wondered what might be preoccupying that young mind besides exams and essays. She had no doubt girls still stole each other's boy friends, still got pregnant, although contraceptives were available in university washrooms. And though abortions were supposed to be no big deal these days, Dorothy didn't for a minute believe they could be lightly undertaken, or could leave a woman unscathed. Abortion had not entered Dorothy's mind, and if her mother had ever considered it, she had not said.

She doesn't know what's she's in for, Dorothy thought, watching the student head off down Portage Avenue as the bus lurched forward. And a good thing, too.

The thick dark hair of Dorothy's son had turned to sunny blond before his condition was diagnosed. "We call it Fragile X Syndrome." The doctor had been solemn, business-like. He told Dorothy's mother, who had accompanied her, that it was rare but not uncommon for a nineteen-year-old such as Dorothy had been to give birth to a child with this affliction.

"What is it?" Dorothy had asked, not overly concerned. Weren't treatments for all manner of conditions being discovered every day? And cures? All the infants she had ever known were healthy, why wouldn't hers be too?

"Let's just say it's a failure to thrive."

Feeling increasingly helpless, Dorothy had watched her son continue to fail to thrive. At first she kept telling herself that next summer Eddie would be playing with the other children in the sandbox and by the following year he'd clamber around on the play structure in the park. He would grow sturdy and tall. But his body remained small and thin, and his mind's slender capacity did not expand. When Eddie had turned seven and couldn't be accepted into a regular school, Christopher's shaken heart had crumbled completely. "I'm sorry Dorothy, I'm sorry," he said when he moved out. Dorothy could see how fractured he had become, how needy, and her supply of emotional energy, though considerable, was earmarked for Eddie. Nothing left for a husband. Where had it come from, that energy? she often wondered.

"You're amazing, Dody," the supervisor of Eaton's Women's Wear used to say. "You do the work of two women."

Through all Eddie's growing up years – Could one speak of growing up in this case? – he was trusting and amiable. Special Ed teachers were uniformly kind. When he was eight they'd helped him construct a Mother's Day card that left her teary-eyed. She still had the card. At the sheltered workshops where he learned to tend plants and package consumer goods of some kind or other, his reliability and thoroughness were praised.

Dorothy loved him.

The group home was a social worker's suggestion. At first Dorothy had fought it, with vigour and with new-found outrage, but when she observed how excited Eddie grew about moving out "to my very own place," she relented. I'm not getting any younger, she had told herself. I have to let him go. In her first report the social worker said "Eddie has settled in very well, and continues to blossom in his new environment."

For Dorothy, solitude had not been easy.

The bus, slowed by a broken water main, passed the McDonald's and the large brick church, proceeded under the overpass and finally approached Polo Park. Dorothy zipped her parka, flipped up the hood. I've reviewed my whole life, she thought, sheepishly, when all I wanted was to figure out THE SEVEN STEPS TO SALVATION. I didn't get far. She hadn't got past "I am a sinner" and something about forgiving.

What is it that I should be forgiving, she wondered? Or be forgiven for? The thought of incompleteness, of work still to be done, wearied her. But she couldn't be sure there wasn't something there that needed attending to. Life with Eddie had taught her that there was always something left to do. One was never done with obligations.

All things considered, cause for blame stuck generously to most people, Dorothy thought. Everyone needed to be forgiven. What else was new? And then another word floated into her consciousness. *Confess*. Or was it *confession?* She had heard the teenager they called Jason reading the word, she was positive, and felt a small rush of satisfaction at having remembered. When she attempted crossword puzzles these days the words were often annoyingly delayed en route.

The bus stopped. She got off with the other shoppers and made her way to the mall entrance. She suspected she was late; Elizabeth would be impatient.

They had started meeting after Christopher died; Elizabeth had surprised her one day with the phone call. "I've moved close to Polo Park. Do you think we could have lunch?"

The periodic lunches that followed were not wonderful, but they were something. Two thin-haired women arguing over a book they had read or a TV show they had seen, or trading home remedies for sore joints and sleepless nights. After a youthful lapse, Elizabeth had returned to her passion for information. She gathered and stored it zealously, and not all of it was trivia. Sometimes they commented on the way things had changed since they were young and Elizabeth would ask what the world was coming to.

"In this changing world," Dorothy would sometimes say, "we've managed pretty well, don't you agree?" and Elizabeth would send her a questioning glance.

There was no talk of grandchildren; neither woman had any. Whenever Elizabeth mentioned Christopher, Dorothy adroitly changed the subject. Although Christopher hovered between them, his presence seemed fuzzy and vague to Dorothy who preferred to leave him out of the conversation. Nor did she speak much about Eddie.

When he'd left her, Christopher had taken his broken heart into the world where broken hearts were too commonplace to be noticed, let alone taken seriously. So he brought it to Elizabeth who accepted it, apparently content to let bygones be bygones.

Stepping carefully along the icy sidewalk, Dorothy was thinking how Elizabeth had made room for Christopher, how that had saved him. Had there been confession when he and Elizabeth were reunited? Had forgiveness been a prerequisite? Could it sometimes be unspoken? She would really like to know, though of course what happened between Elizabeth and Christopher was none of her business. Still, it would be comforting to think reconciliation could happen unconsciously, or sub-consciously, without effort, requiring only the normal passing of time. She thought ruefully of those SEVEN STEPS.

Inside the mall the floor was not slippery, merely mud-streaked. Passing the Sears store Dorothy reminded herself to get several pairs of socks for Eddie while she was here. He was always out of socks and it was a convenient gift when he came for a visit. She hurried toward the escalator and when she reached it, saw the OUT OF ORDER sign. She stepped aside to catch her breath before she headed for the stairs and began climbing. She thought of how effortlessly the teenagers had stepped on and off the bus, how fearlessly they had crossed Main Street. Mike with his arm around the black-haired girl. An observer might think they carried no burdens and were in no need of salvation, even the girl with the acned face.

Elizabeth had finished her cheeseburger and was pouring sugar into her tea. "I didn't wait, Dody," she said, scooping her coat up off the chair she was saving and onto her walker. "I was hungry and you were late." The gaze she directed at Dorothy was a touch severe.

Dorothy removed her gloves, folded them into her pocket, then slipped out of her coat. Instead of blaming her lateness on the bus or the icy snow, as she'd intended to, she said, contritely, "I should have taken an earlier bus. I always assume there's still lots of time. And that's a mistake." Then smiling straight at Elizabeth she added, "At my age." For a few moments the women locked eyes and Elizabeth's face softened slightly.

Taking her handbag, Dorothy made her way around crowded tables to the food stalls. It was tiring, she thought, to be an elderly woman lunching with an acquaintance at a noisy shopping mall. Her life had been ordinary, her achievements unremarkable. But any life could get complicated, even such a life as hers, or Elizabeth's, and there wasn't an easy guide to help you navigate it. You had to persevere, do your best to avoid calamity. Muddle through. And catch those surprising moments of good fortune, or mercy, that were sent your way.

As she waited at the counter for her tomato soup and a cheese sandwich Dorothy thought of her Eddie who was thriving in the group home. His eyes would light up when she gave him the socks. She also thought wistfully of the leaflet carried off the bus by the girl who had said she was a sinner.

Ending With Poetry

On the way to Harbourside, a detour to the 7-Eleven is routine. Today I've got loonies enough for a Big Gulp and the candy bar I've been dying for all day. The loonies come from a jar wedged between stacks of saucers and small plates on the third kitchen shelf. My mother doesn't try to hide the jar. "My rainy day fund," she tells Marlene from next door. "It's always rising and falling. Like a volatile stock market." They both laugh. I don't think Mother's got a clue about stock markets. "Just keep your hands off my rainy day fund," she warns me regularly. Automatically.

Fridays and Saturdays, after Mother and Marlene head for the casino, the jar is empty, but it fills quickly enough. Mother shops as avidly as she gambles, keeping a good portion of Dad's salary in hectic circulation. Spare loonies find their way to the jar. Fortunately. I'm entitled to a bit of extra fuel for my stint at the nursing home. A shot of courage or comfort, call it incentive. I never take too many.

I feed Bernice Mondays and Wednesdays at supper. Regurgitations no longer bother me; I've been in the line of fire from the start. I'm okay with food-splotched pants and shirt, hers or mine. Smells – I can't say smells aren't a problem, but I don't flinch. And I'm totally used to watching nursing assistants manoeuvre Alzheimers with glazed eyes and a shambling gait past me to their tables. Or wheel by with antiques, mostly female, curled into foetal position. A small oriental man wearing white therapeutic stockings rides by me like an undersized emperor in his chariot, gesturing obscenely. It's depressing. A parade of the wounded, whimpering and mostly wordless. A procession that's staged three times a day, seven days a week, rain or shine, year in year out. With a constantly changing cast.

Big Gulp in one hand, half-munched candy bar in the other, I'm heading across the parking lot, revving up for Harbourside, when I run into Kelly, her body poured into T-shirt and shorts, her usual bag of sports gear slung over one shoulder. She's obviously on her way to track practise.

"Hi," she says. She's squinting because of the sun. Or maybe sizing up the extra calories I carry on my body and in both hands.

I return the "Hi."

"You heard about Lesia?" she asks.

"She skipped bio," I say.

"She missed all day."

I hadn't noticed. Since the abortion Lesia's attendance has been hit and miss. I've lost track.

"She's been diagnosed. It's leukemia."

I didn't know she was going to be diagnosed. I thought the abortion screwed her up so she couldn't come to classes.

"It's just so awful," Kelly says, her voice wobbling. "It's devastating."

The drink in my stomach has turned to ice. Of course it's devastating. But nothing comes to mind to say. Nothing that wouldn't sound totally stupid.

"I really have to get going." That's not quite true. I always give myself plenty of time to enjoy the snack en route. But Kelly isn't going to let me go. Says that according to the guidance counsellor Lesia will get chemo regularly. The class is sending flowers, do I want to chip in? She's collecting.

I wedge the Big Gulp under my arm and dig into my pocket for left over change. I give what I find to Kelly who's objecting that I don't have to pay *now*, not *this minute*. I'm embarrassed at my stupidly small contribution.

Every bit of ice in the Big Gulp has melted, the candy bar is soft as cream. Inside me there's a heavy chill. Empty coffee cups and hamburger wrappings bounce across the parking lot, blown by gusts of wind. There's no one on the sidewalk as I press on toward the nursing home.

My decision to become a volunteer at Harbourside isn't entirely altruistic. I'm not what you'd call a do-gooder. Mona Daley, the guidance counsellor, informed our class that summer jobs would become available at the nursing home, and doing a bit of volunteering ahead of time would do no harm. It would give us a 'profile' she said. And we better go in April, before we get bogged down with end of term assignments and exams looming. The response was underwhelming. "Who wants to feed the dying?" "I'll definitely pass." "Me too." "Gloomy." I was the only one in my class to take a stand against majority opinion and I didn't broadcast it.

The volunteer application was no problem until I got to where it said: *Why are you interested in volunteering at Harbourside Home?* The answer to that could be crucial, and I hesitated until I remembered one of the essay topics for our major English assignment. "All People Are Entitled to Equal Opportunity and Respect." I wrote that down.

Gus Lerwick, our English teacher, spent a year volunteering with a relief agency in South America, and our class discussions always veer off toward justice issues. We spend more time discussing fair trade coffee and vanishing rain forests than poetry. Lesia is the only one who agrees with me that that sucks. Last year in spring Lesia and me took our poetry books with us when it was dry and warm enough to eat on the grass beside the school. All poetry texts have sections on nature and war and death. And of course love. Lesia and I used to read the love poems together.

Late as last summer
Thou didst say me, love,
I choose you, you, only you.

So far no one has chosen me.

I don't think I'll write about "Opportunity and Respect." I'm considering "The Poor Among Us." That would please Lerwick, and besides, Winnipeg being the child poverty capital of Canada, I could find lots of examples right here. There's also the topic, "How Much is Enough?" I like the sound of that. I overheard Kelly argue her way out of "Respect," saying she'd prefer to research "Opportunities for Women in Sport." I don't know if Lesia's even thought about the essay. She had to take a few days off for the abortion and after that everything about her became sort of vague.

At Harbourside, old Jakob Krause is already parked in a straight-backed chair opposite Bernice's wheelchair and right next to him sits The Mummy – that's how I think of the withered and preserved-looking resident, a male, with a mouth that's a perfectly round orifice open in the centre of his shrivelled, caved-in face. His eyes are closed. He's asleep in a chair equipped with all these levers and buttons that raise, lower, and tilt the amazing contrivance. The cushioned head and leg rests can be adjusted to any angle. Comfort and convenience available at the flick of a nurse's fingers. Definitely state-of-the-art.

Old Jakob and The Mummy are the only residents besides Bernice not allowed into the feeders' dining room. This trio eats in an adjacent hallway that I call The Fringe. A sort of outer circle for *personae non grata*. Bernice sits beside the TV, the Mummy between the door leading to the nursing station and the budgie in its suspended cage, and Jacob Krause next to him under a gloomy painting of The Last Supper.

Most of the walkers and wheelchairs pass via The Fringe through a wide door to a room with tables set for six. But even though their destination is a rung up from The Fringe, they are "feeders" too. All of them need hands-on help from staff or volunteers. All of them are trapped in the one-way direction of declining years.

There's an even classier dining room for residents who can move on their own steam, with or without walkers or wheelchairs. To qualify, they have to have a certain number of their five wits more or less in working order, their tempers under control and should be able to feed themselves without getting sidetracked by minds too ready to wander. Conversation with table companions is optional, and sometimes actually happens. Plastic flowers adorn the tables, and a full complement of cutlery marks each of the four places.

Old Jakob is a "Fringer" because he's just plain ornery. He refuses his medicine or hides it under his tongue. I've seen him spit out red, brown and tiny white pills as though they're ammunition. Sometimes he makes a fist and threatens to punch the nurse. He insists on eating unassisted and when he's finished his coffee, bangs his plastic cup on the table for more. Every once in a while his face goes pathetic and he'll turn it this way and that as if he's looking for an escape route.

"Vere is Jakob Kr-rause?" he demands. "Tell me vere iss hiss r-room?"

"That's *your* name," a passing nurse says. "*You're* Jakob Krause."

He glares after her.

Last year all three of us – Kelly, Lesia, and me – were on the track teams, indoor and out, running after school every day, keeners all of us, with Kelly the keenest, keeping us revved from her position up front, way ahead in everything. I was the first to drop out.

"You can't," Kelly wailed. "You're getting better." That was kind, but not strictly true.

"It's something we do together," Lesia said thoughtfully when I asked for one good reason for me to stay on.

"We could go to movies," I argued, but Lesia wasn't fooled, I could tell, so I admitted how much I hated running. Hated being a loser.

I had less to do with Kelly and Lesia after that and surprisingly this registered at home. Over dinner, the phone wedged between chin and shoulder, Mother would interrupt her conversation with Marlene to ask about Lesia. And Dad, slumped over coffee, worn out by a day at the accounting firm, would mention "that athletic one" as his hands traced the outline of a slender female body in the air. "Kelly," I'd say, the name suddenly bitter in my mouth.

Bernice's dinner comes in one of those plastic dishes divided into three compartments. A large dollop of something beige marbled with white and roughly textured – the day's entrée – occupies one section; a mound of smooth green paste once parading as peas or beans, the second; and a dark pile of pureed prunes, the third. Soupy brown gravy, too much of it, is poured over everything, even the prunes. The dessert comes in a separate dish and it's always the same: a pale pudding. Could be lemon or vanilla or banana, and always adorned with a white swirl of whipped topping. Bernice gets the diabetic menu, so I can imagine the blandness. Sometimes she objects to the pink terrycloth "clothing protector" I have to tie around her neck. "I don't require a bib," she'll say. But today she submits stoically to everything.

Bernice surveys the plate plunked down on the hospital table in front of her. She says nothing, just stares morosely into it for what seems a long time. Finally she picks up the fork and pokes by turn into each segment of her dinner in exploratory fashion, haphazardly loading the fork. Then she raises it up, up, up past her mouth. When it reaches a perilous proximity to her thin, frizzy cloud of hair, I guide the fork-wielding hand to safer ground. Bernice drops the fork back into the dish. The food slides off.

Her face is deeply wrinkled and her skin hangs in slack folds from her chin. Her nose is thin and sharp, her eyes red and puffy.

"Smells great." I imitate the staff's enthusiasm, determined she's going to deliver food to her mouth with her own hand. At least the first three forkfuls. At least the first two. "How about we get down to business," I say. Brightly.

"I don't know." Her empty hand is heading for the plastic cup of ice water, but at the last moment, draws back. Her eyes have wandered off to The Last Supper.

"How about this?" I point to the prunes. She likes the prunes.

Her eyes return reluctantly. She picks up the abandoned fork and with a display of energy that surprises me jabs it into the green, then into the mashed prunes and finally a bit of the beige. She lifts the cargo, brings it to her mouth. The food enters. I hold my breath and wait for it to go down. I watch her throat for hopeful signs of movement. I listen for a gulp. Bingo. There it is.

"Good girl, Bernice."

"I am *not* a girl."

Sometimes if track practice proved too deflating for me, Lesia and Kelly would suggest pizza afterwards. Hawaiian is Lesia's favourite, Kelly likes vegetarian, and I'm the one who can't get enough of any kind of food. If I had to, I could eat Bernice's dinner. It's pureed to death but blessed with a savoury aroma. Probably tastier than those pre-packaged frozen bags of food they serve in hospitals. Horrible, everyone says, but I suspect I'd eat even those.

I wonder if Lesia will get so nauseated from the chemo that she won't be able to eat at all. I hope to God she isn't heading for a place or state where food of any kind is no longer necessary. People die of leukemia. I am unprepared for that possibility. Even the idea of the possibility. How can a person be prepared for *that*?

The sleeping Mummy eats in The Fringe because his complicated chair won't fit under a table. Where he eats, or if, is of no consequence to him. One day I'll arrive at Harbourside and his obit will be posted on the bulletin board just past reception. That will leave two feeders in The Fringe.

A woman has appeared beside The Mummy. She's straight and slim, a thick blonde braid hanging down the back of her emerald green shirt. Pants to match.

Her presence makes The Fringe glow. She slaps The Mummy lightly on his cheeks to get his attention. "Time for supper," she says. "Are you hungry?" She pushes aside the stool placed there for her, steps close to his chair, her back to me, and gets to work like she's been feeding old men all her life. I haven't seen her before. Must be from a temp agency.

I turn my attention back to Bernice. Bernice eats here because the muscles of her throat are stiffening and she has trouble swallowing. Food placed in her mouth sits there until the necessary muscles agree to contract and push everything down. This takes time. Sometimes the tedious process ends in a dramatic coughing fit and out it all comes like the grungy barrage let fly from the Airfarce Chicken Cannon. Even dazed Alzheimers have to be protected against the feeding habits of Bernice.

Another forkful, mostly green, is en route to her mouth, and again I watch for evidence of swallowing. She reaches for the ice water, lifts the cup. Will the water find the right passage to flow into or trickle down the wrong way triggering a violent spray of mashed peas? Bernice's mouth opens wide, her eyes are tightly shut, she is about to cough. I take the glass from her and quickly place the tip of my finger under her chin, promising that if she closes her mouth it'll all go down. Her face is turning scarlet and for long seconds I'm holding my breath and betting on a choking fit but then her eyes open, her face relaxes and the redness drains from it. I resume breathing. The peas are on their way to their intended destination. May they rest in peace.

She's in no hurry for the next mouthful and I know it's best to wait a while. I use the interlude to consider the essay topics for English: "How Much is Enough?" "The Poor Among Us." Poor in what sense? I wonder. *Blessed are the poor.* That comes from Sunday School. When I was seven I started tagging along with the girl next door. I liked the stories. David with his slingshot finishing off Goliath. All those animals milling about in the ark. Jesus feeding five thousand people with a few loaves of bread and a few fish. *That's impossible*, the boy beside me said. *That's crazy*. But I wasn't so sure it couldn't happen. Eventually I dropped out, bored with sitting on undersized chairs in a basement room. But I still have the Bible they gave me, a real one, not one for kids, and sometimes I read the stories. And of course the poetry.

Bernice is raising the fork to her mouth, empty. I take it from her, pick up the teaspoon, load it with beige entrée and prunes and bring it to her face. She opens her mouth obediently.

"Good?" I ask when she's swallowed.

"Yes. Very tasty. Thank you for coming." She has turned her red eyes deliberately toward me. They are looking straight into mine. These moments of clarity always come as a surprise. And they usually coincide with gratitude which she delivers in very good English. That's not to be taken for granted at Harbourside where the residents are mostly immigrants from Europe and speak with accents, mainly German.

When you arrive at Harbourside there's a reception desk and past it is the obituary bulletin board, and after that a row of seven framed photographs under a gold-lettered sign: THE CENTURY CLUB. All seven are women, two of them still living. Still being wheeled in for supper. It's a well-known fact that women outlive men. At Harbourside they are rewarded for this by having their weathered faces displayed under gold letters. If they haven't had their allotted minutes of fame beforehand, here it is.

Dad disputes vehemently the statistics that support women's superior toughness, claiming he works with guys who are never going to die. Mother and Marlene laugh at him. I've met only a few of his buddies from the accounting firm where he works and they're comfortably lumpy, like Dad. Like I'm getting to be.

Are the members of THE CENTURY CLUB proud when they reach the golden age and get their pictures posted? Do they even know they're there? Do they wish they could start over? Would they like to live forever?

Seema, one of the two nurses on duty, drags a stool over to Jacob, sits down and leans in for a good look at his plate. His nearest arm makes a spastic lunge toward her, knocking over a glass of prune juice. It spills over her white track shoes. "Damn," she says.

"Go avay," Jacob tells her and she does, her shoes leaving a purple trail.

I actually like writing once I've chosen the topic. Maybe I should do "How Much is Enough?" Not because our teacher has poverty stuck in his mind, but because mine is preoccupied with body weight. I am offended with all the junk food around, though you wouldn't know that, looking at me. I could easily write about calories and processing and additives. And about excesses. It might be like doing penance. Some days I swear I can observe the ballooning of my body. It must be visible to everyone. To the nursing assistant in her emerald uniform. To the nurses. The people I pass in the street. To Kelly. When I ran the essay topics by Dad – we were on the deck where he can chain smoke – he said he believed in moderation. In all things. Even exercise could be overdone. And of course there was consumerism. Had I thought of that? No one could accuse Dad of overdoing exercise. And he's not a big spender. But consumerism – that's so cliché. And the way he side-stepped the obvious – overeating – left me annoyed.

Mother has offered no advice, but whenever she looks at me I know what she's thinking. I've resisted the urge to tell her gambling and eating might be parallel ways to destruction. She'd argue there's real life in the Casino, ordinary people doing what they enjoy. What's wrong with that? Everyone has some kind of relaxation, she'd say, and, guess what, it costs something. Besides, she knows when to stop, so I shouldn't be so snooty. And don't I realize I'm getting awfully judgmental for one so young?

Last night browsing the web I came up with this article titled "Enough is Enough." Aha, I thought as I downloaded it.

We have eaten all the prunes, half the peas and most of the entrée and are about to tackle dessert, which usually slides down smoothly, when Seema comes back, shoes wiped clean, and delivers milkshakes all around.

They look like milkshakes, but really they're some kind of energy boosters most residents resist. But not Bernice. She reaches for the glass, brings it to her mouth, and takes a good swig. At this stage of supper she's pretty much filled up, her system tight and tense, waiting like Krakatoa for the chance to erupt, to disgorge all contents, sending a liquid outburst flying into the blessed light of day. The milkshake is too much. Nervous, I grab the edge of the pink bib intending to hold it up like a shield between us. But the volcano beats me to the draw. The explosion is high on the scale. It leaves me peppered from the waist up with beige particles in pea-green slime and showered all over with a spray of second-hand milkshake. Seema watches from across the room.

At this dramatic moment The Floral Woman comes in pushing her walker and grinning like the Cheshire cat. She has finished her dinner in the plastic-flower dining room. She doesn't notice me swiping at Bernice, then at myself, with the pink terrycloth.

"It voss delishus," she announces to the Fringe gathering. "Chust so *good*. Eat, *eat*," she says, beaming encouragement at Jacob. "Ve haf to keep togeder leib und soul."

Jacob is silent. Glares at her.

"EAT," The Floral Woman yells at Bernice, assuming she's very deaf. "I help her at lunch," she tells me with a beatific smile. "Ve aftervards sit togedder."

Pathetic.

Still muttering eat, eat, the woman parks her walker next to me and lowers herself peacock-like into an empty blue chair. I call her The Floral Woman because every skirt and dress she wears is ablaze with roses and bluebells and peonies. Right now her flamboyant presence raises the Fringe population to seven.

"Look, Bernice," I say, still swabbing guck from face and shirt, hers and mine, and looking for some diversion, a reprieve, a time for things to settle. "Why don't we count the people in this room? Start with Jacob. One..., two..., three...."

I point and count slowly, but Bernice won't chime in. She stares blankly ahead. I try again. "Look at that picture, Bernice. Over there. Right over Jacob's head. How many people around the table? Let's count them. One..., two..., three..."

Bernice's eyes are pretty good, I've discovered, but just now she's shifted them back to what's left of the milkshake. It's The Floral Woman who says, "Tvelve. Der voss tvelve eating togedder und vun voss not good, not good atall. He sold Cheesus. Tirty pieces of silber. Dat voss Choodas."

"What are they having for supper?" Bernice asks, her mind suddenly alert, eyes bright as bullets, milkshake dribbling from the corner of her mouth.

The Floral Woman is in a chatty mood. "My Mudder," she says (still smiling, she never doesn't smile), "My Mudder had in tventy vun years tventy children. Vun, two, tree..." She gestures to Bernice to join in.

I try again to wipe Bernice's face, her pant legs, and my shirt with the pink terry cloth. I've heard the woman's story about tventy times. I should have interviewed her in grade six or seven, where they give you the standard assignment on family history. I might have got an A. My genealogy is totally colourless on Dad's side, and Mother refuses to speak about hers.

Seema has just left when Old Jacob's body slumps seriously, listing to one side. Something like a moan rises from it. The emerald temp reacts with lightning speed. Leaving The Mummy to sink back into sleep, she makes a dash for Jacob whose body seems to change size and shape as I watch. It's turning into something unfamiliar. The temp puts her hand on his wrist. All is not well. Seema is called back. She pushes aside the table with the barely-touched food. She feels Jacob's forehead, then runs to the nursing desk When she returns she's got the whole nine yards with her. Beginning with the stethoscope, she gets right down to business. An assistant comes with a wheelchair. The temp watches, ready for action.

I fill a spoon with pudding and bring it close to Bernices's mouth. It opens obediently. Out of the corner of my eyes I watch as nurse and temp slide their arms underneath the armpits of the shape that is Jacob. They lift him up, swivel him around and transfer him expertly into the wheelchair. His head has fallen to his chest. His hands hang open and limp at the ends of dangling arms. I listen for a sound from him as they wheel him past me, but there is nothing. They hurry him away.

The Floral Woman has failed to notice the unfolding drama. She hoists herself up from the chair and wanders off with her walker. Beaming. The Mummy continues to sleep, mouth open. The sun beams its afternoon light in through the window. Outside, the branches of birch trees sway silently like the green skirts of slow dancers and for a while I watch the shadowy patterns they make. There is an interlude of silence in The Fringe. Everything's at peace.

The temp returns to her place beside The Mummy and tries once more to wake him. "He's not doing so good." She means Old Jacob. "You just never know when time's up, do you?"

I am annoyed at the temp for speaking. For breaking the silence. And dissatisfied with myself for being upset. "A girl in my class has leukemia." I say this as if I'm doling out punishment, or blame, to the woman in emerald.

"Oh, leukemia," she says. She has succeeded in waking The Mummy. She's got the spoon halfway to his mouth. "Leukemia calls for aggressive treatment. Sometimes they destroy your immune system. Bring you to the edge. More or less to the brink. And then they introduce someone else's bone marrow into your blood." I'm afraid she's warming up to the subject and will go on and on, but she only adds, so quietly I can scarcely hear her, "Usually it's not successful."

I picture Lesia poised at the lip of a chasm, terrified. There's nothing to hold her back, nothing to keep her from falling in.

Bernice has reached for the spoon and tries to scoop up pudding. The whole tray is a disaster from the recent explosion; I want to look away. My usually steady stomach has turned queasy. I remove the spoon from Bernice's sticky fingers, untie the clothing protector, and push table and tray beyond her reach. She's had enough. We've both had enough.

"I'm glad you came today," she says, as if my coming was a nice surprise. I wipe her mouth one last time.

"You'll see me again soon," I promise, and make my escape. I pass THE CENTURY CLUB and the obit notices. Wave to the receptionist. Halfway out the door I remember the log book, a scribbler kept in the activity room where volunteers sign in and out and write something under COMMENTS. Retracing my steps I think of what I could write. The possibilities are endless:

I enjoyed feeding Bernice today.
Bernice exploded from too much milkshake.
The quality of Bernice's life leaves much to be desired.
I wish I had the temp's blonde hair. And Kelly's figure.

Or I could write those Dylan Thomas lines:

Do not go gentle into that good night,
Rage, rage against the dying of the night.

I pick up the pen and write: *Bernice ate most of her supper.*

June, and I still don't know if I've got the summer job at Harbourside Home. No phone call. No letter. And I don't like to ask. In spite of exams looming I haven't missed a single Monday or Wednesday with Bernice.

One week ago I found her with a huge blue egg above her left eye, bruises on her cheek and a giant lobster-red scrape on her left arm. A bus driver had spotted her sprawled like a sack of potatoes on the sidewalk in front of Harbourside at half-past seven that morning and called for help. The nurses are still baffled. This woman who's been stuck in a wheelchair for ten months and can no longer walk except for a few assisted steps, rises from her bed like the paralytic in the Bible story, and without falling, walks from her room, down the hallway, past the nursing desk, past THE CENTURY CLUB, past the obits, past the reception and out the door. No one sees her go. No bones are broken when she falls. That day I wrote in the scribbler, under COMMENTS: *Good for you, Bernice! Rage on!*

Jacob Krause's obituary was posted for ten whole days. The receptionist said that in winter, with the death count – she didn't use those words exactly – at its highest, obituaries stay up three days max before they're taken down to make room for new ones. Mostly I just look at the picture with the notices, but this time I read the entire short text. Jacob was born in Ukraine and lived as a refugee in Poland and Germany before coming to Canada. He worked in the construction industry until he retired. He's got one daughter, in Vancouver. I read the notice again. It depressed me, and angered me too, that a life can be so neatly encapsulated. And then it terrified me. Can any life, Lesia's, say, or mine, or even Kelly's with all the awards for track she's winning, be one day summed up in so few words?

Before the obit was removed another feeder showed up in The Fringe. Helmie, The Floral Woman. She sits where Jacob Krause sat, under The Last Supper. She broke her hip and had to be hospitalized so they could pin the bone. Now her leg has to be kept in horizontal position. They've got her in a contraption with easily as many bells and whistles as Henry's chair. Henry is the proper name of The Mummy who's hanging in there, I suspect he's planning to join THE CENTURY CLUB. One Monday when they were short-staffed Seema asked me to feed Henry and Bernice both. Like I'm the pro now. A new volunteer, a woman almost as old as the residents at Harbourside, feeds Helmie who eats very little, very slowly, though she has no problem swallowing. She complains that the food is cold, she can't eat it. She accuses the nurses of making her sick. She never smiles. The volunteer whispers to me that Helmie's got a touch of pneumonia. The beginning of the end, she says.

I finally settled on a one-word title for my essay: "Enough." I didn't use any part of the article I'd downloaded from the internet. "Enough is Enough" was about a man who allowed himself only bottled water and bread for a month and toward the end of the month he had some kind of weird experience. Now he's convinced that by depriving the physical body you give space to the spirit. He recommends fasting. I think it was probably just light-headedness from lack of food, but he claims he heard voices and felt a presence guiding him. I can't discount what he experienced. I mean, who knows how Bernice got to the sidewalk in front of Harbourside. And why she didn't fracture a hip and get pneumonia.

My essay was about Bernice, who now wears a security bracelet. How, when her body's had enough, and her throat is exhausted with swallowing, her muscles unable to move, it's time to stop feeding her. I started out padding the essay with all the gross details of supper at Harbourside, but I deleted all that and kept the essay short. I wrote about how her life is narrowed down to the essentials: eating, sleeping, meds and getting cleaned up. How little she needs. How she has totally run out of ideas. And out of people who love her. Gus Lerwick said he'd expected the essay to end as an argument for euthanasia. I'd thought of it, but instead I ended with poetry.

One short sleep past, we wake eternally,
And Death shall be no more: Death, thou shalt die!

I've started bringing bottled water with me on Mondays and Wednesdays and mostly I skip the 7-Eleven. Mother says I'm "doing good." She's surprised how quickly the loonie jar fills up these days. Dad warns me not to overdo anything.

Lesia is almost through her first course of chemo. I know this from Kelly, who came first in the hundred metres and second in the five hundred at the regional track meet. She visits Lesia once a week and tells me how thin she is. Too thin.

So is Bernice. I've started giving her a hug when I leave, a timid hug, because she's all bones, bird bones ready to fracture. I'm scared that one day she'll choke so badly on the pureed meat and vegetables she won't be able to regain her breath. She'll collapse right there in The Fringe, me helpless beside her. Will I be ready for that?

I have this idea – wish, really – that I'll know when I'm hugging Bernice for the last time. I've got a couple of good comments in mind for that occasion. For instance, I could write *Do not go gentle into that good night*, and then cross out the first two words. Or maybe: *Death where is your sting? Grave where is your victory?* But there's something to be said for composing your own comments. So maybe on that day I'll just write: *Bernice has had enough of everything.*

In Such Circumstances

At a window table in the Lockport A&W two men are reading yesterday's *Globe and Mail*, left by the previous customer. The older man – John Deere cap, glasses, short-sleeved grey shirt over navy shorts – holds a section of it close to his eyes. He has finished breakfast, asked at the counter for a coffee refill.

The younger, dark-skinned man has taken a break from his French toast and is reading aloud in a clear, accented voice from *The Globe's* front page: *Nobody could say for sure yesterday why Hesham Mohamed Hadayet had killing on his mind when he entered the Los Angeles international airport on the Fourth of July.* "Bummer," he says. "Can't know what's on a guy's mind, ever. The researchers, they never got to it yet."

The older man grunts magnanimously, as if he would encompass the whole world in that blunt sound.

He sets down his coffee. His part of *The Globe* is folded back to a story with a lengthy headline: *How one man's labour of love is transforming his nightmare into a new world for the poor.* "Now *this* guy," he taps a picture. "Know what's on *this* guy's mind? He turned his sugar-cane plantation in Uganda into an organic farm. Can you beat that? The villagers grow pineapples and peppers. Stuff like that."

"Organic." The younger man leans forward, interested.

"First of all," his companion continues, "first of all this guy loses the plantation, twenty years ago."

The younger nods, and says, "Idi Amin."

"He escapes to Vancouver."

"And gets rich." The younger guesses.

"Rich. And now he gets the estate back and grows vegetables. Organic."

"Organic," the dark man echoes, thoughtfully. "Yah, that's what it needs, this place." He grins and extends his arm in a gesture that includes the booths and the people sitting in them as well as the counter where there's a short line up. "Organic would be good. Would be something at least." His accent, not unpleasant, is obvious to anyone listening, and it is difficult not to, with both men speaking and reading louder than necessary.

The villagers spent two decades in poverty, the older man reads. He stops. Looks up. A van has delivered new customers who head for the order counter. He returns to his newspaper: *There are 84,000 pineapple plants on the verdant land, plus beehives, silkworm and vanilla vines.*

"He's going to hand it over to the villagers," he announces to his friend.

"What?" the younger has returned to his part of the newspaper.

"The farm." The older man has an accent too, east European, not fresh but comfortably embedded. He has farmed in this part of the world most of his life.

The two voices penetrate and draw attention, but the speakers remain unaware that an audience is exchanging glances and knowing smiles before returning to their own table conversation. Their breakfast. Or solitary meditation.

A father with two small children, girls, is too occupied to listen to the news readers at the window. "Finish your fries," he orders the six-year-old as he wipes ketchup from the T-shirt he pulled clean over the tousled head of the toddler less than an hour ago. "I told you to sit down." Tonight when the weekend is over, his daughters returned to their mother, he will regret that he allowed sharpness into his voice.

All week he has anticipated this small outing with pleasure, imagining, in spite of previous experience, a leisurely breakfast with his daughters. They would say amusing things. Confidences would spill from their innocent mouths. There would be gestures to make him smile. Unhurried toast and poached eggs. But the six-year-old has demanded French fries and ketchup and the toddler will not settle for less.

"Are we going to the zoo, Daddy?"

"We'll see. After breakfast."

"Can I do Barbie dot com? I wanna do Barbie dot com." Her voice is piercing and her little sister joins in with a matching wail so persistent her sister pushes away her unfinished fries and claps her hands over her ears.

The dad stabs at his poached eggs. The longed-for weekend with his daughters is suddenly without end. There will be no amusing anecdotes to entertain his secretary on Monday.

The other breakfasters want them to just eat and go.

In one of the booths against the wall, a smartly dressed elderly couple engages seriously with pancakes and sausages. When they are finished they will drive to church; it is Sunday. They are pouring syrup, saying little. The man reaches absent-mindedly with his fork for his wife's sausage. She pushes his hand back, firmly.

"There. On your plate," she says.

Embarrassed, he says nothing.

His business has been a labour of love. The wife looks around, looks up as if she expects to see the words glide by in a cartoon bubble for them to read. Her husband is puzzled. Something in the statement resonates vaguely in his memory, connects with a fragment lodged there, not quite forgotten. He thinks it might be something he taught his first year English students ages ago. The effort of trying to remember interferes with eating. His hand tightens around the fork. He waits for clues. For the fog to clear. And because this is one of the better days, the fog does clear and a clue surfaces: Russian story. Novel. His hand relaxes slightly; he lays down the fork, looks across at his wife who is eating pancakes. He addresses her with tentative eagerness. "Those... those...those patients. With cancer, I mean. That was... that was Russia, wasn't it?"

Sudden and peculiar shifts in her husband's thoughts are nothing new to the wife. She is accustomed to thinking for him, ready to complete his sentences if necessary, but usually she refrains because no one should be too quickly absolved of responsibility. For many years she and her husband read the same novels and discussed them; there were arguments and counter-arguments, praise and critique, and sometimes condemnation. Sharp mental sparring they both relished. She knows the book he is trying to recall.

"You're right," she says, with emphasis. "Absolutely right." And after a long pause that produces nothing, she doles out: "Solzhenitsyn."

"*The Cancer Ward*!" he trumpets.

"Sh-sh-sh." Then, as if to reward him, she offers details. "They were all men. To pass the time they talked about all sorts of things...."

"Philosophical things," the husband interrupts, elated. "Existential things."

He has reached a place of restored confidence. He is like a swimmer coming into his element. A runner reaching full stride. But the assurance quickly falters and a baffled expression falls across his face.

The wife takes pity. "One of the men with cancer

was reading a story by Leo Tolstoy. They were discussing it. Trying to figure out the answer to a question: *What do men live by*?" She pauses. Should she put him to the test? Why not? The morning has gone well. "Do you remember the answer to the question?" She is annoyed to find herself sounding like a school teacher.

"What question?"

"*What do men live by*?"

"I don't get what you mean." His interest has been redirected to his sausage over which he is pouring too much syrup.

Love, the woman murmurs, so softly he can't hear.

There's a lull at the counter. The woman behind it takes the coffee carafe from the burner and brings it around to the tables. The two men at the window accept refills.

"Listen," the younger says, and it is unclear whether he's targeting his companion or the server as he reads: *The FBI couldn't offer a motive for the rampage.*

"That would be in Los Angeles?" the retired farmer asks.

"Where else?"

"Well, I was still in Uganda."

"Oh."

The server recognizes the pair, they come often and she has assessed them as essentially decent men. Not like the sullen truck driver alone in a smoking booth, a regular. "That one's up to no good," she'll tell the manager later.

The trucker hulks over hash browns and ham, his large hands wielding fork and knife as if they are weapons he will use to launch an attack. He catches words from the window table:

"Sounds like he might be a terrorist." The older man is speaking.

Damn right, the trucker mutters, stopping short of going public with his opinion. Damn right. What else does this goddam society ever produce? Though scarcely audible, the mutterings are undergirded by anger held in readiness just below the surface along with a repertoire of obscenities poised for release.

His cell phone rings.

"Hullo." His voice is gruff. Then, as if the sun has at last broken through clouds, his belligerence is replaced by an excited heartiness that requires volume.

"Hey, baby," he says. "Hey, how's it going? Listen. I'm just into ham and hash browns here. Terrible. But I'll finish them off anyway. What? Oh, the A&W. Lockport. Yah, so give me fifteen, twenty minutes."

At the other end a voice asks a question.

"Naw. She don't expect me," the trucker answers. "Baby, believe me. Nothing could keep me away. Hey, I hear you. I'll be there."

He hangs up. Summons the approaching server with an imperiously raised coffee mug, digs into hash browns and grilled ham.

Outside, the world is bright with sunshine. A modest breeze scarcely moves the stiff branches of the dusty potentilla. Three men with fishing rods walk by on their way to the river, their dark slacks neatly pressed, shirts laundered, as if the wearers had started out for church when they were redirected. Oriental families straggle by, a succession of clustered children in all sizes, chattering, laughing, quarreling over rods and bait, bags of snack food.

The window through which all this is visible is spotless. The older man at the window, finished with his section of the newspaper, leans back from his coffee, a picture of well-being.

In the booth directly opposite the Dad and his two daughters a young woman writes in her notebook, pauses to read what she has written, writes again. Biking helmet and dark glasses are parked beside coffee and dry toast on which she will shortly spread marmalade.

She is a university student, and recently enough for it still to be exciting, she's had a story accepted by the student newspaper. A short piece about cycling. In the creative writing class she selected for a spring session credit, the instructor, keen on fiction, has introduced her to the possibilities in story writing. Her newly-awakened imagination is on the alert. She has become a spy.

She is discreet in her observation of the two men at the window whom she is allowing herself to envision as characters in a story. She listens, and whatever they say or read, she records in her notebook.

The truck driver catches her attention by the noisy way he wolfs down his breakfast. She wonders who was at the other end of his cell phone call.

The wife has the car keys in her hand.

"Wait," her husband says. "She hasn't brought the bill." He is peevish. Moves slowly. Fumbles at his pocket.

"We paid at the counter when we ordered," she says.

"I'll have to ask for your keys. I seem to have misplaced mine."

The woman digs in her handbag for something to distract him and finds a photo she keeps there. "Look. That's us when we were engaged. Remember?"

The flag at the nearby gas station is snapping in the wind when the young woman emerges from the A&W, adjusts her helmet and mounts her bike. It is a west wind and comes at her sideways as she heads back to the city. A cloying scent of clover drifts up from the ditch. A dozen pelicans circle grandly above the highway before straightening their formation to follow the river, and their pouched, orange bills north.

As she proceeds south, the would-be-writer watches for familiar landmarks. Four churches in the space of a few kilometres, two orthodox and two Catholic. All of them built by Ukrainian settlers who came to this country between wars looking for a place to make a new life. A safe life anchored in old traditions and familiar worship. Where the trees thin, she can see a fifth church across the river. Anglican.

Last year she observed the demolition of the smaller orthodox church and the progress of its modern replacement. The new structure is set slightly farther back from the highway, giving motorists an improved view – if anyone should care – of the accumulated gravestones in the adjacent cemetery. The cyclist doesn't notice them. She is young, with no experience of death.

There are other landmarks: Lombardy poplars standing sentinel along a driveway; a greenhouse advertising the final sale of bedding plants; an empty gravelled lot that in fall will become a display site for orange pumpkins, huge and so plentiful a good number will be left to rot. And flowers. As summer unfolds its days of heat and rain, cyclists may witness tulips and narcissus giving way to irises and then to anemones, peonies, petunias, daisies. Geraniums and marigolds provide a constant escort of colour.

Before she left her apartment this morning, taking the bike down in the elevator, her boyfriend had made oatmeal porridge, something he rarely does and something she doesn't much like.

"You have to fuel up," he said.

If only he cared half as much about her writing as about her body which he wants her to keep fit. He can't imagine sex with a flabby woman. "An okay hobby," is how he refers to her writing.

The highway's wide shoulder is paved for cyclists. To her left the Sunday traffic passes by in intermittent spurts of cars, trucks, vans and a few larger transports.

A rattling pickup truck pulling a trailer loaded with lawnmowers wooshes past just when the noiseless rhythm of her peddling becomes a dull, ungraceful thumping, the sound coming from the rear bicycle wheel. The world wobbles. The bike becomes capricious, she can scarcely control it as it wavers and threatens to cross the white line marking the traffic lane. A transport coming from behind has scant time to swerve. She grips the handle bar and the bike veers back to the shoulder. For a split second she believes she can remain upright, but control has slipped away. Rider and bike slam down on the gravel at the edge of the road.

After a while she picks herself up. The transport truck has rounded a bend and is out of sight. She is not dismayed, though unsettled, as she moves her limbs to be sure no bones are broken. She feels a trace of blood on her forehead. She tests the tire with her hand. Flat as flat.

The cyclist could walk down one of the driveways and ask to use the telephone. But whom would she call? Her boyfriend's small car has no bicycle rack. Best would be if someone came along and picked her up. Someone with a truck. Traffic continues to stream toward her and pass by on the way north to beaches and cottages where summer is to be enjoyed. The young spy is surrounded by the makings of a story but all she wants is to go home. As quickly as possible.

After he's washed down the last bit of ham and hash browns with the last of his coffee, the truck driver lights a cigarette, takes the first drag and heaves his bulk out of the booth. He doesn't bother to gather up cup, plate, tray and crumpled napkins the way most A&W patrons do, but strides quickly out the door to his truck.

His foot heavy on the gas pedal, he has covered several kilometres when he sees ahead of him a young woman kneeling beside a bike lying on the gravel shoulder of the road. He does not recognize her but his brain – maybe his gut – registers her dilemma automatically and just as automatically his foot moves to the brake, but in the rear view mirror there's a long line of vehicles, the van just behind him controlled by a brainless tailgater who needs his head bashed in. This road stupidity fuels the truck driver's anger and overrides his good intention. Stopping would be difficult under these circumstances.

The young woman trudges south, limping but resolute, leading her disabled bike back to the city, oblivious now to new construction or renovations underway. Blind to the flowers. Her right arm and thigh burn from the abrasive gravel.

At least ten more kilometres to go, but before she has covered one, she is overtaken by two equipped cyclists who apply their air pump, to no avail. Because they are regular, and serious, cyclists, they carry repair kits that contain spare inner tubes. And a compact pump.

The two men at the window table make an unsuccessful stab at reassembling the scattered pages of *The Globe and Mail*. On their way out, they stack their trays and deposit their garbage, smile back at the booths and wave in the direction of the counter.

In the parking lot the father herds his two girls toward the car. The smaller one has stopped wailing for the time being. The older one says, "I wanna go to the waterslide, okay, Daddy?"

In a future that at this moment would seem impossibly distant to the father, the older daughter will receive the Lieutenant Governor's Medal when she graduates from high school. Her father will brag at work. A scant week later, commencement and parties and river boat cruises accomplished, she will be crossing the street when a motorist caught in a moment of inattention will be unable to stop in time. For the rest of her life the girl will travel by wheelchair.

The younger girl will launch a successful legal research business and marry a man who loves her but loves mountains more. The need to conquer consumes him, and each distant peak, it will seem to her, is higher and more daunting than the last. Because she loves him she will be stalked by terror that will threaten to immobilize her. At night she will dream of icy crags, wind swept and littered with empty oxygen canisters. Desperate to keep fear at bay, she will look for ways to fill the hours after work and on weekends.

In a local paper she will read a "volunteers needed" notice and report to the local school where the resource teacher will pair her up with an autistic boy who rocks and rocks and rocks. When the boy is transferred to another school, she will tutor a boy with attention deficit disorder, then a Vietnamese refugee, a kindergarten child with learning disabilities and so on.

"I love my work," she will tell her father when they meet for coffee at the A&W. "But I am always sad." Her dreams continue to be filled with the austere majesty of Mt. Everest and Mt. McKinley. She forces herself to cling to their beauty rather than to their treacherous precipices.

On this clear Sunday morning at the A&W parking lot none of these future circumstances has power to appal the father.

After church, during which the husband listened with determination for ten minutes, then dozed, breathing audibly, the well-dressed couple shakes hands with the pastor.

"Was it a good week?" The pastor's greeting is timid. He is new. He looks young and comically formal in his black clerical gown.

The wife appraises him before she answers. "Yes."

The young man is not satisfied, not convinced. He scrunches his forehead. His eyes radiate curiosity. They will not let the woman turn away.

"Well, there are times and then there are times," she concedes.

The pastor nods.

During his sermon the woman let her mind wander, though not quite unrestrained. Occasionally she turned to observe her husband asleep beside her. She snapped to attention when around her everyone rose for the benediction.

She is embarrassed now that she missed the text for the sermon. She thinks it might have been "For God so loved the world," or maybe it was, "Love is patient, love is kind." She wishes she could repeat the text and prove she was listening. Instead, she repeats the only statement from the sermon that she can remember, "*All of us are better when we're loved,*" pleased that she's retained something at least.

"I can't take credit for those words," the pastor says. He'd spent several hours writing his sermon, but he doesn't mention that. "I read them in a novel. By someone from the east."

The woman and her husband no longer read novels together, and she has turned to *MacLeans* and *Good Housekeeping*.

She doesn't ask for the novel's title or its author, but she repeats the words to herself: *All of us are better when we're loved.* She will write them down when she gets to the car and at home she will post them on her fridge.

It isn't until she is safely home that the student reflects on the providential appearance of the two cyclists. Before she could become desperate, or exhausted, before she had even thought of invoking that spirit of altruism she'd overheard the old farmer read about from *The Globe*, help had come. One man went to work changing the inner tube; the other, after inspecting her bike, scolded her for not carrying a tool kit and a bottle of water. When the job was done, the two rode for a while behind her, then, with a "Take it easy," they passed her and were soon out of sight.

Gratitude overtakes her, belatedly.

Her boyfriend is glad too that she was assisted. The matter has been dealt with, there is no further need to trouble or exert himself over the incident. "You were lucky," he says, takes a beer out of the fridge and picks up the TV guide.

When they make love that afternoon on the sitting room couch, he whispers, "I love you, I love you," but by Christmas, determined to let nothing interfere with her writing, she will have asked him to move out.

After decades on the road, the trucker will announce that he is ready to retire to a quiet place up north, near a lake he knows. His wife begins packing, a slow process that involves much discarding. It is painful. She is certain that at the northern lake her husband raves about she will find herself bereft. Garden, bowling, movies, shopping malls, friends and grandchildren will no longer be within easy reach. She's not sure she can manage under such circumstances. She has all along believed – foolishly, it appears now – that she and her husband would end up comfortably in Tamarack Woods, a stylish retirement complex overlooking an artificial lake.

Her friends will wonder why she remains faithful to a man who has not been faithful to her.

There is good fishing in the northern lake. The former trucker will sit for hours in his boat on the clear water. Sometimes he'll turn his head suddenly as if to check the receding stretches of the Trans-Canada highway in a rear view mirror.

The woman is surprised by the extravagant display of northern lights. When her husband is asleep after a day of fishing, she grabs a jacket and steals down to an outcropping of stones facing the lake. Looking down she sees the moon trapped in the water. Looking up, she sees the darkness lit by a swirling dance of coloured lights. As the dance gains tempo and the colours intensify; she imagines herself in a church where a choir is singing; *Holy, Holy, Holy*. Then the movement winds down, the colours pale and she is left, a solitary watcher beneath the cathedral dome of a black sky seeded with stars. She gazes at them the way humans frequently do – in silent wonder. Some claim they can read the stars; the wife is not one of these. It's the wideness of the firmament that impresses her. And the silence. How much grander than all human achievements and structures on planet earth. How much vaster than rage and infidelity.

In winter the lake grows a thick skin of ice. The pines, sharp and black, stab the leaden sky. Deep cold keeps the trucker and his wife confined to the cabin, to more of each other's company than they have ever experienced.

They survive the winter.

The aspiring young writer will almost have completed her first manuscript of short fiction when the publishing industry falls into economic disarray. The unfortunate delay will allow her to return to a story that has long troubled her. A story about two men who meet regularly at an A&W not far from the city for Sunday morning breakfast. She has decided that one cloudy Sunday – November probably – only one of them will show up. The other is kept away by a circumstance she has not yet been able to pin down. The circumstance, she thinks, will have to be a calamity, perhaps even a disaster, though she has trouble deciding whether it should be accidental or deliberately caused by malice or brought on by human failing or wilfulness.

And which of the two newspaper readers should she select for misfortune?

The older man, the farmer, will be able to endure it, she thinks. Life has taught him patience. He is a good man. But is it fair, after a long life of hard and steady labour? Not to mention his amiable personality and upright character.

She is reluctant to choose the younger whom she will describe as wiry and rather earnest. (Will she be going too far if she says good-looking?) She would like to spare him. As a child born into chaos made by war and famine, he was separated from his parents. As a youth he was arrested for demonstrating against a tyrannical government. He was imprisoned. Tortured. Surely that is enough.

She has not yet worked out how he escaped and fled from that middle-eastern (or was it African?) country and came as a refugee to Canada.

She could flip a coin to determine who should suffer.

She could consult her ex-boyfriend who has been calling her again. His reappearance surprised her, as did his interest, apparently sincere, in her writing. Can he be trusted? Can *she* trust him?

Cycling north, past new houses with three-car garages, vegetable stands, geraniums, petunias, she will turn the matter over – and over – in her mind, wrestling with the complicated burden of choice.

Although her husband's Alzheimers makes each day unpredictable, his wife will continue to take him on small outings. To the A&W for breakfast or lunch. To the Anglican church where he falls asleep while she jots down the young pastor's morning text and waits to hear if he will quote from a novel. Often he does, and if it's not too long she'll copy that down too.

It will be several more years before her husband's restlessness will keep them both home. On their last Sunday in church, the pastor will announce that he is leaving the congregation in order to begin a PhD program at an American university. At the end of the service the woman will bring her husband to shake his hand.

"Thank you for everything," she'll say. "I mean your sermons. I liked them." She doesn't tell him that this is their last Sunday.

The pastor will see how drawn her face has become and he'll notice ketchup stains on the man's white shirt.

On a future fall Sunday the young writer – no longer quite so young – will be cycling once more north to Lockport, accompanied by her boyfriend. She will be elated, not so much by his company, as by the fact that her first collection of short fiction is scheduled for release the following spring. Finally! She has until the end of the calendar year to complete the manuscript, but she's already finished except for the one worrisome story for which she has invented circumstances, supporting characters, weather, plot. She has allowed suffering to befall one of her main characters.

"Which one?' her boyfriend will ask half way to Lockport. It's a question he's asked many times and she has so far refused to say.

"The younger one," she says now.

"So what happens to him?"

"You'll have to wait till the book comes out."

"You're such a tease."

But she isn't teasing. She doesn't yet know how the story will end. If only she could get the outcome right.

At the A&W they will place their orders, take their coffee to a booth and as they settle in the young woman will notice a man hunched over a newspaper at one of the window tables. He wears a crumpled jacket; his hair is grey. A walking cane hangs from the back of his chair and a faded John Deere cap sits on the table near his elbow. She will know at once – at least she will believe she knows – who he is, and will wait with anticipation for the second man, the younger one, to join him. The server will place toast and marmalade in front of her, bacon and eggs in front of her boyfriend. They will eat slowly because it is Sunday, nothing hurries them, and they have learned to be at ease in each other's company.

That Sunday the second man will not arrive, no matter how often the writer looks up from her breakfast to see who has come in, no matter how often she smiles and says "There's still time," when the boyfriend makes a move to go.

The old man continues to bend over his newspaper although she never sees him turn to the next page.

"Let's go." This time the boyfriend means it. He slides out from the booth and picks up both trays.

The writer, more disturbed than she cares to admit, follows reluctantly, unable to believe that the younger man has not appeared. She looks around the parking lot for him. Before mounting her bike she wheels it past the window, but the old man has turned his face away.

On the long ride home the boyfriend will occasionally hum or whistle a tune. He hopes his companion, when he asks her to marry him – very soon now – will say yes.

At this moment, the woman has slipped back into the worrisome story she must complete before the deadline, a story fraught now with absence. She wonders what has happened to the young man, and whether it's too late to save him.

Acknowledgements

I am grateful to Sandra Birdsell for her wise and careful editing of this manuscript and to the editors of the following magazines in which some of these stories first appeared: *Prairie Fire*, *Antigonish Review*, and *Sophia Magazine*.

The words "I want, I want" in "Wednesday is Adoration" are from Saul Bellow's *Henderson the Rain King* (Penguin books, 1966). The songs in "Saved" are by the Medical Mission Sisters ("You God are my Firmament") and Steve Bell "(God our Protector"). In "A Perfect Location" the quoted poems are by G.M. Hopkins ("God's Grandeur") and by Elizabeth Barrett Browning ("How do I love thee"); In "Ending With Poetry" I've quoted Miriam Waddington ("Thou didst say me") and Dylan Thomas ("Do not go gentle"). The line, "All of us are better when we're loved," quoted in "In Such Circumstances" and also in the epigraph, is from Alistair MacLeod's *No Great Mischief*, (MacLelland and Stewart, 1999). Bible quotations are from the New Revised Standard Version.

Photo: Patty Boge

about the author

Sarah Klassen is the award-winning author of one other short fiction collection, *The Peony Season*, and five books of poetry. Sarah holds a Bachelor of Arts degree and a Bachelor of Education degree from the University of Winnipeg. Aside from writing, she has taught English in the public school system in Winnipeg, and at summer institutes in Lithuania and Ukraine. Sarah Klassen was born in Winnipeg, Manitoba, and currently resides there.